everything is sinister

everything is sinister

david llewellyn

seren

Seren is the book imprint of
Poetry Wales Press Ltd
57 Nolton Street, Bridgend, CF31 3AE, Wales
+ 44 1656 663018
www.seren-books.com

ISBN 978-1-85411-469-3

A CIP record for this title is available from the British Library.

This is a work of fiction. The characters and incidents portrayed
are the work of the author's imagination. Any resemblance
to actual persons, living or dead, is entirely coincidental.

The publisher works with the financial assistance
of the Welsh Books Council.

Printed in Times New Roman and Helvetica by Bell and Bain, Glasgow

Lockdown

**coming soon
to a channel near you**

Man is accelerating at an extraordinary rate into a super-technological world...There is something profoundly auto-erotic in this process and... and it's sinister.

Norman Mailer, in conversation with Marshall McLuhan
The Summer Way, CBC Television 1968

west india quay –20:14 | breakfast with sally – 08:32 | edinburgh – 17:42 | ondine – 11:20 | *the voice of the people*– 11:21 | the gym – 12:08 | the deli bar – 12:43 | leicester square – 19:58 | the goldfish bowl – 11:00 | phone call 1– 14:22 | phone call 2 – 18:04 | west india quay – 20:56 | the waste ground – 00:26 | six billion movies – 11:40 | day one – 07:30 | monkey puzzle trees – 10:42 | day three – 08:10 | nigel, apartment 413 – 09:10 | c-fish – 13:21 | email from brian fenton – 18:32 | tinside lido – 23:35 | the confession – 09:36 | *lockdown*, final episode – 21:00 | saturday morning, eleven hours and thirty two minutes after the last episode of *lockdown* series 2 – 09:32 | monday – 10:30 | answerphone – 13:12 | attempt to leave the apartment 1 – 11:32 | attempt to leave the apartment 2 – 17:22 | attempt to leave the apartment 3 – 00:28 | tv now – 11:33 | riots – 22:10 | girl time – 13:46 | behold a gift designed to kill – 13:59 | animals who think they're people –21:34 | trisha smedley – 09:57 | preparations for leaving the building – 11:09 | docklands light railway – 12:08 | ground zero – 12:53 | district line – 14:58 | when i kill colin curtis – 20:21 | the news – 22:00 | soho – 18:49 | cab – 21:06 | shad thames – 21:32 | the next day – 11:01 | the arrest – 12:13 | the fever (i see the future) – 02:31 | galactus.co.uk – 11:45 | dexter wong – 15:49 | book launch – 21:15 | celebricide – 23:09 | overdose blue – 12:41 | signing off – 18:03

"Okay... so what if somebody told you that a hundred thousand Chinese people would die unless you gave up your car?"

"I'm sorry, what's that?"

"If you don't give up your car, a hundred thousand Chinese people will die."

"Where are the Chinese people?"

"In China."

"A hundred thousand of them?"

"Yes."

"Wait wait wait... how long does she have to give up her car for?"

"Permanently."

"So I have to give up my car, *permanently*, to save a hundred thousand Chinese people?"

"Yes."

"How old are they?"

"That's immaterial. They're young and old. There's a hundred thousand of them."

"I'd keep the car."

"You're joking."

"Yeah, you are joking, right?"

"No. I'd keep the car. I've got a fucking Alfa Romeo, Michael. Besides... I'm not being cruel. A hundred thousand Chinese people, that's, like, nought-point-nought-one per cent of the population of China. That's nothing."

"She's got a point."

"Yeah... actually... because I read somewhere that three people die every second."

"Yeah, it's something like that."

"So if there's... how many Chinese people are there?"

"About a billion."

"Okay… a billion Chinese people… and there's six billion people in the world… so that's one in six people who's Chinese. So that's one Chinese person every two seconds."

"Listen to Maths Boy."

"So if one Chinese person dies every two seconds, then it would only take… hang on… let me just use the calculator on my C-Fish… that's one hundred thousand… every two seconds… that's… two hundred thousand seconds… which is three thousand three hundred and thirty three and a third minutes… which is… fifty five point five hours… which is… two point three days. Less than two and a half days. It takes less than two and a half days for a hundred thousand Chinese people to die… whether or not Ondine gives up her car."

"See… I told you I was right. What difference would me giving up my car make? They're dead anyway."

"But if you keep the car, a hundred thousand people will die *as well* as the hundred thousand who will die in the next two and a half days."

"So? It just means a few of them get bunched in together. It all evens out in the end. And I get to keep my car."

"What about you, Ed? Would you give up your car?"

Until this point I have been staring at the strange insect that is gradually making its way across our table, navigating between the used plates and half-empty wine glasses soiled with oily finger-prints. I don't recognise it, and for one brief moment I imagine that I have somehow, inadvertently stumbled upon some new, as-yet-undiscovered species, deep in the heart of London's Docklands. It doesn't resemble any insect I have seen before; this strange creature with its black and orange shell and peculiar, spiky legs.

I hear my name and look up.

"What's that?"

"Would you give up your car to save a hundred thousand Chinese people?"

"I don't drive."

"But if you did, would you?"

"I don't know. I don't drive."

"Ed, you're no fun. Ondine would send them all to their deaths."

"Too fucking right, I would."

"Ondine would drive over their corpses on her way home."

"Abso-fucking-lutely."

The strange black and orange insect stops abruptly as it reaches the edge of the table. It seems to face me, as if somehow aware I have been watching it all this time. The shell opens with mechanical precision, and all at once the creature takes off, rising up, a tiny dancing fleck of post-atomic ash against the fading sky.

"What *are* you watching, Ed?"

"An insect."

"An insect. Ed is watching an insect."

Something's wrong. Something's changed. Everything is wrong. I've been working with these people for years and we do this maybe three times a week but now I'm looking around the table and it's like I don't know them. I know what they're saying but I don't know what they're talking about. Or maybe it's the other way around. I'd put it down to this heat, this unending, unforgiving heat, but I know I'd be lying.

"Why are you watching an insect, Ed?"

"It was just an insect," I say.

My colleagues look at me as if I'm insane. They all laugh through their noses, swig their drinks and carry on talking. I look up at the sky but the insect has gone.

Twenty minutes later I am on the Docklands Light Railway. The air inside the carriage is hot and sticky and smells sickly sweet. A group of teenagers sit in a moody huddle near the door, listening to bass-heavy music blasting from an aquamarine C-Fish. They nod rhythmically, all of them focused on the small plastic device. An elderly woman sitting opposite them rolls her eyes and looks out of the window. In the doorway itself stands a skinhead, he looks about twenty, hanging from the circular overhead bar in a limp cruciform, his cold blue eyes fixed on me. I half expect his expression to change; a smile, perhaps, or even a sneer; but there is nothing.

I realise suddenly that I have missed my stop at Royal Victoria, but rather than get off at Custom House or even Prince Regent I stay, always within view of the young skinhead. When he steps off at Royal Albert I follow him, down the steps and beneath the sweeping concrete artery of the train tracks.

Across the water a Lufthansa flight touches down at City Airport, its wheels screeching against the tarmac, its arrival floodlit by the runway. The roar of the plane's engines and the electric hum of the departing train seem to synchronise in a melancholy harmony, and for a moment I am lost in the noise. A hot breeze that tastes like butter sweeps in from the water, and the sky is full of stars. He has vanished.

I look around, hoping to see a shadow, or a movement, but there is nothing; only the sound of the plane, jets still howling, taxiing around the apron of City Airport and grinding to a halt before the glass façade of the terminal.

I return to Royal Victoria, the train almost empty, and walk around the western edge of the great dock itself. There are motorised dinghies on the water, three of them in all, each one containing four or five armed policemen. They patrol the surface in regular circuits, scanning the edge of the dock with bright torches. There is a weapons fair at ExCeL; the best and brightest from the world of weaponry and munitions collected in one building for the duration of the week. The security alert is high.

For a moment I am caught in the glare of the torch, and I cover my eyes with my hand. The boat turns sharply, spraying water in its wake, and I am in darkness again.

When I enter the building the air is stale but cool, the air-con working overtime to keep the heat outside. The corridors are empty and silent but for the muffled sounds of televisions behind closed doors. No voices, no sounds of movement, just advertisements and the pre-recorded laughter of studio audiences.

breakfast with sally – 08:32

"Here to talk showbiz is *The Voice of the People's* very own Ed Raynes!"

That's me. Ed Raynes. I talk showbiz. That's what I do.

"Ed, how are you this morning?"

"I'm great, thanks, Sally."

I've been awake since half five and the studio lights are hurting my eyes, which had dark grey bags beneath them until they were given "that extra bit of attention" by somebody in make-up. To the audience at home Sally's world is one of brightly coloured furnishings and wonderfully arranged flowers. From where I'm sitting it looks like a big black void filled with strange-looking machines and people wearing headphones.

"So what's been going on this week?"

"Well, Sally, everybody's talking about whether or not Josh and Maria are getting divorced."

I've been appearing on Sally's sofa, or rather the sofa belonging to the studio where Sally's show is filmed, for almost two years, starting only a few months after I got the job writing After Show, my daily column of 'insider gossip and goings on'.

"And are they?"

"It's hard to tell, Sally. All the American magazines are full of stories from Maria's friends saying she wants to settle down and have kids and Josh's friends are saying he wants to play around, so some are saying they will and some are saying they won't."

I used to find this easy. When I used to sound interested it was because I genuinely was.

"And do you think there's any truth in the rumour that he's been having an affair?"

"Well, again, this is all hearsay. There was talk on the set of his last film that he'd been seen out and about with Bridget Kelso, but Bridget claims they are just good friends."

"Don't they always?"

"Exactly, Sally, exactly."

I laugh, and it sounds just like a real laugh. There is a studied, well-rehearsed warmth between Sally and I. You'd think that when we've finished filming we hang out together, maybe even attend the same parties. You wouldn't think that I see her every now and then, maybe once every two or three months, when they need to fill a six minute slot on her show. If it wasn't me sat here it would be a fashion correspondent talking about this season's colour or a holiday expert telling you, the audience at home, exactly where the 'new Ibiza' is going to be.

Sally asks me questions and I answer.

"And what about Qelli Mai?"

"Well quite, Sally, quite." And we talk about the latest 'goings on' in the life of pop star Qelli Mai. I repeat practically word for word everything I wrote about her yesterday and we cut to footage of her walking up the red carpet at a party or a premiere, all artfully smudged eyeliner and big pupils.

We talk about wardrobe malfunctions and grooming mistakes, Sally and I. We talk about backstage extramarital affairs and celebrity face-offs, like ancient Greeks discussing the dramas of

Mount Olympus. Truth be told, I could do this in my sleep. I'm talking ten grand Versace dresses, but my mind is elsewhere.

I'm thinking about a name, a single name, and everything I know about that name. I'm thinking about secrets and promises. I'm thinking about the big black truth that's eating away at my insides like the Ebola virus. And still I'm smiling, and leaning forward on Sally's great big peach-coloured sofa, careful not to brush my microphone with either of my hands in the way that amateurs do when they appear on programmes like this.

edinburgh – 17:42

You kill the first hour in a hotel room that somebody else is paying for by finding out what stuff you've got. Which soaps they've provided you with. Which teabags. Which television channels. How many towels.

You test the mattress, look out of the window. You take pleasure in the fact that this is suddenly your space. You may own your own house, or your own apartment, but you still pad around this little confined world, with its soft furnishings and heavy, sun-blocking curtains, and feel a tiny thrill that in a matter of minutes this space has become yours and yours alone.

You are in a strange city, so you then begin to contemplate the practicalities of bringing a stranger here, impressing them (even though the paper could easily have paid for a better hotel), and then violating them in every which way you can imagine, maybe watching yourself in any one of the abundance of mirrors that are placed around the room.

You masturbate lazily, the curtains slightly open so you feel the frisson accompanying the idea that somebody, somewhere, might just be able to see you. You ejaculate, and this is one of those rare moments when you see the expression on your face as you do, reflected in one of the mirrors. Even then, you are aware that your expression was not spontaneous. You had already noticed your reflection, and begun to assume the kind of expression you have seen in countless pornographic films. This tastefully lit and per- fectly performed moment of pleasure is over all too quickly, to be replaced by those moments when you sluggishly wipe the semen from your belly, and throw the tissue into a plastic-lined waste paper basket in the corner of the room.

You make yourself a cup of tea. The kettle slots neatly into a plastic tray, on which are placed two cups, two saucers, two tea-spoons, and a small bowl filled with individual sachets of sugar and coffee, individual teabags, and small plastic pots of UHT milk. Making a cup of tea while you are naked makes you smile, though your body tingles with thoughts of electrical equipment, hot water, and exposed genitalia being in such close proximity. That same tingle returns later, when you are ironing a shirt while still undressed.

You flick through the limited number of television channels: Two news channels, one channel showing vintage quiz shows, one showing endless re-runs of *You Bet Your Life* and *Ozzie and Harriet*, another nothing but children's programmes. The over-enthusiastic blonde girl in the orange dungarees is showing children how to pretend to play the saxophone, against a backdrop of mottled greens and purples. After a minute or so your eyes begin to hurt, and you find yourself wondering just how you would go about throwing the television through the hotel room window.

You realise that you were actually wondering whether the window would open wide enough for the television, and then chide yourself for thinking in such pragmatic terms. Surely the point would be to throw it through the window while it is shut, to send it tumbling down toward the street below in a glittering shower of broken glass and splintered wood.

You go to the bar on the ground floor. This one is called the Georgian Bar, and every effort has been made to make it look exactly like a Georgian gentleman's club, as imagined by a tourist in the twenty-first century. The walls are adorned with hunting scenes and portraits of people that nobody remembers, every chair is upholstered with red velvet. The carpet is subtle, but austere.

The barman is from somewhere in Europe. You aren't good with accents. When he asks you if you want ice he holds eye contact just a split second longer than he should. You wonder whether if you ask him to charge the drink to your room he will somehow take that as a hint and show up in the early hours of the morning.

As you sit alone in the bar, sipping your drink and reading through a complimentary magazine on nearby tourist attrac-tions, your C-Fish rings. It's the photographer, telling you where you can meet him. A small part of you fantasises that he is not a photographer and you are not a journalist; that you are in fact a secret agent, and that you are here on some kind of undercover mission. Only the sudden appearance of American tourists in khaki shorts disrupts this brief reverie.

The taxi drives you the short distance into the city's West End where you meet the photographer at a café bar. You could have walked, only it's still in the thirties and you don't want to have visible sweat patches when you get to the party.

The photographer is a veteran with thirty years in the business. Even before he decided to ravage his body with a scorched earth policy of forty cigarettes a day, a penchant for vodka, and an addiction to fried food, he was afflicted in the womb with strawberry birthmarks that traverse his face in an archipelago of angry red flesh. He has been married, though the marriage was apparently brief, and he very rarely sees his children, who now live in Birmingham.

You drink an Americano while he drinks a vodka and coke, and you check your plans for the evening ahead. You will be going to a club called Nefertiti's for the homecoming party of *Lockdown* contestant Nicki Santos. Nicki, a twenty-four-year-old air stewardess from Leith, was 'paroled' out of the reality TV show last Friday. After a weekend of publicity work and press junkets she is back in Edinburgh, and tonight is her night.

The party itself is exactly as you expected it to be. Not a party in the truest sense of the word, more a brief pageant in which no moment goes without being photographed or filmed. Nicki, groomed in the last three days no doubt, gives banal answers to your banal questions.

"So, what next?"

"Well, I'd really like to get into the music industry. I've always loved singing."

While other guests quaff bottle after bottle of Moët and stumble around on the dance floor, Nicki Santos nurses a glass of sparkling mineral water, mindful of the photographer's ever-watching lens.

"And will you be on the lookout for a boyfriend?"

"Well, I don't know if I'll have the time! I'm too busy for a boyfriend right now, though I did meet Nathan Cox at a party on Saturday… he's very sexy, so I wouldnae mind meeting him again!"

A coy chuckle, and a humming chorus of approval from her friends gathered around the table at the very mention of former boy band member, Nathan Cox, who you know for a fact is gay.

The camera flashes. Nicki smiles. Then she moves to the dance floor, where, instead of dancing, she strikes dance-like poses while the photographer shoots another twenty or thirty pictures. Caught in the middle of a throbbing crowd she makes a strange tableau vivant; a breathing waxwork begging to be immortalised with every sudden white strobe of the flashbulb.

After the interview you and the photographer stalk the party, looking for familiar faces. In one corner of the room you see one of your newspaper's former 'Page Four' models vomiting into a plant pot. The camera flashes again. When she passes you at the bar you notice a light dusting of white powder on her top lip. She recognises you and smiles, her eyes barely open, before heading into the ladies' toilets.

Another taxi, with a different driver, takes you back to the hotel. The European barman in the Georgian Bar is no longer on duty. You fantasise, briefly, about him waiting in your room, sprawled naked on your bed. You are disappointed, though not surprised, to find your room empty when you get there.

You wake a little too early and manage to eat perhaps half a breakfast after packing your things into the overnight bag you brought with you. You look at the notes you've written on your laptop. You wonder if there was any real reason in them sending you all this way, when all you managed to glean out of Nicki Santos were such *bon mots* as, "I was never in it to win it," and "I'm not bothered about being famous, I'm just enjoying this while it lasts".

Did you really need to travel four hundred miles for that?

A taxi driver who looks like the actor and playwright Sam Shepard but who talks a little like Sean Connery picks you up outside the hotel and drives you to the airport.

All airports are essentially the same; all regional airports, anyway. So much so that if you've been to two or three of them, you can usually navigate your way around the rest without having to follow the signs. The girl at the departures desk smiles and looks at your passport, which has almost expired and shows a younger, somehow happier you with more hair and better cheekbones. She studies it for a moment, adding ten years to the photo with all the malice she can muster, until she comes to the satisfactory conclusion that yes, with less hair and a fuller face the person in the photo would look exactly like the tired, slightly deflated-looking human being in front of her.

You place your suitcase on a conveyor belt where it passes through a metal detector and joins another conveyor belt, with all the other suitcases. The thought crosses your mind that it will take some other journey around the labyrinth of the airport before hopefully arriving at the same destination as you. It will enter the cold confines of the luggage hold, where it will be sandwiched between the suitcases of strangers. This leads to thoughts of what those suitcases might hold. Negligee bought especially for that second honeymoon, perhaps? Pornographic films. Sex toys and cigarettes. Concealed drugs. Or maybe there is just as much pleasure in imagining the mundane items: the plastic sandals and cheap jewellery; the duty free perfumes and fridge magnets with pictures of dolphins on them, bought as gifts.

The departure lounge is one of those places blighted by the same tension and anxiety that afflicts any transient space. Heads are craned back, gazing intently at the monitors announcing each imminent departure. Children run in circles around piles of hand luggage, far too alert and excited for the early hours of the morning. Men in suits, business travellers waiting for internal red-eye flights, drink coffee from recyclable paper cups with plastic spout lids while reading broadsheet newspapers.

Everybody tries not to think about terrorism.

A pre-recorded voice apologises for a delay. Another pre-recorded voice advises you not to leave your luggage unattended, adding the ominous warning that any unattended luggage may be destroyed. A flight is announced, and a group of people enter into a sudden migration toward a certain gate, dragging their children and hand luggage behind them.

They call your flight. The screen above you changes. You join the migration and walk toward your gate. A smiling boy with plucked eyebrows and splashes of blonde in his otherwise dark hair tears your ticket and you walk down the long telescopic tunnel that takes you to your plane. Twenty minutes later they are showing you how to put on an inflatable life-jacket, and you wonder what use the life-jacket will be on a flight that never once, in its journey from one end of the country to the other, passes over a significant body of water.

Five minutes after the demonstration you are pinned back in your cramped seat by the sudden thrust of acceleration, and you peer out through the tiny porthole to see the landscape surrounding the runway and the airport tip violently on its side before getting smaller and smaller.

From thirty thousand feet the earth becomes an abstraction. Towns containing tens and even hundreds of thousands of people are reduced to unremarkable grey puddles; the people and cars, the very traces of human life, too small to be visible. From thirty thousand feet cities become a little less like themselves, and a little more like their maps.

Eventually the world is drawn back into focus. There are cars, and there are people, and all at once there is another, seemingly identical runway.

Another tunnel.

Another airport terminal.

Another taxi.

And home.

ondine – 11:20

Ondine looks kind of strange, framed against our panoramic view of the Isle Of Dogs. If I squint just enough it looks like she's floating over the city, her head framed by clouds, her neck neatly bisecting the sharp u-turn of the grey Thames and the sprawling industrial estates of Millwall. Her hair dances on the artificial breeze from her desk fan, which is whirring away at full speed. The whole office buzzes with a chorus of identical fans, but most of the time it just feels like they're moving all the hot air around.

Ondine cradles her telephone between her head and her shoulder, rolling her eyes impatiently and chewing the end of a ballpoint pen.

"So they're not going to be there?" she says to the telephone. "So where *are* they going to be? We were told he was going to be at home with wifey and the kids. We *weren't* told he was going to jet off to his villa in the Algarve. No, Tony… I'm sure this has come as a surprise to you, too. The question is *why* has it come as a surprise to you? Yes, Tony, I *know* you're only human, but this is… this is schoolboy stuff, surely?"

She's talking about the Home Secretary, a married MP who's been shitting on rent boys. She's talking about the fact that her tipster, a shadowy figure by the name of 'Tony', told us that the MP in question would be spending time at the family home while he re-evaluates his career and his private matters. She's talking about the fact that she, and one of our photographers, were all set to drive up to the family home in Cumbria and join the small army of reporters and photographers who will be waiting at the gates.

"Well what about the rent boy? Do we know who he is? You do? And what do you think the chances are of... "

A pause. Another roll of the eyes.

"How much are they offering him?"

She shakes her head, putting her hand over the mouthpiece.

"The fucking *Mirror*," she says. "I can't believe it. Okay... okay... so Tony... were there any other rent boys? There *were*. And do you know any of them? No. Okay... well... what say you toodle on down to Soho and see if you can find out. What do you mean they don't hang out in Soho? Where *do* they hang out? On*line*? Well... I don't know... hang out online, then. Yes. Yes. Okay, Tony... less talky more findy. Goodbye, Tony. Goodbye."

She slams the phone down and physically *seethes*, the tendons and veins becoming pronounced on her thin, baby sparrow neck, her eyes bulging in their sockets.

"God," she snarls. "Is it really too much to ask that these people do their fucking jobs? We're sat here with our hands up our arse. The *Mirror* are giving that little he-slut seventy fucking thousand. Where's Brian?"

She's referring to Brian Fenton, our editor, and the man who will have the final say on whether or not we can better the *Mirror*'s offer of seventy thousand for this rent boy's story.

"Where the fuck is Brian?"

She stands, sending her chair rolling back toward the window, before pacing across the newsroom, breathing noisily in and out of her nose.

I return my attention to the monitor and my half-written account of Nicki Santos' homecoming, with accompanying images by our man with the strawberry birthmarks.

I should have written a template for this kind of thing a long time ago. Young newcomer to the world of celebrity has party, maybe drinks a little too much, but 'keeps it real' by still bothering with her old friends, the friends from before the time when everyone in the country knew her name. It's become a kind of modern fairy tale with its own subtle variations depending on who's telling the story, but ultimately it's the same story, time and time again.

I've got thirty minutes to finish this, but still I'm procrastinating by occasionally scanning the profiles on theboyshop.com, when nobody in the vicinity has a clear view of my screen.

hornysteve82

up4afuk

gagging4cock

Sultry eyes gaze out of home-made, semi-pornographic images but, behind their attempts at amorous desire, traces of something more melancholy are visible. Imagining the scenario in which they came to take the photograph; positioning the camera, setting the timer, tilting an angle poise lamp just so; only adds to the sense of fruitless longing.

Ondine reappears, this time accompanied by Brian.

Brian Fenton is almost forty, but seen in soft focus could pass for a teenager. There's something about his proportions, the scale of his head in relation to his body, and his slight frame, that suggests adolescence. Close up, of course, the illusion is shattered. He smiles almost constantly, to such an extent that the thought of him becoming suddenly, perhaps violently angry is quite terrifying. There is something perverse about his smile, exposing his perfectly symmetrical, teeth while forcing out his bottom lip like the spout of a jug.

In addition to the smile, Brian Fenton laughs far too much; a braying, near-hysterical laugh that carries across the newsroom. I am sure that the smile and the laugh have both been honed by years of shaking hands with people he finds neither interesting nor funny. It's an award-worthy performance, and a useful smoke-screen for his notorious boardroom reputation. The legend still persists that when one sub-editor created a legal stir for his last paper, *The Sunday Gazette*, he forced her to eat a whole box of frozen fish fingers in the boardroom in front of every other sub.

"Seventy thousand," says Ondine, shaking her head, and still breathing heavily.

"And is this the rent boy he actually shat on?" says Brian, puffing through the corners of his mouth; the effortless, somehow dismissive variation of his normal laugh.

"Yes… Tony seems to think so."

"You see… we don't want to shell out on a story if it's just going to be some lad he's picked up for a quick hand shandy, now, do we?"

"No… no, of course not."

"I want the boy he shat on. Nothing less," says Brian. "Tell Tony we can go up to eighty. No higher."

"Okay."

Brian holds his chin, nods, turns on his heels and moves at great speed to the other side of the newsroom.

"Yes!" says Ondine, slamming her hand down on her desk triumphantly. "We'll have that little fuck on page one."

Eighty thousand pounds. A jump of ten thousand in the time it takes most people to decide what kind of coffee they'd like. Ten thousand pounds generated from whichever bank account it is we use to pay these people. The former glamour models and 'high class escorts' and jilted lovers and washed up celebrities with stories of personal degradation to share. Ten thousand pounds that in any other walk of life might seem like a lot of money, but here seems like spare change.

Ondine picks up her phone and punches Tony's number into its battered keys. There is a long pause.

"Tony. Get me Mr Shit. We can go up to eighty," she says, grinning from ear to ear.

the voice of the people – 11:21

The Voice of the People began life in 1905. It was founded by the journalist, and one-time MP, Henry Boardman, whose intention was to
produce a newspaper that '(spoke) to men of all classes, encouraging
the pursuit of knowledge, truth, and liberty'. Between 1920 and 1939 it
was Britain's second most widely read newspaper. This changed with
the advent of World War II, when the paper's support for the Nazi regime
in Germany and its policy of appeasement throughout the late 1930s
saw many branding it a 'pro-Hitler paper'. Despite a change in editor, its
sales would not truly recover until it was bought by the newspaper
tycoon Lord Keynsham in 1969. Keynsham turned the paper into a
tabloid, and it was under then editor Roger Dunstan that the decision
was made, in 1972, to include a semi-naked woman on page 4. By
1979, following its support of the Conservative Leader Margaret
Thatcher in that year's election, *The Voice of the People* had become
the most widely read newspaper in Britain.

Since 2006 *The Voice of the People* has been a part of the K-Media
Group (which includes The New York Press, Big TV and Television One)
formed by Lord Keynsham's youngest son Sebastian Keynsham
(husband of the television producer Trisha Smedley). The current editor
is Brian Fenton (former editor of *The Sunday Gazette*).
In 2009 it was announced that *The Voice of the People* had become the
most widely read English language newspaper in the world, with daily
sales of more than three-and-a-half million, and an estimated readership
of more than ten million, meaning that on average, one in six Britons
reads *The Voice of the People* every day.

(taken from www.megapedia.com)

the gym – 12:08

I hate it when Brian Fenton is in the gym at the same time as me. I've always liked being left alone in the gym, it's not one of those moments I like to share. Maybe it's knowing the kind of facial expressions I'll pull or the kind of noises I'll make. Maybe there's something a little too sexual about it for comfort. Whatever my problem is, I really hate it when Brian Fenton is there at the same time as me.

I'm on the running machine when he appears by my side carrying a plastic bottle full of water and a Dolce And Gabbana hand towel.

"Good work up in Edinburgh," he says, mopping some of the sweat he built up on the cross-trainer from his brow. "I know what you're thinking… why the hell did they send me up there in the first place? It's all about presence, Ed. You know this. Trisha Smedley's very keen for us to maximise our role as the official *Lockdown* newspaper. Never mind *The Sun*. We'll be getting the exclusives, and that means your face being at all the parties, wherever they are."

Brian Fenton could easily afford the membership at any one of the gyms in Docklands, and indeed probably has a gym at his home in Kent, but he chooses, more often than not, to use the one on the thirtieth floor of our building. It keeps him close to the newsroom and in amongst his workers. I think he secretly judges us on our stamina and our strength.

"I can see you playing a very important role in the future of K-Media," he says as the rhythm of his running machine increases from a heavy plodding to a low, throbbing whirr. "Trisha Smedley's taken a shine to you. And if she's taken a shine to you then Seb will be doing likewise. Like peas in a pod that pair. Peas in a pod."

He pauses only momentarily. I find myself hoping he is out of breath and unable to continue. Each time he has spoken I have been physically unable to answer him. I can only hope he is now in a similar state.

"Did I ever tell you my theory about the Ultimate Headline?" he asks, dashing my hopes.

I shake my head and manage to say half of the word 'no'.

"I suppose it's the aim of every editor, if they're honest with themselves. It's that front page, that headline, that defines an epoch. The one they'll be talking about for decades to come. They don't come along very often, Ed, and they don't happen to every newspaper, but when they do they're sealed in concrete. Preserved for eternity."

Another brief pause. He swigs from the bottle and mops his brow.

"The trouble is we just don't have the stories any more," he says, dolefully. "Everything's a remake these days. Wars like the wars we had last year. Murders like every other murder. Some hookers get stabbed, we call the killer 'The Ripper' because we don't know what else to say. Where's the new story, Ed? Isn't that where the word 'news' came from in the first place? We need something *new*. I don't know when it'll be, Ed, but I can just imagine the headline!"

I step off the running machine, sweating and unable to breathe properly, and Brian simply nods in a way that is almost self-congratulatory, as if he feels he's won something. When I've drunk almost half a litre of water in a matter of seconds and I can breathe again, I take to the free weights, while surreptitiously watching some of the others in the gym, or their reflections in the mirrors.

What interests me about the gym, other than my personal goals of fitness, vanity, and a concern for my own health, is the way in which it transforms people.

The short guy with the thick glasses and charcoal-coloured hair who works for the legal department and always smells of Joop enters the changing rooms a buttoned-down-collared office worker and leaves it a strutting centaur in a grey vest. His eyes scan the equipment and the other members, sizing each one up in turn. His entire body flexes; veins jumping out of his arms and his shoulders, as he warms up with fifteen kilo dumb-bells.

In another corner the young lad from marketing who usually looks so unassuming in his ill-fitting suit and over-polished shoes slams his gloved fists repeatedly into a punch bag, sending it reeling back against the wall. His expression is one of almost unimaginable violence, the lips drawn back to reveal both rows of teeth, his eyes glowing and fierce beneath a heavily furrowed brow. He grunts each time he punches the bag, as if genuinely caught up in an act of retribution.

In another hour these people will be back at their desks, peering into the glow of their monitors, their bodies composed, but still tingling with the echo of violence.

the deli bar – 12:43

I could always leave the building to find lunch, but I don't. That would mean taking the elevator down to the ground floor, leaving the building, and then dragging my heels around Canary Wharf until I find the sandwich bar, delicatessen, or snack booth that fits the bill. Sometimes too much choice can cancel out the act of choosing, like when you go into some four-storey book shop and come out with nothing. It's much easier to go to the deli bar.

Today the deli bar is manned by the squat, funny-looking guy who bears more than a passing resemblance to the film actor Peter Lorre. He always looks at me like he's scared, but that's okay because I think that's the look he gives everyone; like he's perpetually startled by the world.

I ask for a pastrami and wholegrain mustard sandwich on rye bread.

"We haven't got any pastrami," he says.

"You don't have any pastrami?" I ask. It's a fatuous question, but I'm pumped up with endorphins and feeling confident.

"People just weren't buying it," he says dismissively.

"I was buying it."

"Every day?"

"Nobody eats pastrami every day," I reply.

"Exactly."

I tell him I'll settle for garden-variety ham and wholegrain mustard on rye. He tells me they don't have any rye bread.

"Because people just weren't buying it?"

"Exactly," he says. "We've got white bread."

"Okay, I'll settle for white bread."

"Nothing wrong with white bread." The voice comes from my right and, when I turn, I see Bruce Albion and I smell whisky.

Bruce Albion is our number one columnist, appearing every Thursday. We headhunted him from *The Herald* three years ago, instantly making him the best paid columnist in Britain. He's one of those people you like to think is nothing like the character in his column. You read what he has to say, and you think it's all an act, like the bad guys in the wrestling. You look at his photograph, all sneer of cold command and bulbous, thyroid eyes, and you think he can't possibly be like that in real life, but he is. If Bruce Albion didn't have his column, if he'd never become a journalist, he'd still be sharing his opinions with anyone who cared to listen.

"I grew up on white bread," he says. "Never did me any harm. All this bollocks about carbo-frigging-hydrates. Load of bloody nonsense. D'you think Churchill gave a fuck about carbohydrates?"

I'm trying to work out quite what Winston Churchill's personal tastes in bread have to do with anything when the Peter Lorre look-alike behind the deli bar hands me my sandwich, wrapped in white paper. I pay for it, and am about to walk away when Bruce Albion holds my arm.

"It's all this brown bread that's making people soft, you know." He says. "In the head. It's what's making people weak. Like all that poncy shite you write about. Nobody gave a fuck about any of that before brown bread. And people call it brown bread because it sounds so politically correct and wholesome. You know what I call it?"

I shake my head, feeling anxious and uncomfortable in my own skin. He's still holding my arm.

"Coloured bread," he says. "I call it coloured bread."

leicester square – 19:58

To either side of the red carpet there are banks of photographers, and before them the screaming crowds of onlookers. The flashes explode several times each second, creating a rippling sea of light that passes over those making their way toward the cinema. We, that is the guests, file in first. I spot our man in the crowd, nod briefly, smiling at a few other cameras even though I know it won't be my picture they show in tomorrow's papers.

There's something horrible about attending a film premier on your own.

The garden in the centre of Leicester Square has been decorated in preparation for tonight's premier for almost three days. Life-sized waxwork figures of Marilyn Monroe stand beside trees in poses familiar from her films. It's a wonder that none of them has been vandalised. I wonder if this is because there is something sacred about her image; something that places her beyond deface-ment, as if such an act would be sacrilege.

The curious thing about tonight's performance is that the star herself will not be present, having been dead since August 5,

1962. Norma Jean Baker, known to the rest of us as Marilyn Monroe, will be portraying herself in the film, *Something's Got To Give*.

"The film is an account of her life, from her unhappy childhood in Los Angeles orphanages and foster homes, through to her rebirth as the most famous woman on the planet. It has taken a team of computer animators and sound artists over three years to create a digital Marilyn based on thousands of hours of footage and audio recordings."

That's from the press release. Of course, the main draw of this film is that we finally get to see her die. To an audience already as accustomed to Warhol's screen paintings as it is to the cross, the swastika, or the McDonald's 'M', this is the real deal. The money shot.

My presence here feels almost unnecessary. I've been to these things before, and usually I watch the film, and then turn up at the party. Sometimes, if I'm lucky, I'll have my photograph taken with the stars of the film so that I can be seen socialising with the A-List. Tonight there is no chance of me being photographed with the star. The star will not be arriving by limousine, by helicopter, or in a flourish of pyrotechnics. The star is still quite dead, buried at Corridor Of Memories #24, Westwood Memorial Park, Los Angeles.

This hasn't stopped a rival of ours from using a TV clairvoyant to conduct a series of interviews with Monroe, in which she has so far revealed that she is a 'big fan of Madonna', remains 'friends with Sinatra and the Kennedys', and would have 'liked to have made a film with George Clooney'.

There are other actors appearing in this film, of course, but none of them are as famous as Marilyn. They will talk, in their publicity interviews, about how difficult it was acting with the stand-in (a professional Marilyn Monroe look-alike) who would be on set each day, knowing that in the finished film they would be up on screen with the 'real thing'.

After the film I am driven to the party at a club in Farringdon where I rendezvous at the bar with our photographer, whose name is Carl. Carl is young and beautiful. His saturnine features would be feminine if they weren't framed by a square, lightly stubbled jaw. He wears a t-shirt that fails to cover his lean brown stomach and jeans that almost reveal the northernmost suburbs of his pubic hair. I feel a slight wave of resentment when he talks to me as though I am old enough to be his father. I'm only five years older than him.

We are among the first to arrive; the real stars of the show, apart from Ms Monroe, are most likely still outside the cinema. I ask Carl whether he enjoyed the film and he shrugs.

"Once you've seen one film you've seen them all," he says. "And who gives a shit about Marilyn Monroe, anyway? I didn't even know who she was until Steph told me."

I almost choke on my drink and tell him that surely Marilyn Monroe is one of the greatest cinematic icons of all time.

"So how many of her films have you seen?" he asks me.

I pause, and realise that I have only ever seen *Some Like It Hot*, and maybe a few scenes from *Niagara*.

"Exactly," says Carl. "It's the twenty-first century. We've got new icons."

"Such as?" I ask.

"Ted Bundy... Hitler..."

I am about to tell him that both Ted Bundy and Adolf Hitler died in the twentieth century when the doors open, and perhaps thirty or forty Marilyn Monroe look-alikes enter the room.

"Now I've seen everything," says Carl. "I mean... *really*. What the fuck is *that* all about? Could she *be* any more dead?"

By the end of the evening I will have been photographed standing in the middle of a crowd of eighteen Marilyn Monroe look-alikes, smiling for the camera as if all of my dreams have come true. In reality the heightened drama, the music, the light slush of alcohol in my bloodstream, and the visual quality of these Xeroxed film stars is more akin to the kind of nightmare you have when suffering a fever.

"I'm going now..." I hear Carl say through the growing haze of too many complimentary mojitos. "This place is full of dead people."

Minutes after Carl has left I spot the pop star Rob Rascal leaning against the bar, resting his upper lip on an oversized glass of red wine. I curse the fact that Carl has gone, realising there was a photo opportunity to be had here, but at least I might be able to get a little side piece out of it.

ROB RAT-ARSED.

WHERE ARE THEY NOW? No 1: ROB RASCAL.

I'll think of something.

Rascal, real name the more ordinary Robert Phillips, was the lead singer with early 80s electro band Belsen Beat. They had a few top twenty hits and maybe a number one, though the only song that seems to get shown on any number of vintage music channels these days is their song 'Digital World'.

In the video to 'Digital World', Rob Rascal looked like he was not so much born as created in some factory of the distant future. His face was artfully airbrushed blue and silver, his hair sculpted to perfection, his body clad in a silver body stocking. All very dated now, of course, but in 1981 he looked like the future. He looked as if he never needed to eat, sleep, or indulge in any bodily functions. If he ate, one could only imagine it was with gold cutlery, or that it was astronaut food, served to him by androgynous flunkies in modernist glass houses with views of vast, twinkling cityscapes.

If anything killed the career of Rob Rascal it was reality. By the mid-1980s people did not want pop stars who literally looked out-of-this-world. They did not want androgyny, or ambiguous sexuality. They did not want the alien, or the bizarre. They wanted aspirational figures to represent their own desires; pop stars who looked like well-groomed investment bankers and millionaire playboys.

In addition to this change in tastes, Rob Rascal's life soon became too real for him to handle. Addictions to alcohol, cocaine and heroin saw the façade of futuristic glamour slip. Anecdotes began to circulate about him soiling himself on transatlantic flights and vomiting backstage at awards ceremonies. Rob Rascal was suddenly a human in clown's make-up; funny and tragic, an object of ridicule or pity, but no longer beautiful.

A quarter of a century after he was last a household name, Rob Rascal strikes a bitterly comical figure. His attempts at remaining youthful have been seriously undermined by his addictions; so much heavy make-up and badly coloured hair. I wonder how he came to be invited to this party, though I imagine it is only through these events that he has managed to maintain anything of his former life.

I approach him cautiously, and say his name softly.

"Who're you?" he slurs, peering at me with one eye open.

I tell him my name and he grimaces.

"The fella who writes After Show in *The Voice of the People*?" he asks, putting his glass down on the bar, but almost missing it, spilling some of his wine on the floor. "You here to do a story… "

he says, "about the fucking pop star, or what?"

"No, I'm here for the film," I say, though of course the reason I am talking to him now is because yes, he was famous once, and yes, he is drunk.

"Fucking film... " he says, trying to nod sagely. "Fucking film... yeah... what was it called? Fucking *Some Like It*... no... hang on... fuck it." He stands away from the bar, swaying on his feet, and steps toward me.

"Listen, mate... " he says, in conspiratorial, hushed tones, "I don't mean to be cheeky, but have you got a few quid you could lend me?"

The question shocks me to such a degree that at first I wonder if I've heard him correctly.

"Just a few quid... thirty or forty quid... only it's my niece's birthday... and I want to take her to see Kylie... you know... in concert... and the tickets... they're, like... twenty quid each. You couldn't lend us thirty or forty quid...?"

I lie, telling him I don't have any cash on me.

"I'll pay you back... " he says. "In the morning... I just need to buy the tickets tonight, like... and I've left my wallet in my flat... "

I shake my head, feeling a sudden wave of melancholy, before turning and walking away.

I am taken home in a hire car. Travelling across London in a car is a very different experience to using its public transport. On the tube, or the DLR, you are a part of the city, a tiny cog or spring in its clockwork heart. Even when passing landmarks that are familiar from postcards or television images, you find them transformed by the reality of the rush of traffic or the chattering voices, the desperate yelling of drunks or the apocalyptic rumbling of descending aeroplanes. In a car you are hermetically sealed off from the grim brushstrokes that transform London from a theme-park of iconic buildings into a living, breathing city. You peer out of the window, kept cool in the sultry night by the air-con, the angry snarls of the city drowned out by sweeping strings or gentler horns from the car's music system, and watch the streets drift by like the images in a vast zoetrope.

Canary Wharf has the quality of outlandish science fiction when seen from Aspen Way. On one side the slick auto-piloted carriages of the DLR glide along elevated tracks, while on the other the light on top of the obelisk of One Canada Square blinks through wraiths of steam escaping its ventilation shafts. To the south, these buildings appear to dance around one another, as if floating in a vast sea. To the north, in the ruins of the Lea Valley, stand cranes; gargantuan sentinels above the floodlit foundations of the Olympic Village.

Velocity House welcomes me with motion-triggered illumination. It feels almost like an embrace. Even though I left the balcony door slightly ajar when I left, the apartment is still warm. One of the thin white curtains dances on a light breeze, but even the breeze is hot.

It occurs to me that leaving the door unlocked and open was a foolish thing to do, but then I remind myself that I am ten storeys above the dock, with so many balconies and obstacles to stand in any potential intruder's way. This building isn't a domicile, it's a fortress.

And yet, when I look down at my laminated wood-effect floor it's an intruder that I see: crawling slowly from one side of the room to the other, a woodlouse, or pill bug. What kind of journey could have brought a creature like that this far?

Even though I'm still reeling from the mojitos I'll try to get a thousand words written and emailed in the next hour. I'm fuelled now. Fuelled by the booze, fuelled by the night. I'll write about the premier but I'll also write about Rob Rascal. I'll tell the world how he drunkenly asked to borrow money from 'one guest' so that he could buy tickets to see Kylie. I'll make some sly joke about how I've never heard the euphemism 'seeing Kylie' before. But first I'll just watch a little TV.

I lift the remote control from my coffee table and hit the standby button. The screen flickers into life and I automatically find the Television One news channel. A late-night presenter is looking at tomorrow's headlines.

The Independent... 'How many roads must a man walk down?'... *The Times*... 'Immigration not a Race Issue warns Bennett'... In the redtops, the *Mirror*, 'Beaten to death'... that's the story, of course, about the ninety-three-year-old woman who was beaten to death... *The Sun*... 'Insanity: Asylum Seeker given Ferrari', and *The Voice of the People*... 'Utter Filth: Confessions of a Rent Boy', regarding the accusation that Home Secretary Phillip Mackenzie had relationships with male prostitutes. More about that story later, of course, but first we go to Katie and the weather. Katie... even more hot weather to come, is that right?

Yes Tom... as you can see we have two fronts here over the south of England This very high pressure which has been making its way north over the last few days, bringing all the nice weather we've been having, and this band of very low pressure coming down from over Ireland and Wales. This means we can expect quite a few thunderstorms and some heavy rain in the south-west over the next day or two, so you'd better take that brolly out with you! But it's still going to be very, very hot, even after the rain. Meanwhile, in the south-east the good weather will continue over the weekend, and throughout next week, with temperatures reaching the mid-thirties by Friday.

On the floor the woodlouse has somehow ended up on its back, kicking its fourteen spindly legs in a vain attempt to turn itself over. I think of Kafka, and remember my father once telling me that woodlice are nocturnal crustaceans, and breathe through gills, hence their attraction to darkness and moisture. With no moisture in the vicinity the woodlouse will die if it remains on its back. I stare at its frantic movements, the drone of Katie's voice still telling me about heavy rain in the north-east and Scotland until, eventually, it dies.

I decide to forget about Rob Rascal.

the goldfish bowl – 11:00

Morning conference takes place in the Goldfish Bowl; a glass box, two storeys high, situated in the centre of the newsroom. It's like an oven today, or maybe a blast-furnace. My colleagues sit around the table, fanning themselves with sheets of paper and folded newspapers. In each corner of the room is an over-sized monitor on which the two main news channels, Television 1 and NOTM24, and the two main sports channels, T1 Sport and NOTMS, play silently. While we sit around the edge of the colossal round table decorated liberally with this morning's papers, Brian paces the perimeter, thinking out loud.

"Tristan... what's happening online?"

"Good stuff on the Mackenzie story," says Tristan, a gaunt kid of twenty-five with a voice like the talking clock. "People love filth. They love talking about filth. It *is* starting to get a little bit homophobic on some of our discussion forums… "

"So?"

"Well, exactly. But basically they're lapping it up. First decent sex scandal in a while, I guess."

"Great. Then we go with more of the same tomorrow. That's you Ondine… anything you didn't put in last time, in it goes. Within reason, of course… we are a family newspaper." He turns back to Tristan. "And the Arsenal lad?"

"Lots of speculation. Lots of people think they know who it is. Some of them are *saying* who they think it is, so we're kind of snowed under taking out anything that's legally… well, you know… "

"Great. Nihad… I want more on this. We need to start putting a bit of pressure on the abortion clinic… fuck the Data Protection Act… manila envelopes under the desk… somebody somewhere is going to snap. Now what's this drug everyone's talking about? Synth or something? Should we be doing a piece on that?"

"It's not our readership," says Tristan. "It's your whole Kings Cross club set. Hasn't hit the suburbs."

"Okay. Well in that case we'll wait til some teenager dies. Ed… good stuff on *Lockdown* as usual. I've read the piece on the Marilyn Monroe premier… it's good, but next time don't get too pissed at the party. There were no fewer than thirteen typos, and we could only find one picture of you which didn't have at least one eye closed. "Sport… sport… Tristan?"

"Liverpool, this week. Rogers, Lombardi or Basilevsky."

"Basilevsky's never gonna manage Liverpool, so I think we can rule him out. Carl… talk to Rogers' people… talk to Lombardi's people… find out what the fuck's going on. Now did somebody say something about an earthquake?"

"Yeah, it was just on Reuters," says Mike. "Something in Pakistan."

"Mmm… Pakistan," says Brian, grimacing. "Are we talking hundreds or thousands?"

"No numbers yet, Brian."

"If it's hundreds page seven it… if it's thousands page five, unless there're any Brits involved, and then we'll play it by ear. And see if we know anyone over there. Sophie… I'll give you that one… check Reuters, but I don't want it clogging up a whole page. Not unless there are dead Brits. Oh yeah… Ed… it's the Jupiter Music Prize next week. Who's favourite to win?"

"Qelli Mai," I reply. "Or maybe Carnal Spanner."

"Okay. Qelli Mai's got more… you know… "

"Tits?" says Ondine.

"Pizzazz," says Brian. "See what we can get… even if it's just her with friends sipping mochas in Soho… also… there's a new series of *Celebrity Autopsy* starting in October… do we know who's on?"

"Someone said Carol Vorderman's signed up," says Mike.

"Yeah, and I heard that Gary Barlow was a shoe-in," says Nihad.

"Well less discussion here and more finding out… Ed, you're in charge of that, but if we can all keep our ears to the ground… I think that's us done for now. Today is going to be our day, people… "

And with that he's gone. The door closes behind him and a murmuring starts up amongst my colleagues.

"It's a fucking abortion clinic… " says Nihad. "They're, like, the Fort Knox of information or something. They don't give anything away. And she's thirteen. They're so not going to give out her name."

"Time to ring Tony… " says Ondine.

"It's going to be Lombardi," says Carl.

"Thirteen typos, eh, Ed?" says Nihad, playfully punching my shoulder. They file out of the room, their chatter growing louder. The glass door shuts with a hollow clank, and they are rendered silent, their mouths opening and closing but making no sound.

I am alone for no more than a minute when the door opens once more, and Shardul, the cleaner, walks in, carrying a vacuum cleaner.

"Oh… very sorry… " he says.

I tell him it's fine and that he can carry on cleaning.

Shardul is of an indeterminate age, anywhere between thirty-five and sixty. His hair is neither brown nor grey, but a strange shade of bronze. His face is always impassive, with recessive cheeks, and eyes that are obscured behind tinted lenses. He wears a large, gypsy-like earring in his left ear and a gold chain on which hangs a pendant in the shape of a tiger's head.

"Very hot day," he says, pointing out beyond the office to the glaring sunshine of the world outside. I nod and murmur in agreement. "Twenty-nine degrees in the shade," he says, shaking his head. "Very hot day."

"Do you read newspapers, Shardul?" I ask. He looks up from where he is plugging in the vacuum cleaner and frowns. When he frowns his heavy, brown/grey/bronze eyebrows bunch together.

"I'm sorry?" he says.

"Newspapers... do you read them?"

He laughs, a dry smoker's laugh. "No no no... " he says. "No. They are all full of the same old same old. Once you've read one you've read them all."

phone call #1 – 14:22

"Ed! How are you?" She doesn't wait for me to reply. "Great. Listen... it's kind of looking like Colin is going to win."

I'm being C-Fished by Trisha Smedley from Big TV, the producer of *Lockdown* and wife of Sebastian Keynsham, and my heart is suddenly in my mouth.

"Really?" I ask her. "I mean... *really*?"

"Yes... the audience loves him. I just wanted to make sure that... you know... the hatches are battoned down as it were. Regarding... you know... "

"Yes. Yes, of course they are."

"Good. Good. Because I don't think we've got any leaks at this end. I think we should be able to coast through about a month of aftermath before anything gets out, and by then his contract will have ended, and we'll be starting the promos for series four."

"But... can't you *fix* it? I mean... the phone votes...?"

"No can do, Ed. No can do. Not after last year. You let one Downs Syndrome girl win and everyone cries 'fix'. No... this year it's all being done *in-de-pend-ent-ly*. We think seven million people are going to vote for Colin Curtis, which means he is going to win, and the next day his face is going to be plastered all over every newspaper from one end of the country to the other, and there is nothing we can do about it. Except keep schtum, of course. I can trust you to do that, can't I Ed? To keep schtum?"

"Of course you can."

"Thank you, Ed. You've always been my favourite. You know that, don't you? Forget that cunt on *The Sun*. She's a booze-drenched harridan in cheap mascara. But you... you're a *friend*."

phone call #2 – 18:04

"Your father and I are converting to Islam," says my mother, as calmly as if she were telling me they were thinking of buying a holiday home in Bulgaria. I don't respond, something which I am sure annoys her, because her tone becomes more stern.

"Well, I'm sure that doesn't fit in with what you or your newspaper have to say about the tenets of the world's fastest-growing religion… "

Rising to the bait I ask her why they are converting to Islam.

"Out of sympathy for Muslims around the world. They've had a very tough time of it lately."

"But you're atheists."

"I hardly think that's got anything to do with it. There's a Muslim group that meets in Exeter once a fortnight. We've started taking Arabic lessons. Reading the Qur'an in English just isn't the same. It's merely an *interpretation* of the Qur'an. Your father is hoping to be a Hafiz by Christmas."

"What's a Hafiz?"

"Somebody who has memorised the Qur'an, in Arabic, in its entirety."

"But why?"

"Because it's *important*. Really, Edgar, I would have hoped for a little support, but I suppose we shouldn't expect any better. That newspaper of yours was going on about immigrants again the other day. It was all rather ugly."

"Mum… "

"Ed… really. You're a man in your thirties. Don't you think 'Mum' is a little childish? You *can* call me Catherine, you know. Although we are thinking about changing our names."

"To what?"

"Well your father was thinking Yusuf, you know, like Cat Stevens, and I was thinking Kameela. It means 'most perfect'. Would you like to speak to your father?"

Before I have had a chance to answer her I hear my father's voice.

"I know what you're going to say, Edgar, but your mother and I are adamant. Only if there are a significant number of white, British Muslims in this country will the government take notice of our plight."

"Whose plight?"

"The Muslims, Edgar. I really don't think you're listening to a word we say sometimes."

"But we aren't Muslims."

"No… you might not be, but we are. And we're not going to take their bullshit any more."

"Whose bullshit?"

"The government, Edgar. The government. Of course this has made things a little awkward down the club. Your mother pointed out that there weren't any Halal options at the Summer Barbecue last Sunday and Cynthia Brandon was devastated."

"Does Lola know about this?"

"Yes."

"And what does she think about it?"

"Well… I don't think she's really bothered either way. She's been acting very strange lately. You can hardly get a word out of her. Have you spoken to her?"

"Not in a while, no."

"Well you should. It's her birthday soon. Don't forget."

"I won't… "

"Okay, son… well… we've got to go now. We're going to the Al-Sharaf's for dinner. Lovely couple. From Syria. Did you want to say goodbye to your mother?"

"Um… no… no. That's fine."

"Ma'a salaama."

"What?"

"Ma'a salaama. It means goodbye."

"Goodbye Dad."

west india quay – 20:56

"So who do you think would win?"

"Stalin, probably."

"Nah… not Stalin… "

"Hitler?"

"Fuck Hitler… he was a little fella, had loads of storm troopers to do his dirty work for him. No… not Hitler… Hitler was a fucking ponce."

"Well, Stalin then. He was a big fella."

"No he wasn't. They just always photographed him to make him look taller. He was five foot four. A fucking midget."

"So who do *you* reckon would win?"

"Idi Amin."

"Idi Amin? Who's he?"

"You don't know who Idi Amin was? He was the president of Uganda in the seventies. He was a former heavyweight boxing champion, for fuck's sake. On top of that, he ate people."

"He did *what*?"

"I said he ate people. Straight up. If I'm gonna put my money on any dictator in a fist fight, it's got to be Amin. He'd kick the shit out of you, and then *eat* you."

"What about Mao?"

"Nah. Mao's a pussy. Used to get soldiers to wank him off to help him get to sleep. Nah... Idi Amin any day of the week and twice on weekends. See... they don't make them like that any more. It's a shame... "

"Shhh... shhh... shhh... it's on. It's on."

All eyes gaze up toward the HD television on the other side of the crowded bar as the opening credits of *Lockdown* begin.

We've come here for two reasons. One is to watch this week's "parole", the other to celebrate Ondine's story being the talk of the country since the paper hit the shops. Early indications are that we've hit our biggest sales spike in two years.

Ondine is slumped in her chair, her lips tinted overdose blue by the cocktails she's been drinking since four o'clock this afternoon. She hasn't spoken in over an hour.

"Ondine... *Lockdown* is on," says Mark, nudging her gently. She stirs slightly, looking up at the screen and nodding without properly paying attention.

"We need to get her some coke," says Nihad, reiterating a point that has been made three or four times in the last half hour alone. "Or maybe some of that symph. I haven't tried it yet. Has anyone tried it yet?"

"Fuck no," says Mike. "My mate tried it at some warehouse party up in Hackney. He said he saw himself die. Fucked him right up, it did."

"Yeah... " says Kirsty. "It all looks a bit scary. Some guy in Manchester jumped in front of a train, and... I don't know... that kind of thing just freaks me out."

"Okay, then, pussies," says Nihad, "Who can we get coke from?

Does anyone deliver?"

"Jason delivers."

"Not Jason."

"Why not Jason?"

"Because... I don't know... he's just a bit too real for my liking. A bit too East End. We're past that whole gritty realism thing, aren't we?"

"So who?"

"Marcus?"

"Marcus has retired."

"Marcus? Retired?"

"Yes. Since that whole thing where his nose fell out and he had to get it done. Doesn't even drink any more."

"You're fucking kidding."

"Ed... do you know anyone?"

Attention turns to me once more and I shrug. What the hell am I doing here?

"Oh come on, you *must* know someone. There must be a dealer in your building. It's Scally City in there. It's like a fucking Triga movie. All the Essex wideboys moving to the city. There must be *someone*."

I tell them there isn't. I should just leave. Or maybe if I sit here and say nothing they'll forget I'm here.

"Well what about Richard?"

"Oh yes. Richard. Richard will deliver. He's always about on a Friday."

"Okay... I'll C-Fish Richard."

"It's okay, Ondine. Nihad's going to C-Fish Richard."

Ondine looks up again and nods as a reflex action to the sound of her name.

On the television screen a crowd has amassed outside the disused HMP Crowmarsh on the outskirts of London. The grey stone walls of the Victorian edifice are lit up by projected images of the *Lockdown* logo; the letters L and D embossed on black and white prison bars. The crowd stands either side of the runway leading from the prison gates to the temporary studio where tonight's parolee will be interviewed. They carry banners showing their support or disapproval of each 'inmate'; some pledge their undying love, others their burning hatred. Taken out of context, their near-hysterical screaming is not unlike the sound I imagine the witnesses to a mass terror attack or presidential assassination would make.

Nihad takes the bright green C-Fish from his jacket pocket and starts tapping at the keys.

"How many do we want, people?"

"Four?"

"Five?"

"Do we need as many as five?"

"Five?"

"Four?"

"I say five."

"Five?"

"We'll get five."

He taps the keys again and hits send. Within thirty seconds there's a synthesised whoosh sound followed by a fanfare.

"Great. He's only round the corner in Bar Basra. He'll be here in ten."

With our eyes still on the television we reach into our wallets and start throwing money down onto the table. Nihad gathers the notes, counts them, and pockets them.

"It's okay, Ondine… Richard's going to be here soon."

As if Richard were an emergency service, which, to all intents and purposes, I suppose he is. Like a St Bernard with a barrel of brandy around his neck. I guess that's the way we do it these days. You get yourself incapacitated by one drug, you take another to balance things out. Forever stacking up chemicals on either end of the pharmaceutical see-saw.

On *Lockdown* the build up is almost unbearable. Who is going to be paroled? Ronny? Jessica? Calum? Colin?

When Richard arrives it is thankfully during a commercial break, so he doesn't interrupt any of the programme. Richard used to work at *The Voice of the People*, as a junior reporter, until he discovered that the side-business he had in providing his friends and colleagues with cocaine was infinitely more lucrative. He's a local boy, born and bred in Plaistow, who always seemed like he belonged more in the old East London than the new; as if he were somehow marooned in the desert island of a newspaper office, and that he truly belonged on the streets, hawking fake Rolexes and Louis Vuitton handbags. When he enters a room it is as a sudden burst of energy; something elemental and unpredictable. He ruffles Mark's hair and kisses Kirsty on the lips. He points at Ondine and starts laughing.

"Look at Ondine. She's fucking mullered."

Scanning the bar quickly to ensure that no-one outside our group is paying attention, he reaches into his jacket and produces a small manila envelope, which he places on the table beneath one of our plates.

"Five, yeah?"

We all nod, like infants. Nihad hands him the money.

"It's good stuff, too. Mate of mine knows a pharmacist. It's practically pure. Fucking rocket fuel, I'm telling you. Anyways… must fly… people to go, places to meet."

He exits as briskly as he entered, seeming to leave a vacuum.

"Fantastic," says Nihad, retrieving the envelope from under the plate. "Come on, Ondine. Time for your medicine. Kirsty… Take Ondine for a line, will you, and sort out the grams?"

Ten minutes later Kirsty and Ondine return to the table. Ondine is doing a little dance in time with the music to a car advert in the third commercial break. When she reaches the table she wraps one arm around my head and croons, "Ed Ed Ed… I love you… "

"Somebody's back in the land of the living," says Nihad. "Come on, Ed. Ready for half time refreshments?"

I frown.

"I'm not on about fucking oranges," he adds, before putting one fingertip against his nose and sniffing twice. "VC spotted in the woods, twelve o'clock. Come on."

I'm not convinced the code is necessary. The Owl And The Pussycat is populated, almost exclusively, by people far too absorbed in their own worlds to be listening in on ours. It is one of those curious places where people go in the hope that somebody, anybody, will look at them. We sit in these places, wanting some degree of privacy, in our sectioned-off booths and private rooms, but what we really want is to be noticed. Bars and clubs are theatres for the soul, the venue for an endless talent show without any real judges. As your gaze passes across the room each new act comes to the fore and is praised or dismissed in turn. The slightly nervous-looking kid with the pronounced Adam's apple and cluster of angry spots on his chin, possibly too young to be drinking. He looks like he would smell of too much aftershave and thank you if you fucked him. The wide-boy in a Ben Sherman shirt narrowing his eyes and scowling at his audience as he picks at his teeth with the nail of his little finger. The only woman at a table of six who isn't laughing at the joke that one of them is telling. The older man near the vaguely incongruous fruit machine, one hand in his pocket, clutching a pint of beer to his chest.

Though I observe him for only a second or two I know he's not waiting for anyone; he's alone. Perhaps he came to this pub in the days before the skyscrapers and the apartment buildings. Maybe he was a regular when the pub was filled with the smell of stale tobacco and a carpet steeped in beer, when the soundtrack was one of tinny rock music blaring from a dilapidated juke box in the corner. I imagine that he came here all the while when it was transformed into a wine bar, at the turn of the 1990s and started serving overpriced cocktails to a soundtrack of acid jazz. He stood his ground through all the incarnations that would follow; the brief time in which it became a minimalist experiment in conceptual design, basing itself on the interior of an airport departure lounge, or perhaps an operating theatre; the Cold War-themed vodka bar with portraits of Lenin on every wall; the critically acclaimed 'gastro-pub' venture of a celebrity chef that went bankrupt after eight months despite the praise that was heaped upon it. Through all those years he remained a constant, as resolute as the footprints on the Moon, until finally The Owl And The Pussycat was transformed back into a traditional British pub, albeit one with HD televisions and a semi-respectable wine list.

Nihad and I leave the table and head into the gents toilets. The cubicle is barely large enough for one person, let alone two, and it's a heat trap. Nihad and I are practically pressed together in a way that borders on being erotic. I find myself staring at the sweat on his top lip, which he licks away as he produces the bag of coke from his pocket. He quickly sets about dipping in one of his keys and lifting out a small mound of the white powder.

"There you are... " he says, putting the end of the key under my nose. "Get that down your neck."

I sniff and feel a chemical jolt hit the back of my throat. Nihad dips the key back into the bag and takes a hit, and for a moment he holds my gaze, grinning mischievously, almost flirtatiously. I can feel the heat off his body. He licks his lips once more, mops his brow with the back of his hand, and then opens the cubicle door.

Cocaine is, for the brief time when its effects can be felt, a kind of fine-tuning for the senses. We return to the table wired, alert. When I breathe in it feels like I am taking in every last bit of oxygen in the room. If I hold my breath I half expect the others in the room to drop to the floor, killed by a sudden, violent asphyxia.

"We had to say 'an act too disgusting to be described in a family newspaper'... "

Ondine is back on top form. Her eyes are like sapphires.

"So what *was* the act?"

"Oh, Mike, for fuck's sake... don't you know *anything*?"

"I've been busy this week. I haven't got time to keep up to speed on everything."

"It was shit."

"What was shit? The story? But the story was *great*... "

"No, not the story. Well, yes the story, but not that the story was *shit*... just that the act involved shit."

"Shit?"

"Yes. And double fisting."

"Christ. Double?"

"Yeah."

"Make mine a double ha ha ha ha ha ha ha ha ha ha ha ha..."

"That's just... surely that's impossible."

"Yeah, I mean... yeah..."

"Which way round was it?"

"Was what?"

"The double fisting? Was he double fisting the rent boy or was the rent boy double fisting him?"

"The rent boy was double fisting him."

"Jesus... how much does someone pay for something like that?"

"Double what you'd pay for one fist, I guess... "

On the television screen we return to *Lockdown*. The crowd is now screaming at full volume, the presenter in a state of quasi-derangement. The loud chattering of the patrons in The Owl And The Pussycat ceases abruptly.

The person to be paroled from the *Lockdown* prison this week... is... Ronny!

On screen Ronny, a hard-looking but artfully unkempt Liverpudlian who has had some kind of sexual contact with no fewer than five of his female inmates stands behind the bars of his cell, and shrugs. The experience of seeing a prisoner disappointed by their imminent release is unsettling.

"I can't believe it's Ronny."

"Are you kidding? *The Sun*'s been running a fucking character assassination piece on him every day this week. Ex-girlfriends, the half sister he never speaks to…"

"Yes," I say, the first word to leave my lips in perhaps an hour. "But that's because she's a hooker."

All eyes turn to me.

"Go on, go on… " says Nihad, his already-wide eyes opening a little wider.

"One of my tipsters… he told me. We might run something on her next week… "

"So who's gonna win then?"

"Calum," says Ondine.

"No way. He's a fucking pussy."

"Not Jessica. Women never win."

"Colin, then."

"Yeah, I suppose. All the housewives love him."

Oh God… I don't want to be the one to tell them.

I close my eyes like I'm waiting for an explosion. I wipe the end of my nose, leaving a thin trail of powdery white snot along one finger, and knock back a mouthful of wine in an effort to remove all thoughts of Colin Curtis from my cluttered mind.

Within an hour of *Lockdown* ending Ondine is dancing on a table, and Nihad has ordered three bottles of champagne. Their yelling and cackling becomes incoherent, like some terrifying foreign language. I feel nauseous, as if their every action were part of a disgusting pantomime, designed specifically to disturb me.

"Hooray for double-fisting!" shouts Nihad, holding one of the champagne bottles above his head.

"Hooray!" the others shout, as a chorus.

I make my excuses and leave.

the waste ground – 00:26

On the DLR I see the skinhead again. He is sitting this time, gazing through the window at the firefly streetlights that flit past, and the neon towers of Canary Wharf dancing their slow dance in the distance. After a while he must realise that he is being watched, because he turns his head to look at me, and he smiles.

Once again I find myself staying on the train, stepping off at Royal Albert, and following him down toward the edge of the great dock. On the other side of the water a Swissair MD-11 is taking off; its nose leaving the runway and pointing skywards, its rear wheels suddenly breaking away from the ground in a breathless leap.

The skinhead is silhouetted against the bright guide lights of the runway, walking away from me with practised indifference. Only when the plane is high up in the air, and the lights have dimmed, does he look back at me and smile again.

I follow him down along the waterfront, the only sounds our footsteps and the water lapping at the dock's edge. We pass a vast, empty office building, its windows filled with declarations of floor space, and eventually reach the rusting gates and the waste ground.

I've been here before.

Not with the skinhead, but with others. Here, in the middle of this landscape scarified by industry and commerce, nestled between the dock and the train tracks, there is a waste ground, perhaps a hundred metres in length, closed off on all sides by decaying wire fences. It consists of little more than overgrown grass and weeds, and broken concrete. I don't know what was here before the waste ground. Perhaps once, in the last century, it served some purpose; perhaps it was a part of the docks, occupied by a warehouse or a ship yard. Now it is a void, between purposes. No doubt before the decade is out it will be the site of a leisure complex or an office building; a hotel or a gated compound of luxury apartments. But now it is a waste ground.

Anyone who knows the waste ground can tell you that the rusting gates at either end serve no practical purpose. The lock was removed a long time ago, and the gates open with ease. Once you are on the other side of the fence there is a strange sense of freedom that washes over you, as if you have somehow removed yourself from the city, taken yourself out of its absurd equation, and entered some other place, far away from it.

The skinhead walks along the makeshift path that winds its way between the shoulder-high weeds and grass. When we are drowning in the shadows he turns around.

"You want me to suck you off?" he says. I feel my pulse quicken and hear myself breathing a little louder. I nod, and begin undoing my belt. As I awkwardly lower my trousers to my knees and feel a warm breeze on my hard cock a billion stars explode in the right side of my face and for a few seconds the world turns silent and black.

When my senses return I am suddenly aware of noise and pain. I am on the ground, my back on the hard broken concrete, my arms over my face. A booted foot slams into my side, possibly breaking a rib, before swinging again to hit me in the side of the head. I close my mouth and feel the crunch of broken teeth, nerve endings shredded by a sharp intake of breath.

He is on me at once, his hands grasping my head, shaking me violently.

"I know you!" he says, spitting in my face. "You write that column in *The Voice of the People*. Fucking After Show. I know who you are. You and all the other fucking parasites. Brainless rubbish for the plebs. Mental garbage to stop anyone thinking about anything that's fucking real. Well none of this is real, d'you know that? None of this is fucking real. None of it fucking matters. How do you live with yourself, cunt?"

He kicks me again and I think I hear another bone break. Then I hear his footsteps as he walks away.

I lie there, the only real sensation one of pain, for what could be forever. I think about dying here, wondering if it's possible to will yourself to death in a place so detached from what you laughingly refer to as the real world. I wonder if I'll drown in my own blood. Perhaps blood is filling my lungs right now, unseen but slowly killing me.

My morbid reverie is interrupted by the throaty rumbling of a boat's engine and the sound of a man's voice asking me if I can hear him. The bright light of a torch puts fire behind my eyelids as the engine and the voices get louder.

six billion movies – 11:40

Every time you step outside your home you see six billion movies. You don't think so, but you do. The people you see as you're walking around, or sitting on the tube, or standing on an escalator, all seem like extras in your own private movie, but what you have to remember is that to them you are the extra.

You might try to work out their narrative, the reason they are in the same place as you at the same time. Where are they going? Why are they having that conversation on their C-Fish? Why do they look happy? Why do they look like they're about to cry? You could try to catch up with that story but it's too much. This isn't some TV series with a brief synopsis of the story so far at the beginning of each episode. This is their movie, and it's a movie that started years and maybe even decades ago.

I step out of Velocity House and walk around the edge of the dock. All around Royal Victoria the sound is one of descending planes, a diminuendo of jet engines. It's like the sound of the world falling. The air here smells chemical, man-made. It has a bitter-sweet quality, a tang that is somehow familiar and yet unlike anything you've experienced before. It took me a long time to work out what it was. When they began the construction of another hotel on the other side of the dock the smell grew more intense for a few weeks. It was the smell of builders' glue.

I take the DLR to Canary Wharf, and the carriage is full of movies. You can see it in their faces. These people aren't simply being paid to sit there and populate my reality. They aren't waiting for some unseen director to tell them when to get off the train or when to check their C-Fish for messages. Their faces are animated, even when still; the slightest eye movement hinting at a raging sea of thoughts. The only thing any of us has in common is that our lives, however different they might be, brought us to this time and place so that we could share the same enclosed space.

Canary Wharf on a Saturday afternoon is a virtual ghost city. There are occasional groups of tourists, marvelling at the sky-scrapers and at the emptiness of it all, but little more.

The tube station is like a subterranean cathedral; a Notre Dame to the city beneath the city. Its vertiginous arches and glass domes seem to drag the sky down into the bowels of the earth, somehow tainting it with concrete artificiality.

At the bottom of the escalator an old man in a court jester's hat sits in a wheelchair, playing a Bontempi keyboard and a harmonica. The melody is bizarre, discordant; a synthetic bossa nova beat accompanied by the mournful wailing of the mouth organ. It rises and echoes from the weird, afflicted little man, filling the colossal interior of the station and echoing along its platforms and thoroughfares.

I stand on the edge of the platform, inches away from the glass barrier, and watch the lights of the incoming train reflected off the black tunnel walls. The train enters the station with an electric hum and the two sets of doors open in perfect synchronisation.

I'm not sure how long I stay on the train because I'm not really sure where I'm going. I suppose in my movie the director is absent, or the script simply ran out of pages. I look at my reflection in the darkness of the opposite window, and I occasionally glance at the other passengers. Without exception they look angry and hot, some fanning themselves with newspapers, others sticking out their lower lips to blow cool air over their own faces. Some of them look at me briefly, with vague curiosity, before quickly looking away. My injuries must speak of violence.

Last night the police asked me what had happened and I told them it was nothing, really. They reminded me that I was trespassing, and I nodded dolefully.

"You don't want to maybe go to the station and have a word with somebody about this?" they asked. They were armed with submachine guns. I told them I'd rather not, and brushed the gravel from my suit.

After taking a very brief statement and giving me a verbal warning, they took me home across the dock in their small motorised dinghy and I felt the warm night breeze on my face as I watched the lights of Velocity House get bigger and brighter.

Sat on the train, aware of the chary glances of my fellow passengers, I realise I've slipped outside the boundaries of acceptability. I look different, a divergence from the norm. People see me, and then look away, as if to deny what they've seen. I've become a ghost.

And still, wherever I get off the train, there are movies.

In Canning Town a man sleeps, slumped over in his wheelchair, a mixture of snot and vomit dribbling from one corner of his mouth. The stench of piss around him is overwhelming.

Near the Cutty Sark a woman shouts at her children, shaking one of them violently when he spills a drink on the pavement and screaming, "What are you doing? What are you doing?"

In Greenwich Park a man sits on a bench hugging himself while staring into space. His teeth are chattering, and as I pass him he smiles at me and nods.

Outside Borough Market an old woman is selling necklaces made of human teeth.

On Tower Bridge Road an elderly man is wrestled into the back of a police van by four officers. He is screaming so loud the veins in his neck look like they might rupture, "I don't want to die! I'm alive! Alive! Alive! Alive!"

On the steps at Tower Gateway a girl sits clutching a baby to her chest. Beside her there is a cardboard sign on which the words "AIDS NEED MONEY" are written in black felt-tip pen.

On the DLR a man starts talking to the rest of the carriage.

"So… what do we think of this weather we've been having? Hot enough for you?"

There is a long pause. Nobody says anything.

"Nobody talks any more," he says, with a tone of genuine regret. "Do they? Nobody talks. My dad died this morning. He was a cabby. Drove a cab for best part of forty years. Died this morning. I'm like him, see? Outgoing. But nobody talks any more."

Everybody looks everywhere except at him. Suddenly it's as if everyone can share my anxiety, this thing I've been feeling lately. Suddenly it's like everyone understands, and it's not just me. There's something wrong. With people. With this city. With everything.

I return to my apartment and go online. I have three emails. One is from my sister, Lola. It's her thirtieth birthday soon, and she has noticed the film *Logan's Run* on television no fewer than six times in the last month alone.

> Their entire society consists of those under 30. They don't need anyone over that age, because when it comes down to it, we don't.

The second email is from Serge. He tells me that his company has just landed a major contract to organise the UK publicity for Jesus Vs Satan, the evangelical action film that's just opened in the States. He and his boyfriend Dan have just returned from a fortnight on a sun-kissed Greek island. He includes a photograph of them on the beach.

The third email is from Brian Fenton, telling me that I have to be at a party this evening to celebrate the nineteenth birthday of Qelli Mai.

> If all this stuff about the Jupiter Prize is on the mark it would be a wise move to be there

says the email.

> And make sure the photographer focuses on her tits. She's nineteen now so it's all fair game.

I stare at the email for a long time trying to absorb the meaning of the words and put them into some sort of context, but I can make no sense of it. This email could not have been sent to me, not to the broken person who people chose to ignore on the underground, not to the person who was found face down on concrete by armed police.

I look at my schedule for the week and I see parties and press junkets, photo opportunities and free dinners. I see a world of physical events that are as ephemeral as snowflakes, lacking in reason or meaning, completely and utterly without gravity. Names and faces that flicker between turned pages, incongruously filling the spaces between stories of global carnage and disaster.

I feel nauseous again and run from my computer to the bathroom where I suddenly and violently regurgitate my breakfast into the toilet bowl. My body shudders and heaves again but there is nothing.

I return to my computer, a warm breeze from an open window suddenly chilling the cold slick of sweat that covers my skin. I look at Brian's email again. I hear his voice saying the words. Hastily I begin typing a response. I tell him about the attack, only this version of the story reads more like a synopsis of a porn film. In this version the skinhead slaps me in the face with his cock and then fucks me against the cold hard concrete. I carefully leave a certain degree of ambiguity, so that it's up to Brian to work out whether or not the act was consensual. I decorate my story with every telling little detail I think Brian deserves, right down to the drying spunk in my hair, and I end it with the line, "And if you gaze for long into an abyss, the abyss gazes also into you."

Then I hit send.

I can't face going out again. I see the faces of all those passengers on the tube. I see their disapproval. I hear the desperation in that man's voice, practically begging someone, anyone, to just talk to him. All those raging emotions. All those narratives blindly crashing into one another. All those desires and dreams smashed together like so many motorway pile-ups.

If I could just stay in this apartment and never leave. If I didn't have to see any of these things again; the little telling details that make this whole sorry mess so fucking painful.

I walk around my apartment, as if to test its limits. How many paces take me from the kitchen to the bathroom? Thirteen. How many from the bathroom to my bedroom? Eight.

If I stayed in this apartment, would the world miss me? I imagine my colleagues sat around a table outside The Owl And The Pussycat, and I remove myself from that image. Is there any change? If I'm not in the newsroom, will it drastically alter its dynamic? We're all interchangeable now. Like spare parts. Our culture is like the salamander: cut off the tail and it grows right back. Soon enough, nobody will notice the difference.

So if I stay in my apartment, and I don't leave, what difference will that make to the rest of the world? Nothing? No difference at all? Perhaps a ripple on the surface of the pond, but soon enough that ripple will fade to the outer edges, and all will be tranquil once more.

I can stay in my apartment, where the only other people will be two dimensional and will shut up the minute I hit 'mute'. I can stay in my apartment, where the only noise can be drowned out with music of my own choosing, or by closing the French doors that open out onto my balcony. I can stay in my apartment and treat life as a video clip that I can pause, fast forward, or stop altogether as and when I see fit. Why didn't I think of this before?

I stand in the centre of my apartment and I activate the television using the remote control. On my laptop I open a number of windows and log in to megapedia.com, theboyshop.com, megaearth.com, galactus.co.uk, and cumcoveredfarmboytwinks.com.

One last splurge, I think. One last gluttonous overdose of information. One last Bacchanalian digression, as I feast myself on images, sounds, and words.

On the television, a programme about a cat hospital in the Midlands. A smiling blonde woman stands beside a veterinary surgeon who is attempting to remove a small .22 calibre pellet from behind the left ear of a four-year-old Siamese cat.

What Martin's trying to do is remove the pellet, causing as little damage to the surrounding tissue as possible.

I gorge myself on information, as if every word and image is the last drop of water before I embark across a desert. I look at pages and pages of information about characters from history; Saladin, Marie Antoinette, the Borgias, Gilles de Rais, Delphine LaLaurie. I look at images of naked men penetrating one another and covering themselves in semen. I check out how many times my blog has been read on galactus. I look at satellite photographs on Mega-Earth.

On the television the blonde woman says

Cassie won't wake up for a few hours, and Martin will have to fit her with this special collar to stop her from trying to scratch out the stitches...

Delphine LaLaurie was a New Orleans socialite who, along with her husband, Dr Louis LaLaurie, tortured her slaves and performed a number of bizarre medical experiments upon them. Following a fire at their home, firefighters found one slave who had been subjected to an attempted sex change, while another had had her arms and legs broken and reset at such alarming angles that she was only able to move around 'like a giant crab'.

Hotboi1988 says: hey m8... Looking 4 a fuk?

Saladin or Salah al-Din (1138–1193, Salah al-Din meaning The Righteousness of the Faith) was a Kurdish Muslim warrior from Tikrit, in present day northern Iraq. He was responsible for founding the Ayyubid dynasty of Egypt, Syria, Yemen, Iraq, Mecca Hejaz and Diyar Bakr. He was also renowned across both the Middle East and Europe for his mercy and his chivalry.

Now what's wrong with Archie?

Well... Archie's got gingivitis...

Gingivitis? Isn't that something humans can get too?

Yes, Fiona, it is...

Horny young twinks r waiting for you to shoot your hot load all over them!!!

Gilles de Rais was the French military leader, nobleman, and national hero who, in 1440, was found guilty of the rape and murder of between eighty and two hundred children of both sexes, aged between six and eighteen. According to his testimony, he did this under the direction of a man called Francesco Prelati, as part of a sacrifice to a demon called 'Barron'. It was not uncommon for de Rais and his servants to line up the severed heads of the children they had killed in order to judge them on their beauty.

Now, it could be that Archie's allergic to something, possibly bacterial plaque, which would make him plaque intolerant. Alternatively he could be allergic to a certain type of food, or perhaps fleas, though this would probably manifest itself not only in the gingivitis, but also in skin and gum lesions called feline eosinophilic granuloma…

Fit4fukin – 23 yrs old – Plaistow – Act/Vers – 9" – up 4 a meet now.

I see a satellite image of Barcelona, as an astronaut might see it from a space station or a shuttle; an impossible grid of seemingly identical blocks spread out above the ramshackle mess of the Barri Gotic.

Your blog has been read 9370 times.

MICKEY LOVES BUKKAKE.

There are a number of ways we can treat this… either with the application of fluoride… antibiotics… corticosteroids… but the most important thing, if this is not allergy-based, is a good diet and good oral hygiene.

I feel a surge of tingling pleasure pass from one end of my body to the other; a slowed-down re-enactment of an electric shock; a spasm that trips along my spine and seems to focus all of its energy on my cock. I masturbate, my gaze passing from the television to the computer screen, over each image and word, forming my own montage, my own pornographic catalogue of data. I close my eyes and clench my teeth, the exposed nerves in each broken molar exploding suddenly like a sensory firework. When I ejaculate I am thinking about cold concrete.

day one – 07:30

Like a pre-programmed machine I wake at exactly seven thirty. Once I am awake there is no chance of me falling asleep again, it's too hot, and so I rise and walk around my apartment naked, first making myself a cup of coffee, then turning on the television.

The screen shows images of missiles falling upon civilians in some distant, half-imagined city. Minimalist '70s apartment buildings burn next to jagged, half-demolished minarets. Black plumes of smoke and red tongues of fire erupt from the shattered golden skull of a mosque's qiblah. Women in chadors wail over the piles of rubble under which their presumably dead children are buried. I switch on my computer and see that I have an email from Brian:

> Ed, in light of what you've told me, I think it might be best if you take a little time off work for now. We'll have to skip Monday's After Show. I'll get Toby to cover from Tuesday. I'll tell the others that you have family problems. You say you've spoken to the police already. Is it possible any of the other papers might know about this? The last thing we need is that bitch from *The Sun* getting her hands on this. They'd have a fucking field day with it. Hope you're bearing up. Brian.

I imagine him saying the words out loud and realise it is impossible to invest any sympathy in it. The last sentence was an afterthought, hastily added in the seconds before he hit send. Besides, I don't want sympathy.

I stand on my balcony looking down over Royal Victoria Dock. The first commuters swarm out of Velocity House and make their way toward the DLR station, the sound of their shuffling feet audible even from the tenth floor. It is eventually drowned out by the sound of a descending airplane, which passes over the dock at an altitude of only a few hundred feet. I watch its reflection pass over the undisturbed grey water before silently hitting the peninsula of the runway.

The old machine of the city continues with its daily chore of moving its inhabitants, guiding them along train tracks and runways, pavements and dual carriageways. The sound of its machinery is constant, unending. Ten storeys below me the suited office workers and hotel staff move, blissfully deluded that they do so through free will, as if the city were not simply using them as its fuel. From this vantage point it is possible to see the patterns that they form, and therefore consider their movement not as random coincidence, but as a mathematical inevitability, like the motion of the planets around the sun, or the rising and falling of tides.

Within twenty minutes there are no more commuters. The last of them, a man in a grey suit with a laptop bag bouncing at his side, runs from the building, almost stumbling on his way.

For a moment the dock falls silent. No people are visible. The electric blue sky is a grid of disintegrating vapour trails. Another plane howls into view before coming in to land at City Airport.

I return to the living room. On television, the Home Secretary Phillip Mackenzie is making his way through another airport, on the other side of the city. He holds a green folder in front of his face in a desperate attempt to shield himself from the gaze of so many lenses. He looks hunted, as I imagine an animal caught in a snare might look as it contemplates gnawing at a trapped limb in order to escape.

A second email arrives, this time from Ondine:

> Hey Ed, are you okay? Brian says you're taking some time off. He's going to get Toby to write After Show... Toby's a fucking idiot.

I delete the email without replying to it, and pick up the remote control for the television. I flick through dozens of channels, scanning each one's output for no more than a few seconds.

...eighteen thought to be dead, with up to fifty seriously injured...

Listen Columbo, just for a minute how about we stop pretending that I'm brilliant and you're simple!

For the dog who has everything...

There may be some thunderstorms over the Channel and along some areas of the south coast, but inland this hot weather is going to continue, with plenty of sunshine and temperatures reaching as high as thirty-four degrees in London and parts of Essex.

...which was when you decided to have the gender realignment surgery?

I'm horny... horny horny horny...

Let me guess. You're a French aristocrat, she's a simple girl of the people, and she won't even give you a tumbrel. Hah!

Shots were fired from a rooftop less than a hundred metres from the main square...

What have you got for an opening act this time? A Chinese gorilla dancing ballet?

This dazzling diamonique bracelet, only seventy-five pounds, is perfect for any occasion. Weddings, dinner parties… if we could just look a little closer here… I don't think you'll tell the difference between this and real diamonds…

…in Shahr Park a mother cradles her dead son…

A million onlookers crowded the highways and beaches surrounding the Kennedy Space Centre to watch the launch…

I see images of explosions and death juxtaposed suddenly and violently with ones of launching space rockets and glittering bracelets. Fragments of vintage films collide with the gaunt and terrified features of Phillip Mackenzie, forever swimming against a tide of camera crews and reporters. Game shows and talk shows are interwoven with the repeated images of a burning city and its screaming citizens. Seen at this frenetic pace there eventually ceases to be any kind of contrast. Patterns seem to emerge from the seemingly random symbols and images, as if to create their own abstract process of cause and effect. Occasionally there are chance meetings between the frames; the circumference of the bracelet finding its echo in the crater left behind by a teenage boy strapped with explosives; the smile of a game-show host and the grimace of a grieving mother.

The French dramatist whose life was fictionalised in a play by Edmond Rostand was Cyrano who?

…bodies lay in the gutter outside the Ministry of Justice… police struggled to control the crowds…

…would be suitable for formal functions, as well as more casual parties… This really is something you could wear at…

…won the 1982 Nobel Prize for Literature?

Feros. Take a walk on the wild side.

Don't you know that you're toxic?

…awash with the blood of…

…in the family Lucanidae…

…it's butter. Can you?

…really is amazing…

…gunfire from the…

…screaming and…

…in June 1988?

…explosions…

…for only…

…I can't…

I hit standby. The television falls silent, the only sound in my apartment the low drone of the computer. For what feels like an age I sit in the room and listen to its incessant hum.

Eventually, in a few hours time, I will return to the balcony. I will watch the commuters return from their places of work, marching back toward the building from the other side of the dock. They will be different creatures from the ones I saw leaving this morning. Their ties will be a little looser, their shoulders slumped, their hair a little untidy. The city will spew them back out into the sultry evening like swirling clouds of exhaust fumes.

I will watch the dying light drag long shadows out over Royal Victoria Dock, and glint off the reflective arches of the Thames Barrage. I will watch as City Airport comes to resemble a vast alien landing site in the gloom of the night, its runway lit up on both sides by white lights converging in a distant vanishing point. Perhaps I will sleep there, suspended high above the city beneath a blanket of stars, for all the world floating in infinite space.

monkey puzzle trees – 10:42

The Mapuche are the indigenous people of central and southern Chile, and northern Argentina. The Spanish settlers named them the *Araucanos*, and they include a wide range of ethnic groups held together by a common social and religious structure and language.

Following Chile's secession from Spain the Mapuche were able to co-exist with their Chilean neighbours, though there were occasional skirmishes between the two parties, which were eventually brought to an end, with force, by the Chilean army in the 1880s.

The central figure of the Mapuche community is the Machi, a shamanic figure, often an old woman, who performs various ceremonies to cure diseases, ward off evil spirits, and pray for rainfall.

The sacred food tree of the Mapuche is the Pehuén tree. It is, perhaps, one of the hardiest species of conifer in the genus Araucaria, can grow up to forty metres in height, and live for almost two thousand years. It will grow in many temperate regions, not only in its native South America, but in parts of Britain and the United States, able to survive temperatures as low as -20°C.

Its common English name, the Monkey Puzzle Tree, originated in 1850, in the town of Bodmin, Cornwall, fifty-two miles from the town where I was born. Upon seeing the exotic tree, with its strangely curved branches and prehistoric, scaled leaves, a visitor to Pencarrow Garden remarked, "It would puzzle a monkey to climb that".

By 1985 the Monkey Puzzle Tree had become a common sight in the British Isles, and to me was a symbol of white, middle-class suburbia. Of course, I had no real concept of 'white middle-class suburbia' at the time, but I knew who we were. We lived in neither the town nor the countryside, but somewhere in between. A short drive from the cities of Exeter and Plymouth, but close enough to the countryside for a day-trip to be hindered by tractors and flocks of sheep being moved from field to field.

We had money. I never heard my parents arguing over money. I remember Richard, in his days when he was still working at the paper, telling me how his mother, and his friends' mothers, would often visit his school on weekends to pick up unlabelled tins of stewing steak and blocks of butter; EU surplus handed out to lower-income families. I couldn't imagine anything worse. Had my mother ever had to queue for free tinned stewing steak she would probably have written a rather stern letter to *The Observer* declaring a national state of emergency.

Having a Monkey Puzzle Tree in your garden denotes a number of things. First it establishes that you have a garden large enough to grow a Monkey Puzzle Tree. Secondly, it signifies that you would not settle for something as domestic as a Cricket Bat Willow or Leylandii. The Monkey Puzzle Tree is vast, and exotic, and the one in our garden towered above the surrounding flora, an incongruous visitor amongst the rose bushes and rhododendrons. At night I would stare out of my window at its majestic, jagged silhouette, and imagine that it were some kind of giant, forever advancing upon our house, waiting to reveal long reptilian arms that would crash through my windows and pluck me from my bed.

It seems a common feature of childhood for the most innocuous of things to be rendered sinister. My parents warned me not to stray too close to the goldfish pond in the shade of the Monkey Puzzle Tree, and so I became convinced that it were somehow bottomless; its murky depths reaching deep into the ground; a suburban Mariana Trench decorated with lilies and elegant orange fish.

A child from our town, a boy by the name of Steven, went missing one day while playing in a field of luminous yellow rapeseed flowers. The sky was alive with police helicopters, the first time they ever flew over the town, and I remember watching the lines of local men combing the fields from our classroom window as the teacher attempted to distract us with our nine times table.

Eventually talk of Steven's disappearance extended beyond the regional television news, when his image appeared above Trevor McDonald's left shoulder and we heard the newsreader say his name. By this point Steven had probably been dead for more than a day, buried beneath a mulch of dead leaves in woodlands about three miles from where he had last been seen.

My parents were reluctant to tell me what had happened to Steven, saying that he must have had an accident and fallen, but in the playground there was talk of strangers. A stranger had killed him. The same kind of stranger that our parents, our teachers, and all those television ad campaigns had warned us about. The person in the car offering sweets or the opportunity to see a puppy. The man with the easy smile and cloying charm whose real intent was never made explicit.

Suddenly the streets of our town were quiet on those hot summer evenings. The fields of rapeseed flowers, rich with the scent of honey, went untarnished by the feet of children, and in play parks the swings creaked idly on the breeze.

There was an air of suspicion over the whole town, with fingers pointed at every loner and eccentric. Neighbourhood watch became more than an opportunity for residents to gather and talk about the problem of graffiti. Despite these efforts, whoever it was who had snatched Steven away in the middle of a sunny afternoon was never caught. It was as if the field itself had taken him and left him in what could barely be described as a grave.

Perhaps it was that which would eventually drive me toward the cities; first Plymouth, then London. Cities have order, and geographies that obey, or at least seem to obey, rules. There are streets and there are buildings. There are tunnels and roads. For all its darkest secrets the city will never harbour an unknowable infinity within its limits; the bottomless pond or the infinite field of shoulder-high flowers. Every inch of the city, from the flickering lights on top of skyscrapers to the deepest recesses of the Underground, has been designed and placed there by Man. When it rains the water falls upon concrete and glass and runs in streams into conduits created exclusively for the purpose of directing all that water into the dirty grey graveyard of the Thames. It's as if the city absorbs nature, and then rejects it as a body will eventually reject a virus. Any evidence of nature within the city; its parks and ponds, its tree-lined avenues; are little more than token gestures; a decorative simulacra of nature placed there to give the illusion of nature's triumph over the man-made and the artificial. This is, of course, a self-perpetuating illusion: artificial nature, planted to distract from the artificiality of the city itself. A tree planted in a city is as alien as the Monkey Puzzle Tree at the bottom of my parents' garden.

day three – 08:10

I am on my balcony, watching the morning commuters, when it occurs to me that I haven't eaten in almost thirty-six hours. My stomach occasionally lurches and grumbles, and I have experienced moments of lethargy at unusual times in the day. The nature of my work dictates the contents of my kitchen: UHT milk to add to my morning coffee, and packets of dust and dehydrated vegetables that magically become food when mixed with boiling water. I bring my laptop out onto the balcony so that I can continue watching the commuters while I place my order with an online supermarket, but as I sit down on one of the plastic chairs I notice another figure on one of the lower balconies.

It is a tall, blond-haired man, perhaps forty to forty-five years

old, leaning against the rail and looking down over the dock. I
don't recognise him. Though there must be hundreds of people
living in this building, I would recognise many from the morning
journey to Royal Victoria DLR. Perhaps he's a newcomer. I watch
him for five minutes or more before he looks up and notices me.
I expect him to look away in that nervous way that people do
when they make eye contact with strangers, but instead his gaze
remains firmly on me, and though he is quite far away I am sure
that he smiles. In unison, it seems, we turn our attention once
more to the commuters and their dawn exodus into the city, as
content as men watching a sunset.

The shopping list that I compile consists largely of foods that I
am led to believe are nutritious, foods that will supply long term
sustenance without the need to replenish supplies too soon. I
order malt loaf, and pasteurised orange juice; cured meats and
boxes of cereal; tinned vegetables and a variety of multivitamins.
I enter my credit card details and I hit 'purchase'. My order
becomes at once a series of zeros and ones travelling through
miles of cable to an unknown, virtual destination. Somewhere,
perhaps a hundred miles away the order is received within a split
second, processed and sent to a depot where it ceases to be
abstract data and becomes the physical process of locating each
item and placing it into a cardboard crate with all the other goods.
The crate is carried from the depot to the waiting van. The van
leaves the depot and makes its way around East London, presumably making other deliveries before arriving at Velocity House's
car park gate. The driver leans out of his window, cursing himself
for not pulling up a little closer to the intercom, before typing my
apartment number into the keypad. He waits, listening to the
scratchy dialling tone for the few seconds that it takes me to walk
to the door and pick up the handset. The driver tells me that he has
come here to deliver my shopping, and I hit the button that opens
the gate. He pulls up in one of the visitor parking spaces in front
of the main entrance, gets out, and unloads my shopping from the
back of the van.

Meanwhile I am at my door. There will be too much shopping
for him to carry to my apartment, and so it will be necessary for
me to go down to the entrance. I place my hand against the door
and take in a deep breath, feeling suddenly nauseous. It has been
four days since I last left these rooms. When I open the door my
apartment breathes out with a sigh.

I make sure I have my keys before stepping out into the corridor and closing the door behind me. Even so I check again before I reach the elevator, and for a third time once I am inside the elevator and descending toward the ground floor.

Ground floor, says the elevator's pre-recorded female voice. The doors open, and for some reason the reflected light from the tiled floor and the stark white walls is almost blinding. Through the glass of the door I can see the driver's blue uniform and his unkempt, mottled blond hair. He smiles a formal, practised smile. When I open the door he smiles again, but it fades suddenly, as though he is somehow shocked by what he sees.

"Oh, right, yeah… " he says. "I thought I recognised the name… After Show in *The Voice of the People*. My girlfriend's reading it all the time for all the gossip off *Lockdown*. I almost didn't recognise you. If you could just sign here…"

He holds out a small black plastic pad in the centre of which is a grey LCD screen, and hands me a plastic pen-shaped instrument. When I sign, the resulting scrawl looks nothing like my normal signature.

"Yeah… she wants that Colin to win. I think everyone does, though."

"Colin… " I say, feeling another wave of nausea.

"Yeah, well, he's a bit of a lad, isn' he? All the girls love that, and blokes like that too, so everyone's gonna vote for him, at the end of the day. Not like that Calum. He's fucking wet. And Jessica's fit, but all the girls hate her, and it's girls who end up voting, isn't it? Nah… I reckon it's gonna be that Colin. Not that I watch it mind you. It's just a blatant rip-off of *The Clink*, if you ask me, only without the celebrities and that, but the missus has it on all the time."

I nod without saying anything, and he starts carrying the boxes over the threshold.

"You want a hand with these?" he asks. "There's loads here. You preparing for World War Three or something?"

He's right. There are four cardboard crates filled with supplies, and each foodstuff will remain in edible condition for months and possibly years to come. This is apocalypse food. I tell him I'll be fine.

"Suit yourself. I'll tell the missus I met you. She never misses your bit in *The Voice of the People*. She loves it, all that celebrity gossip and that. Can't get enough of it."

I nod and attempt a smile.

"Anyway, cheerio," he says, closing the door as he leaves.

It is only when I return to the apartment that I see what it was that elicited the driver's initial response. I haven't shaved since Friday. My hair is a mess. My eyes seem to cast their own shadows. I bear little resemblance to the picture that appears above my two-page spread: Me, tanned and smiling, wearing a dark blue Ozwald Boateng suit and an open-collared Vivienne Westwood shirt. I'm amazed he recognised me at all.

What has changed? I struggle to remember a time before my view of the world became so jaded; a time when I was able to pose for that photograph without a trace of irony. There were parties and there were interviews. People know my name and they associate it with a certain brand of frivolity; the news stories that add nothing to the world and take nothing away, that make no impact upon the geo-political map and yet somehow manage to scar the world. I am the medium. A vital, if reluctant, cog in the machine that churns out the images and words.

I think about what the skinhead said.

"Mental garbage to stop anyone thinking about anything that's fucking real."

Is that what I've done with my life? Is that what I contributed? I find myself wondering if there is an afterlife, whether they keep some kind of tab of all the things you did that added to or took away from the sum of human happiness. What will my bill look like? Will I be in credit? The delivery driver tells me his girlfriend loves my column, but what does she love about it? Is her enjoyment of it based entirely on Schadenfreude? If so, am I not simply spreading human misery thin enough to make it appear like a fine glaze?

Who the fuck am I?

nigel, apartment 413 – 09:10

On the television a young couple, eyes filled with optimism and the thrill of being on television, are shown around a suburban semi-detached house by a celebrity house expert.

This would make a great nursery, or even a guest room. There's plenty of light, and they've decorated it in neutral colours, so there's not really a lot of work to be done in here...

I eat a breakfast of malt loaf and concentrated, pasteurised orange juice, along with a handful of vitamin supplements. I take tablets that contain concentrated vitamin A and vitamin D. Tablets that contain vitamin B12, vitamin C, folic acid, niacin, riboflavin, and thiamine. Vitamin A and D are fat-soluble vitamins that would normally be found in food such as butter, dairy products, liver and oily fish, but are here found in the form of small grey capsules. The others are water-soluble vitamins that would normally occur in the fresh fruits and vegetables that I haven't bought for fear of watching them rot.

Debts bringing you down? Credit card payments too much to bear? Call now and answer the following question and you could win up to two thousand pounds! Which of the following is a country in Europe? Is it A... France? B... South Africa? Or C... Mongolia? That's A... France. B... South Africa. Or C... Mongolia. Call now for your chance to win up to two thousand pounds!"

Coming soon to Television One...

'You might be a pop star over there, sonny, but out here you're expend-able! You are a worthless little worm! Now get in that ******* helicopter!'

Ten celebrities... one real-life conflict. Celebrities At War. Friday at nine.

It is as I get up from the sofa that I notice the envelope beside my door. I cross the room and pick it up. Written on the envelope are the words, 'To the man on the balcony'. My curiosity waxing I tear it open and find inside a handwritten note:

Are you a refugee from the plague? I see you in the mornings, watching the sufferers go about their business, blissfully unaware of the contagion they carry. The illness is not terminal; we simply haven't found the cure.

Nigel, Apartment 413

I sit and contemplate the note for a while. It's clearly from the man I saw on one of the lower balconies. I wonder what he means by plague, and contagion. Does he mean a literal virus?

My mind circumambulates around the suburbs of an elaborate fantasy world in which Nigel is a biochemist or perhaps a virologist. He has, no doubt, spent the last eight years working on a weaponised virus in a top secret laboratory. The virus has somehow been stolen and released, and now he sits on his balcony, waiting for the first symptoms to manifest themselves in the public.

On the television a young woman with her hair fashioned into gravity-defying spikes is talking to the fashion designer Hector Q. Interspersed with moments of the interview are clips of Hector Q's latest catwalk show in Milan, where statuesque models stride toward the camera wearing t-shirts splattered with brown, congealed bloodstains.

It took us approximately twelve months to collect all the blood that was needed,

says Hector Q in a clipped north-of-England accent reminiscent of a young David Hockney. He is holding a cigarette that has been pixelated to avoid the on-screen promotion of smoking.

My physician warned against giving blood so regularly, but what is art without sacrifice? Then it was simply a case of applying my blood to the t-shirts and treating each one with a solution that would prevent it from washing out.

More models in more blood-spattered t-shirts, each one looking like a re-animated murder victim; their eyes glazed, their make-up cadaverous.

I sometimes wonder if some future collector of fashion might be able to create clones of me using the DNA in each bloodstain

says Hector Q, allowing himself a wry giggle.

There could be hundreds of me. I'd be pret-a-porter.

Another chuckle, and the pixelated blur of his hand leaves a trail of smoke in front of his face.

Should I ignore the note, and perhaps avoid the balcony? If I respond, what kind of paranoid fantasy will I be exposing myself to? In addition to this, the air is different out there. I discovered this when I went as far as the ground floor to collect my shopping. The air is different beyond my door, tainted as it is with the smell of other people's cooking, or the lingering traces of morning perfumes and eau de toilettes left as the residents rushed from their apartments. Beyond my door it smells of people, other people, in abundance. Inside my apartment the air I breathe is somehow more pure, as if there is comfort in inhaling dead skin cells and traces of carbon dioxide from previous exhalations. If I open the door to my balcony I can smell and taste the tang of builders' glue drifting from the new hotels and apartment complexes.

How can I make it as far as Apartment 413 when the outside has become such an assault upon the senses?

And the light. The light is different now. Forever shimmering in a mirage and scorching, as if focused through a magnifying glass. Everything is visible, as if the sun leaves no shadows.

c-fish – 13:21

For the first time in several days my C-Fish makes a whoosh-and-fanfare noise. I pick it up and read the message. It's from my sister.

Fish, and plankton, and sea greens, and protein from the sea. It's all here. Ready! Fresh as harvest day!

I decide now to allow my C-Fish to die. Where once I would feverishly recharge the thing the minute it was down to two bars of power, now I will simply watch it wither away and die. I will listen to its electronic whimpering, see the flickering blue light next to its screen, and I will wait for the moment when it finally falls silent.

"Oh God… I don't know how I ever managed without it."

How many times have you said that?

"It makes Blackberry look like parchment and fucking quill."

"I know… can you imagine? How did we cope? It was like the Stone Age or something."

On television there is a travel show.

"Vorkuta is over a hundred miles north of the Arctic Circle. Traditionally a mining town, it has a population of just eighty-five thousand, but has recently opened itself up as a major tourist resort. For the princely sum of three hundred pounds a night you too can experience the horrors of Stalin's Gulags by staying at the newly renovated Vorkuta Prison Camp. Opened in nineteen thirty two, the labour camp at Vorkuta was the biggest complex of prison camps in European Russia, serving as the administrative centre for the neighbouring camps in Kotlas and Izhma. We met some of those staying at the Vorkuta Prison Camp, and asked them what it was that had drawn them to this perfect reconstruction of a Stalinist Gulag...

Well... we've always wanted to come to Russia, isn't that right, Harv?

Yeah... we'd always wanted to come to Russia.

But we saw this advertised, and we just thought it was so, I don't know... *zany*... I mean, how many people do you know who've stayed in a concentration camp? We've been to Auschwitz... but they don't let you stay there. They don't even sell souvenirs.

No souvenirs. Not one. Not even a pencil.

The blue light on my C-Fish flashes once.

But here... you've got everything. T-Shirts... pencils... they got these little Stalin dolls...

It emits a high pitched bleep.

And they've got actors playing all the guards... it's so realistic...

The blue light flashes again. Another high pitched bleep.

This feels vaguely sacrilegious, as if I am breaking some kind of modern taboo, or committing a strange new act of cruelty. On the screen of the C-Fish appear the words – BATTERY LOW – PLEASE CHARGE.

It said 'please', as if imploring me to attach it to the mains, to feed it. It flashes and makes another bleeping sound. I pick it up, and contemplate attaching it to its charger in the corner of the living room. I hold strong, staring down into its tiny LCD screen as it grows dim and the battery symbol in the corner begins to flash. Another flash of the blue light, another bleeping sound, and the screen becomes suddenly blank. I breathe out.

I wonder whether there will be a time when all the lights go out. How much time have I got with the money that I have? The paper will only pay me for so long before replacing me completely. Then it will simply be a case of dwindling resources. Eventually there will be no more money to buy food, or to pay the bills. The cupboards will be empty, the bulbs will die or the electricity will be cut off. I will sit starving in the darkness until eventually I too flicker briefly and die, just like the C-Fish.

email from brian fenton – 18:32

A few hours after the death of the C-Fish, and its consignment to a grave full of crushed packaging, empty milk cartons and rotting food, I receive an email from Brian Fenton.

Hi Ed,

Listen – we've put the feelers out, got on the phone to some of our moles at *The Sun* and the *Mirror*, it doesn't look like anyone's got wind of your current 'situation'. So we decided to follow it up ourselves, see how much information there was, see if anyone from the Met knew anything. Funny thing is, Ed, nobody knows anything. We got one of our best insiders to check the records, and there's nothing about anyone being picked up that night in the condition you said you were in. It's all very odd. Is there any chance you could come in to the office some time this week so we can have a chat? I did try calling you but you seem to have your C-Fish switched off.

Also – we've come up with a temporary solution to your absence. Something that will fill in for After Show while you're away. We've picked three kids (a boy and two girls) from Enigma, you know, the modelling agency? We're going to send them to all the parties and what-have-you, and Toby's going to ghost-write the column. We haven't thought

of a name yet – we're not launching it until Friday. Let me
know if you have any ideas.

Brian

I very nearly laugh as I read the words, not entirely sure what
they mean to either of us. The change of tone, even in blank and
plainly punctuated text, is palpable. His quasi-genuine concern
has transmogrified into something a little harder. I sense anger.

"The condition you said you were in."

And now there are three young models ready to take over the
column. I think they will never even see the inside of the newsroom, but they will be ever-so popular with the people at
K-Media. It was Seb Keynsham who kicked out so many of the
old-school journalists and hired Brian Fenton after the turn of the
century. Is that what's happening to me? Is the contrast between
my vacuous smiling picture and the reality of my bloodshot eyes
too much for them to bear? These three models will look right at
the parties. When they are photographed with celebrities they
will blend in; a kind of aesthetic camouflage, so that the readers
might not be able to tell the difference between the reporter and
the star.

How long, I wonder, before it becomes necessary to erect a
wall that will divide the beautiful people from the rest of the
world? Within their compound the beautiful people will be able
to eat, drink, dance and fuck; though constantly being filmed and
photographed, while the ugly and obese, the deformed or the dis-
abled, will sit outside, eyes fixed upon flickering television
screens, silently worshipping their idols. Beautiful journalists
will interview beautiful actors and actresses, beautiful models
and beautiful pop stars, in beautiful surroundings.

I reply to Brian's email:

Brian,

I will be unable to come into the office for a chat...

Many apologies for the inconvenience. Something appears to
be changing. I'm not sure whether this has been noticed out
there, but it is becoming increasingly noticeable here.
Something is wrong with people.

Glad to hear that you have found a replacement team to cover After Show in my absence. You ask whether I can think of a suitable name for "their" column. Nothing comes to mind immediately, though perhaps something along the lines of 'Which One Is Brian Fucking?' might be suitable. Just out of interest… which one *are* you fucking?

Ed

I hit send, and start laughing hysterically, until there are tears rolling from my eyes. The laughter eventually sounds more like sobbing, but I'm unable to stop. The tears roll down my cheeks and my chest begins to hurt from each loud and forceful exhalation. My career is over.

tinside lido – 23:35

Smeaton's Tower was the name given to the third Eddystone Lighthouse, nine miles off the coast of Cornwall. Two previous lighthouses had occupied the same site; the first, an octagonal wooden structure, was built by Henry Winstanley in 1698 before being destroyed by a terrible storm five years later. The second was built by John Rudyerd in 1709. This tower survived until 1755 when its timber frame burnt to the ground. When the civil engineer John Smeaton began work on the third lighthouse he did so using hydraulic lime, thus ensuring a sturdier, longer-lasting building.

Standing eighteen metres in height, Smeaton's Tower served as the Eddystone Lighthouse for one hundred and eighteen years, until it was discovered that the rocks on which it was built were gradually being eroded. The tower was dismantled in order to make room for James Douglass' fourth lighthouse, and partially rebuilt on Plymouth Hoe, in a place overlooking the Hamoaze, where the rivers Tamar, Tavy and Lynher converge and enter Plymouth Sound.

Situated at the base of the limestone cliffs below Smeaton's Tower is the 1930s lido known as Tinside Pool. For several years the pool lay empty and derelict; a rather sad and poignant reminder of some happier time when it wasn't covered in graffiti and home to nothing more than empty bottles, dry leaves and dirty needles. By day it was the home of screaming seagulls and bored teenagers. By night, with the brow of the cliffs held in stark silhouette against the orange glow of the city, the area around Tinside Pool became the scene of midnight trysts; illicit assignations between strangers.

I had lived in Plymouth for little more than two months before I found myself there. I wondered immediately why it is that ancient ports seem to give birth to these places so quickly, bringing with them an undercurrent of potential violence, like something out of Genet.

A married man stood in the gloom, his face pressed against concrete, his white buttocks exposed by the moonlight. He said nothing as I covered my cock in lubricant and pushed it into him. Soon a crowd of other men gathered and watched, masturbating in the shadows, murmuring words like a half-whispered mantra, "Fuck him… fuck him… fuck him… "

At the point of climax I looked up at a canopy of stars that were barely visible through the broken terracotta clouds and it seemed, for just one moment, that I could hear the sound the world makes as it turns.

I returned to the lido on a number of occasions, always alone, always enjoying its peculiar dichotomy: the sepia-tinted location of family days out in a bygone age, and the Stygian scene of consensual and mass voyeurisms in the modern night. Though a small and very provincial city, Plymouth seemed to contain so many random possibilities and chances that the contrast was not entirely jarring. On a Friday or a Saturday night the thoroughfare of Union Street would be filled with drunken students and sailors on shore leave. Military Police patrol vehicles crawled up and down its neon promenade looking so much more fierce and imposing than their civilian counterparts.

The Military Police were a necessary presence in the city. On arriving at the university, the wide-eyed, small-town boy, I heard half-remembered stories, never properly confirmed as truth or urban myth, of drunken marines gang raping teenage girls and leaving them for dead. These stories couldn't help but add extra frisson to my nocturnal visits to the lido.

The last time I visited the Tinside Pool was shortly before my graduation. It was a night when even the breeze coming in from Plymouth Sound did little to counter the oppressive heat of summer; a night that promised storms. I walked down to the lido, and through the shadows, spotting the occasional silhouettes of strangers; the firefly-like tips of cigarettes hovering in the darkness.

Though I could barely see him, he didn't look old, perhaps nineteen, a little younger than myself, dressed in council estate leisure wear and gold jewellery.

"Let's go somewhere else," he said.

Within minutes I was face down in one of the secluded shelters alongside the promenade, his hand around my throat, as he roughly forced himself into me. The notion of consent had long ceased to have any meaning. He told me I was a 'fucking queer' and that I liked 'this sort of thing' and then he came and he punched me in the side of the head and he left me in the shadows.

I walked home along Union Street, wiping the dried blood from my lip and brushing the embedded bits of gravel and broken glass from my skin. A green Landrover pulled up at the side of the road, and a red-capped officer leaned out.

"You okay, son?" he said.

I nodded, though I could feel tears burning behind my eyes.

"Who did this? Get into a fight, did you?"

I shrugged.

"Was it squaddies?" the redcap asked.

I shook my head.

The redcap sighed and said something to his passenger and they drove away.

Weeks later I left Plymouth and endured eighteen mercifully brief months living with my parents and writing stories about jam festivals and foot-and-mouth for the local newspaper. After those eighteen months I moved to London, and a job as a junior reporter, writing stories about random and forgettable acts of violence and the kind of inexplicable events which are boxed away as single paragraphs: the Chinese woman who ended up in Torquay instead of Turkey, a record attempt at the most clothes pegs on a human face, a dog that thinks it's a monkey. You know the kind of thing I'm talking about. At the time it felt like an ascension, but now I'm not so sure.

Ten years after my last visit to Tinside lido I come in from my balcony, where I've been watching police helicopters cast their search beams down over the eastern suburbs of the city, and I re-read

Brian Fenton's last email. Then I walk to the bathroom and I stare at my reflection in the mirror. The bruises are beginning to fade. The scabs are drying out and falling off. I remember seeing myself the day after I was raped beside the Tinside Pool. I looked so broken, like there was something damaged inside, something irreparable. Something damaged, but something put in its place. I think about the email I sent Brian, telling him of my fictional rape beside Royal Victoria Dock, and if I think about it long enough, I'll realise with tears in my eyes that I wish I hadn't been lying.

the confession – 09:36

I think it's Friday morning. After a breakfast of malt loaf, sunflower seeds, vitamin supplements and water, I check my emails while listening to the planes.

Even with all the spam filters in the world there are still offers of college diplomas, offers of Viagra, offers of free porn for those of every sexual orientation. In amongst these loud advertisements I see an email from Ondine.

> Hey Ed,
>
> How are you doing? The office is dull dull dull without you, and Brian appears to have hired three toddlers to take over After Show. Big mistake. Big. Huge. They're going to call it something like Red Carpet. I mean… *Red Carpet*? It sounds like some sort of communist rug shop. And they won't even be writing it… Toby's going to be doing all the hard work. The reason I'm emailing you is just to check you're okay, and see if you fancied joining us tonight. It's the last *Lockdown* (like you didn't know already!) and we're all getting out of Docklands and going to watch it on a big screen in Bar Number 2 in Bishopsgate. You know… the converted underground gents toilets? Apparently very cool and you can't smell piss or shit or anything. I love the way that even these really cool places are getting so post-ironic that they're showing *Lockdown*. I can't wait for the tide to change when we can all go back to saying how much we hate it again. Who

do you think is going to win? All the bookies think it'll to be Colin. Let me know if you can make it.

Ondine xx

That name again. Colin Curtis. The hot favourite to win this series of *Lockdown*. My stomach turns. My hands shake while hovering over the keyboard, and I type my response.

Ondine,

I'm afraid I am unable to join you this evening. I have made a number of attempts, both mental and physical, to leave this apartment, but it does not appear to be possible. Something is wrong with people.

On the subject of Colin Curtis, I have little doubt that he will win this series of *Lockdown*, though I feel obliged to tell you, both as a colleague and a friend, that the man is a paedophile. Prior to his entering the *Lockdown* prison he served five years in a real prison for sexually molesting his six-year-old niece. I'm not entirely sure how, but Big TV has managed to keep this out of the other papers so far. The only reason we haven't covered the story is because of Trisha Smedley.

K-Media is selling the public a paedophile, and the public are buying him, and there is nothing we can do about it.

Ed

Thirty minutes later I receive a reply from Ondine.

I love it. Very dark, a bit weird, but so funny. Imagine if he was a paedophile. That would be crazy! See if you can make it tonight. It should be fun.

To which I reply.

No. He really is a paedophile. He molested his six-year-old niece. Big TV only found out about it during week one, but he has proved popular with the public and when they carried out a poll in week two they found that sixty-five per cent of viewers said they were only watching it because of him,

hence the decision to block the story getting out at every
turn. I think they may even have bribed the family. This is a
disaster waiting to happen. It could all go down in flames…
the company, the paper, everything. I've seen the court transcripts… it was horrible. When the rivals get wind of this it will
be finished. All of it.

Ondine replies after five minutes.

Okay, Ed… ha ha ha. I get the joke. Maybe see you later?

They won't see me later. They might never see me again. Like a
dumbstruck tourist on a beach, watching the coming tidal wave,
the best I can do is close my eyes and hold my breath.

lockdown, final episode – 21:00

I can feel the heat closing in.

On television the opening credits of *Lockdown* roll and the
camera pans up to the floodlit walls of what used to be HMP
Crowmarsh. The crowd screams. Cameras, hundreds of them,
flash in a machine-gun strobe.

It's the last one!

screams the presenter.

The last *Lockdown*. Can you believe it?

The audience screams. The presenter screams. If I could summon
up the energy I'd probably be screaming too, albeit for different
reasons.

We are treated to a montage of the day's events, accompanied
by a droll, monotonous voice-over. Calum and Colin have had
an argument over cigarettes and Jessica is missing Ronny (with
whom she had a number of sexual encounters) terribly. All three
appear haggard and withdrawn, as if twenty-six weeks in the
confines of this artfully dilapidated Victorian edifice have
finally begun to take their toll.

I don't know what freedom will be like,

says Jessica, walking around the exercise yard with her hands in the pockets of the overalls she has worn for a hundred and eighty days.

I can't remember freedom. I can't even remember what rain feels like.

For just one moment, in amongst all the flashing cameras, designer editing and screaming crowds, we are given a brief disturbing window into something that transcends primetime TV. It passes almost as soon as it has begun, dissolved and absorbed in a maelstrom of noise and bright colours.

Suddenly we are in another commercial break.

The C-Fish 32-L. What do *you* see?

Feros... Take a walk on the wild side.

One of them was the Son Of God, sent to Earth to die for our sins. One of them was the Fallen Angel, cast into Hell, and looking for revenge.

'I renounce you!'

'Yeah? Well renounce this!'

Jesus Vs Satan... released July nineteenth...

There follows another fifteen minutes of tension outside the disused prison on the outskirts of London, the presenter gripped with paroxysms of ecstasy, as she announces that the next person to be paroled from *Lockdown* will be...

Calum!

The crowd erupts in a Biblical wail. We cut to the interior of the prison where the cell door is flung open, and Calum steps out into this new kind of freedom. He is guided dramatically to the prison's entrance where one of the guards (an actor who you may recognise from toothpaste commercials) hands him his belongings before opening the door.

After four thousand three hundred and sixty eight hours inside this building Calum is suddenly frozen in the strobe of a thousand flashing cameras. The presenter rushes to his side and guides him along a catwalk, between two vast seas of hands reaching up to him as if he is suddenly imbued with something messianic. As Calum and the presenter step into a studio at the far end of the runway we go to another commercial break.

Are you or a loved one addicted to crack cocaine? Is it beginning to affect your family life, your job, your *finances*? Then call Crack Users UK. We can provide confidential advice on how to beat your cravings and sort out your life. Get back on track... wave goodbye to crack.

'How can I possibly go to Carol's wedding? I mean, look at my nose. I should have had something done about it years ago, but it's too late now. The wedding's only two weeks away.'

'You should try The Face People.'

'Who are they?'

'The Face People specialise in facial cosmetic surgery. Noses, chins, cheeks... they're the experts. Not only that, but The Face People guarantee one hundred per cent healing with no bruises or scars within ten days of surgery.'

'Really? That's amazing!'

'And not only that, but if you're a first-time customer, The Face People give you the offer of free collagen injections, electrolysis, or any number of other beauty treatments.'

'Great... I'll phone them now.'

'The Face People, because beauty really is skin deep.'

As we return to the show, the main attraction, I begin pacing frantically around my apartment. My breathing becomes erratic, syncopated with the frenetic beating of my heart. I need to speak to somebody, I need to tell them what is about to happen.

On television the presenter is interviewing Calum. She is telling him about ten million votes and people watching this live in twelve different countries. I grow dizzy thinking about the zeros and ones that are currently dancing through the ether; the phone calls and the C-Fish messages that are scrolling across the bottom of the screen.

WE ❤ U CALUM

CALUM UR THE BEST .

NICE 1 CALUM

Inside the prison we see the faces of Jessica and Colin, behind the bars of their cells. They look restless, anxious, waiting for the voice to tell them which of them has won the prize of a quarter of a million pounds and at least a month's worth of instant celebrity. To them, at least, it's instant. To the outside world their faces have been in magazines and newspapers on a daily basis. They have entered the fabric of our everyday lives. Their names have become brands.

The interview with Calum ends. He stands and faces the crowd to another almighty scream and another bombardment of flashing cameras. We go to another commercial break.

Worried about the coffee you drink and the chocolate you eat? Well embrace your guilt right now with Unfair Trade. Unfair Trade is a company dedicated to selling you goods produced by the exploited workers of the world without the deception and conceit of other brands. Unfair Trade coffee is picked by child labourers in Colombia who often work up to nineteen hours a day for seven days a week. In return for this they are paid the equivalent of only twelve pounds a *month*. Our chocolate is produced by the finest cocoa beans, harvested in Ghana by children as young as four.
Unfair Trade… the guilty pleasure.

The C-Fish 32-L. What do you see?

Feros. Take a walk on the wild side.

Aaaaaaaaaaaaaaaaaaaaaaaaaahhhh! Has anyone seen my Joo-Joo?

The new Tri-Turbine K from Aquinas. The perfection of power.

We return to *Lockdown*, and now I am in a state of abject panic. I want to bite off my fingers. I wonder what kind of satisfaction that would give me; the incredible, absolute pain coupled with the satisfying moment when my teeth meet and are clenched together, my mouth filling up with blood that tastes like old coins.

A crane shot looks down at the prison building, at the throbbing crowd caught in a dozen war-time spotlights. The twinkling orange lights of London look like a toy city on the horizon.

The votes have been counted...

says the presenter.

The world becomes silent, the screaming stops, as if everybody on the planet is holding their breath at the same time.

And we can now announce...

Why am I even bothering to watch this? This is like watching a car crash, or perhaps being able to witness your own death, but filmed in slow motion.

That the winner of this year's *Lockdown* is...

My fingers dig into the upholstery of my sofa. The leather squeaks and groans as if about to burst.

Colin!

A scream like you might hear on a passenger jet that's stuck in a terminal nosedive.

Inside the prison Colin's eyes grow suddenly wide, and he starts hollering and jumping up and down while Jessica does her best to smile and play the part of the good loser. Her cell door opens and she, like Calum, and Ronny, and every other contestant on this show, is taken to the entrance of the prison and offered to the public and the press like a fresh sacrifice.

I put my hands over my eyes and try and block out the noise, but it's useless. It's as if I can taste the chaos.

Jessica is led to the studio at the end of the runway, and interviewed, and grilled about her relationship with Ronny.

It all got very steamy in there!

says the presenter. The crowd laughs, whistles, and howls. Jessica blushes. I find myself fantasising about a sudden explosion, or perhaps a plane crash; an incident of such violence and disruption that it will be played on TV endlessly for years to come.

We wave goodbye to Jessica, and now it is the turn of Colin Curtis to leave the prison. When the doors open the sky erupts with innumerable fireworks. Combined with another almighty scream from the multitude is the cacophonous rumble of simultaneous explosions. If hell sounded like anything, I imagine it would be this.

Colin Curtis stands at the end of the runway, hurled into the spotlight. A smile appears on his face that others might take to be one of humility, or gratitude, but to me it's sinister. Colin Curtis must be wondering how on earth he has won this. I wonder whether he has spent the last twenty-six weeks waiting for his secret to be revealed to the public outside, for him to be launched into the outside world an overnight villain; the focus of an entire nation's hatred and outrage.

Instead he is greeted by worship.

I watch him smiling and I listen to the fireworks and the screaming of the crowd for a few more seconds before hitting the standby button on my remote.

saturday morning, eleven hours and thirty-two minutes after the last episode of *lockdown* series 2 – 09:32

On Saturday morning there are fewer commuters. It's possible to hear the sound the DLR train makes as it passes across the northern side of Royal Victoria Dock; the sounds of the city seem more individual and less a part of one almighty, sinister chorus. I have been out on the balcony, endlessly watching the footage of Saddam Hussein's hanging, but with spoof subtitles, when I notice Nigel from Apartment 413 standing on his balcony, only this time he has company.

With him is an elegant blonde in a slightly dated trouser suit that may have been more at home in the early 1990s, but still carries a certain amount of class. She looks somehow famous, perhaps as a result of my distance, and the surreptitious way in which I am watching them. They look out from the balcony, across the dock and toward the airport. Nigel speaks intermittently, pointing in the direction of different buildings. When there is an occasional respite from the sound of descending planes or passing trains it is possible to hear his voice as a distant mumbling. Her voice is strange, feminine but with a coarseness to it; not the voice I had imagined such an elegant woman to have.

Suddenly Nigel sees me, and though I want to duck out of view I wave politely, as a suburban neighbour might do from one side of a garden fence. He smiles warmly and waves back, before gesturing to his female companion. She turns and also smiles and waves, and I breathe in so suddenly I get a sharp, stabbing pain between my ribs.

The woman on the balcony with Nigel is Princess Diana.

Inside my apartment, standing very close to the window, I attempt to absorb what I have just seen, but it's no good. My version of reality, the only version I will ever have, appears to be failing me. Perhaps this is all merely a symptom of the phenomena going on in the rest of the city, indeed the rest of the country. Perhaps I was foolish to think that I could avoid it by staying inside these four walls. Then I am struck once more with a blinding revelation, something which causes me to breathe in until it hurts and hold my breath for fear of making a sound.

I know what Nigel from Apartment 413 meant when he referred to a plague. He was talking about these, the phenomena. I had assumed he meant a virus, a contagion; something tangible, albeit on a microscopic, sub-cellular level. Perhaps he did. I was brought up and educated to believe in a scientific reason for everything. The God preached and taught outside our atheist detached house in Devon was simply a God of the gaps, created by frightened children to explain away thunder, volcanoes, and infinity.

Newspapers (*The Voice of the People* being one of them) talk about moral decline and the death of human decency, as if these things were chosen by the people or voted for in a referendum. Where was I when the vote was cast?

No, this is something else. This is Nigel's virus. This is something we couldn't see or smell or even touch, but we could feel it on a very intimate bio-chemical level.

It is becoming increasingly clear that I need to find some way to leave my apartment and establish proper contact with Nigel. Perhaps there are others in this building.

Princess Diana.

No, it wasn't Princess Diana. I did not see Princess Diana. What I saw was perhaps a memory of a famous face reflected in the features of somebody with a passing resemblance. Why though, if that were the case, had such an effort been made to perfect the hair, the clothes?

I find a notepad in a cluttered drawer full of stationery, along with a black ballpoint pen, and I try to make a diagram that might explain all this to myself.

First there was… first there was what?

First there was the insect. I remember seeing an insect. And people were talking.

Before that. There was something before that. Or maybe after that. The skinhead. I saw the skinhead on the DLR and he smiled at me. But *did* I see him on the DLR? I saw him near Tinside Pool, but I was younger. He hit me and shattered my teeth. He fucked me while I didn't scream.

When did *this* happen?

When *did* this happen?

Did this happen?

I look at the word 'skinhead' scrawled on the notepad. I don't even recognise my own handwriting. The near silence of my apartment is interrupted, shattered by the loud buzzing of the intercom. When I answer it I hear a familiar voice that almost makes me weep.

"Ed, it's Ondine. I need to speak to you."

"Ondine… " I say, her name almost choking me with happiness. I buzz her in and within a minute she is stood at my door.

"Oh God, Ed… " She says. "What… what's happened?"

I ask her what she means.

"You, I mean… what's happened?"

Still unsure what she means I shrug. "No work… no play," I say, hoping to string together a familiar phrase but failing. "Things have… been getting a bit on top of me lately."

I invite her into my apartment and even with my somewhat clouded senses I can still see the look of vague disgust as she surveys my room full of litter; empty envelopes, bottles, cartons, scattered around the room. For some reason it is the first time that *I* have noticed any of these things. I almost laugh.

I tell her to sit, but seeing no clear space on any of the sofas she shrugs apologetically and remains standing at the balcony window.

"We need to talk," she says.

"What about?" I ask.

"Colin Curtis," she replies. "The email you sent me." She starts shaking her head and pacing back and fore in front of the window. "It was all true, wasn't it?"

"What do you mean?"

"About him being a convicted paedophile. He is, isn't he?"

"Yes."

"Oh God, Ed, why didn't you tell me?"

"I *did* tell you. In my email."

"Before then. Why didn't you tell anyone?"

"Because it was the truth."

She stops pacing and looks at me, her eyes becoming suddenly wider. She fumbles in her handbag for her cigarettes and a lighter.

"What the fuck is that supposed to mean?" She asks. "Look at you, Ed. What the fuck has happened to you? We don't see you for – what – two weeks? You haven't shaved. You look like you haven't changed your clothes. Are those *bruises* on your face? Then you send me this email… and I was worried. I was actually worried about you. I'm *still* worried about you. But the email was *true*?"

"How did you find out?"

"*The Sun* has got something on it. The victim's cousin. Somebody Big TV didn't pay off. Somebody outside our reach. It's going to be on the front page of Monday's paper."

I start laughing softly.

"It'll be beautiful," I say.

"What do you mean, beautiful? It's going to make us look like idiots. It's going to kill *Lockdown*, which is going to kill Big TV, which might just kill K-Media. Jesus… this fucking kiddie fiddler might just be the end of us."

"Like dominoes," I say. "Beautiful."

"Would you stop saying 'beautiful', Ed? You don't care, do you?"

I smile, trying for just one second to make it look like I *do* care, but it's impossible.

"How do we sort this, Ed?"

"Why are you asking me?"

"Because I don't give people glowing reviews, Ed. I don't build people up. I don't make people look good. I upset people. I destroy them. I plaster pictures of them stumbling out of brothels all over two-page spreads and I do it with pleasure. How do we rescue this? If we savage Colin Curtis we savage the show. If we savage the show we're savaging Big TV and K-Media. It'll be like biting at a loose fingernail only to end up chewing our fucking arm off. We can't do this. We *can't* do this."

"You could always try to make him look good."

Ondine looks at me as if I have just performed some obscene act or said something blasphemous.

"Are you insane?" she says. "Make him look good? He's a pae-dophile, Ed. He has abused children. We can't make this look good. It's impossible."

"Not impossible," I say, shaking my head. I realise that when I speak out loud I have started slurring, a possible side effect of having spoken to only one person in over two weeks. "We decide who they love and who they hate, not them. Tell them they love Colin Curtis. Everybody loves a bad boy."

Ondine is now walking toward the door, a thin trail of blue smoke following her cigarette.

"You really are insane," she says. "I'm sorry, Ed, but there's too much going on out there. I can't deal with this right now. There's too much happening. First Bruce Albion, now you."

I ask her what has happened to Bruce Albion.

"He was on *Night Talk* on Thursday. Started ranting. I think he was drunk, or maybe on something. He used the N word. What's *wrong* with people?"

"I know what you're talking about, Ondine." I say. "I've felt it too. You think it's me. You're probably trying to blame me right now, but trust me it isn't. Something's wrong with people. A virus or something."

"Goodbye, Ed."

"No, Ondine… you need to believe me. You need to tell the others."

She walks out through the door and into the corridor. I try to follow her but become suddenly nauseous from the smell of cooking and the citrus tang of old sweat. She looks back at me just once before boarding the elevator. She looks as if she is crying.

monday – 10:30

And I suppose the question many are asking is just how much did the producers of *Lockdown* know before they let him in the prison?

Well, Graham, that's an interesting point. Having worked in television I can say quite confidently that the producers were aware. It's curious that no immediate member of the victim's family came forward while the show was on television; though obviously there are all manner of legal reasons why this can't be explained right now. I suppose it does raise a lot of interesting questions regarding the ethics of a television programme like...

...the news that *Lockdown* winner Colin Curtis is a convicted paedophile only recently released from a genuine term in prison has come as a shock to many in the...

Mr Curtis is currently a resident at the Savoy Hotel in London, courtesy of Big TV. It is thought that the other *Lockdown* contestants were also staying at the hotel, but that several have left in protest. Of course, they are contractually forbidden from stating their reasons at this moment, but those contracts will only be valid until...

Curtis, thirty-four, served a five-year sentence at Dartmoor Prison for sexually assaulting a six-year-old girl. He was originally sentenced to eight years with the possibility of parole after five...

Of course, everyone's talking about Colin. Having won the series with so many votes I imagine there are a lot of people out there asking themselves some very difficult questions. Especially people with families.

Interesting to see *The Voice of the People*'s front page this morning... of course they were the official *Lockdown* paper and had exclusive rights to interview Colin on his release from the show... The headline this morning: '*I served my time*' and under that, '*I am so, so sorry for what I did*'. I suppose that raises the question of whether these people can be rehabilitated, and if they can how we should treat them and react to them?

Yes, absolutely... It's true that he served five years in prison, and already we are getting reports that while in prison he did receive a pioneering treatment previously tested in Denmark...

...that a convicted paedophile has won the country's number one reality TV show... unbelievable... just unbelievable. I mean...

Mr Curtis was seen leaving the Savoy Hotel with a number of security guards before going to The Ivy where he had dinner with a number of *Lockdown* producers and executives from Big TV. No word yet on what was being discussed at...

Well I just think it's shocking.

So, Doctor Yager, could you tell us a little about this treatment? What does it involve?

Well, you see, the client… we always refer to them as the client and not the patient, or the prisoner… is placed in the programme for up to twelve months. In that time they will go through cognitive therapy, psychotherapy, and a drug treatment, the dosage of which can be reduced as time goes on…

…and the only word from the victim's family has come in the form of a very brief statement through a family solicitor, making it clear that they do not wish to make any kind of statement. Mixed reports coming from other family members who have spoken to the press… talk of bribery from certain key figures, though obviously none of this can be conf…

One has to ask whether any of this really matters. It's a little like the rapist who won the lottery. Those protesting against such things are clearly missing the point of a lottery. There is no right and wrong, it is a game of chance, and so it is with reality television. The watching of such shows is not compulsory, we do not demand the same levels of honesty and openness as we might require from politicians or those in positions of power…

We can confirm that Mr Curtis has now left The Ivy and has returned to the Savoy Hotel, though he has not yet issued any kind of statement other than his interview with *The Voice of the People*, an interview which appears to have tipped public opinion somewhat. In an opinion poll carried out only forty-five minutes ago, three out of five people said they think a person's prior convictions should have no bearing on their life once they have served their time, providing they do not re-offend.

That's very interesting.

Very interesting indeed, Tom. We asked some people here in Leicester Square what they thought of the matter…

I think they should lock them all up for life. They're perverts, the lot of them.

Well, he has done his time. And he says he's sorry in the paper… Maybe he means it. Who are we to judge?

I don't know and I don't care.

Who's that? Oh, him off that programme? Yeah, I was reading about that in the paper this morning. I don't know… all a lot of fuss over nothing, isn't it? I mean, the girl's family haven't said anything about it… let sleeping dogs lie, I say.

Well, he seemed like a really nice guy on the show. You can't fake that, not for twenty-six weeks. Maybe he is a changed person.

They should have chemically castrated him and thrown away the key.

Torture's too good for people like him.

I don't know… I voted for him. He's got a cheeky smile.

Doesn't make a difference to me. It's what's inside that counts.

Seems like an alright bloke. I was reading that interview with him in the paper.

People can change. The girl was probably too young to remember anything, anyway.

Yes, and you know what young girls are like these days… they're just as bad.

Everyone deserves a second chance.

Well, he seems to be making a go of it.

I am breathing too quickly. My heartbeat is irregular. I imagine Ondine stumbling from my building on Saturday morning; sickened by the state she has seen me in, by the disaster zone that is my apartment. She would have put out her cigarette before hastily lighting another one. Then she would have tentatively made her way back to her car (an Alfa Romeo if I remember correctly) and driven back to Canary Wharf. Despite it being a Saturday there would have been a skeleton staff sat around the newsroom, including a palpitating Brian Fenton, all of them with bags under their eyes, chewing nicotine gum and frantically drinking vending machine espressos.

She would have sat in silence for a while as the others talked about damage limitation before she finally found the courage to say something.

"We… we could always try to make him look good," she would

have said, and the others would have looked at her with that same look she gave me. Then, slowly but surely, they would have started nodding. Brian would have started nodding too.

In true MGM musical style he might have even said, "It's a crazy idea, but it might just work".

By that evening they would have contacted Colin Curtis at the Savoy and arranged to interview him. By this morning it would have been front page news:

I SERVED MY TIME

answerphone – 13:12

You have... one... new message.

Hi Ed. It's Serge. I'm just calling to see how you are. I guess you're there but you aren't answering, huh? God, I hate these things. I always sound like such an idiot when I'm using them. It's so weird, don't you think? When you think about your voice echoing round an empty house or an empty flat. It's like the loneliest sound in the world or something.
Anyway... I saw Ondine. She looked kind of stressed. Busy in work, I guess. She looked kind of... what's the word you use? Wired? Is wired the right word? Anyway... she looked kind of crazy. She said... well, never mind. I just thought I'd call you. She said you were taking some time off from work. I thought maybe you might be ill or something. So if there's anything you need, any shopping or anything like that, I don't know... maybe you need me to get you medicine or something... I don't know...
We should meet up some time. For dinner or something. You know, if you're feeling better some time.
Okay... well... I'll, um... I'll see you around, I guess. You know if you need anything you can call me. You still have my number. Bye.

End of messages.

attempt to leave the apartment #1 – 11:32

I have decided it is entirely necessary for me to leave the confines of my apartment. My sense of geography has become warped in recent days. I visualise the city as a grid beneath my window. I imagine phone wires passing over and above the ground like communication tunnels, all of them leading to my rooms. In this vision my apartment is a control hub at the centre of a vast network of blinking lights and streamlined circuitry. My seclusion has left me a little egocentric perhaps, and I am not convinced that this is good for the soul. I need to reconnect, but with who?

My first idea is to fashion some kind of device that could physically pass handwritten notes to the balcony of Apartment 413. If I could establish two-way contact with Nigel then this might enable me to engage with the outside world in a way that isn't virtual. Then, and only then, will my perception of what is real have any relevance.

I quickly realise that it will be impossible to pass handwritten notes to Nigel unless he is complicit in the plan from the start. I do not have any kind of string or rope, not even cotton, with which to make a line that I could pass to his balcony. Furthermore, his balcony is not only below mine, but several apartments away and at a vaguely obtuse angle, Velocity House being roughly the same shape as a tick.

My only real option is to leave the apartment and travel down to the fourth floor. Just thinking about this makes me nauseous. The thought of human interaction in itself is disturbing. My elation at seeing Ondine would appear to be an anomaly, as when I consider talking to any other people I feel physically ill and want to lock myself in a darkened room.

Even so, I know that I need to leave the apartment. I managed to do this when the shopping was delivered, I am sure that I can manage it again. On that occasion the light was different, somehow brighter when I walked out of the door. More intense. And the human smells were overwhelming. It was as if I could smell every pollutant leaking out of every human body. Every drop of saturated fat, nicotine, and alcohol. Every last bead of amphetamine-laced sweat, every breath laced with coffee and tobacco smoke. I could smell the rank ammonia stench of urine and the sickeningly sweet smell of sugary faecal matter.

I remember something about using a damp cloth placed over the mouth to reduce smoke inhalation during a fire. Perhaps the same rule would apply for this new kind of pollution. I soak a clean kitchen cloth under the cold tap and place it over my mouth. I can still breathe.

Concerned that any new kind of virus might be communicable through the soft tissue around my eyes I root out the swimming goggles I bought when they started over-chlorinating the swimming pool at my old gym. I clean the fingerprint-smudged lenses, and put them on. I contemplate protecting my skin in some way, as you might against the harmful rays of the sun, but realise I have nothing to hand.

When I open the door my apartment breathes out again; a sudden gust of air as if the outside world were a vacuum. I stand in the doorway for some time. The breeze passes over and around me, sweeping in from the balcony, through my apartment, and out into the hungry corridor.

What I can hear is the sound of televisions, multiple televisions, and people talking. They chatter into their telephones and C-Fishes, but nobody seems to be having a conversation with anybody who is in the same room as them. What I can see through the blue plastic goggles is the short corridor and, at the far end, the dull silver of the sliding doors. What I can smell is rotting flesh.

I try to regulate my breathing, drops of water leaving the cloth and landing on my tongue every time I inhale. When I put my foot down in the corridor it feels suddenly electrified. My breathing quickens again. I think I can hear children's voices from a neighbouring apartment.

If the children leave the apartment and see me breathing through a cloth and wearing swimming goggles they will tell their parents and their parents will assume it is all a part of some kind of bizarre autoerotic-asphyxiation ritual. They will call the police, the police will come here, arrest me, and take me to a station. The station will involve far too much exposure to whatever plague it is that Nigel has identified. If this plague genuinely is spreading then I can only imagine that it is hospitals and police stations that are bearing the brunt of it. I will have to sit in a cell that might already be contaminated with DNA-rich samples such as blood, spit and semen. The neighbouring cells will be filled with those already infected with the virus, and if it's airborne it will filter out under each heavy iron door or through each observation grill, through the corridors and into each neighbouring cell. A passing police officer breathes in, the virus enters his or her lungs via an airborne nuclei of evaporated droplets containing infected micro-organisms, or perhaps through infected dust particles. The police officer finishes the shift, and they go home on the tube. Every time they breathe out, a new batch of infected particles swarms through the air and into the body of a neighbouring passenger. It spreads like a viral Fibonacci along the carriage, and on disembarking from the train each and every newly infected passenger will pass it on to all those they come into contact with.

I step back into my apartment and slam the door behind me.

attempt to leave the apartment #2 – 17:22

I am at the door again. It's open, but now the corridor is quiet. I can no longer hear the voices of children. Earlier I discovered a packet of elastic bands in a drawer and I have used those to hold the damp cloth to my face. My appearance is still possibly a little strange, but I can't help but think that the image of me holding the cloth to my face with my hand would have more closely resembled an act of sexual perversion.

The cloth amplifies the sound of my breathing, which is measured and slow. I check my pulse, and it too is more regular than during my last attempt. I've placed small pieces of cotton wool in my nostrils so that I can no longer smell the awful stench that now infests the rest of the building.

I place one foot into the corridor, and then the other, without closing the door behind me. I take a very deep breath.

The thought occurs to me that a door on this corridor could open at any time. I realise that one of my neighbours, perhaps one of the lipstick lesbians from 1005 or the French guy from 1006 might step out into the corridor and see me with this makeshift filter wrapped around the lower half of my face, the elastic bands digging creases into my skin. They might react to this in a completely unpredictable way. With the contagion spreading as it is, who can say what their reaction will be?

They might step back into their apartment, closing and locking the door before telling a loved one what they've just seen. This delay in them leaving their apartment might then have further repercussions. Just a nanosecond's difference in timing might mean that they will not be driving along Silvertown Way at the precise moment when a heavy goods vehicle jack-knifes, its trailer skidding across every lane, taking the tops off several vehicles, including that driven by my neighbour. Their resulting non-death could then have all manner of further consequences. A child might be born who was never meant to be born; a child whose very existence might have a profound effect on the world for centuries to come.

My leaving the apartment, looking as I do, at this very moment, could be the most calamitous event in world history, and nobody would know except me. Although the eventual outcome might happen many years after my death, I would always know that the world was a different place because I chose to leave my apartment, to expose myself to the physical actions of every other human being on the planet. I would have participated in the great, chaotic circus of human events, something I have practically sworn not to do.

Every second that I am standing in this corridor, facing the elevator doors, the risk of me becoming a complicit agent of chaos increases, just as your risk of an untimely death must surely increase every time you attempt to walk along a tightrope or swim with great white sharks.

I step back into my apartment once more and close the door. The relief this brings about is almost indescribable, as if news of a loved one's death had proven to be premature; a case of mistaken identity. I am out of the corridor and back inside my territory. I am no longer an active cog in the chaos machine. The burden of complicity has been lifted from my shoulders.

I settle in front of the television.

Next we'll be looking at some patriotic squirrels in Wisconsin, and a cat that has survived on nothing but rain water for two weeks, right after this break.

... reaching the mid-thirties by around lunch time tomorrow...

... Take a walk on the wild side.

The sounds and images are my panacea. In these rooms I am safe. With my involvement with the outside world limited to a one-way flow of information I am happy. But still I know I need to leave this apartment.

attempt to leave the apartment #3 – 00:28

I wait until after midnight. No more planes landing at City Airport. No more DLR trains. No more nearby traffic sounding like the washing of waves against a shore. The neighbouring apartments fall silent also. I watch them from my balcony as one by one the lights go out. The dinner party on a lower balcony finishes with a round of espressos, quickly followed by lazily smoked cigarettes, before moving indoors. Soon the whole of Royal Victoria Dock is possessed by an eerie silence.

It isn't a true silence, of course, for there is no such thing, but it is as close as a city can come to it. The sounds I can hear are travelling great distances. They are isolated, lonely somehow; echoing over the great grid of the eastern parts of the city. A distant siren. A distant train. A plane passing over at an altitude of thirty or forty thousand feet.

Now I can face it. The outside world, I mean. Now it's as if somebody has simply put the world on standby.

I open my door, holding the dampened cloth to my face, and this time (after checking for the third time that I have my set of keys) I close the door behind me. I edge my way along the corridor, listening in at each door that I pass for any evidence of activity on the other side. There is nothing. When I finally reach the brushed metal doors of the elevator I reach out and touch the cold steel. This in itself is an achievement. I hit the button with the downwards-pointing arrow and I wait.

On the other side of the doors I hear a pre-recorded female voice say, Tenth floor. Doors opening. When the doors open I step into the elevator, and I press the button marked '4'. The pre-recorded woman's voice says, Doors closing. Going down. Seconds later she announces the fourth floor, and the doors open again. It strikes me that if it weren't for that initial feeling of motion the experience of travelling in an elevator would be quite disconcerting, especially in a building such as this. The doors open and, seemingly, nothing has changed. I am in an identical corridor, with identical walls, doors and carpet. Only the numbers have changed.

Stepping out onto the fourth floor I wait for the doors to close again before proceeding along the corridor, checking each door number, until I reach Apartment 413. I ring the doorbell. From the other side of the door I hear footsteps and then the jangling of keys. When the door opens it does so by only a few inches, a short chain preventing it from opening any further. Nigel appears in the narrow gap, studying me carefully with his narrow, piercing blue eyes before smiling. He's taller than I'd imagined when I saw him from my balcony; tall and angular, with long, slender hands like Akhenaten. His skin is weathered with fine lines, though his face retains a certain boyishness. His mouth is feminine and sensual.

"I knew you'd come," he says eventually, his voice soft and calm and as soothing as the crackling of a log fire. "You're a very brave man."

He rattles the chain free and opens the door fully.

"Come in."

I follow him into the apartment, which is based on exactly the same plan as mine, but in terms of décor could not be more different. The rooms smell of tobacco smoke and incense. The walls are lined with either bookshelves or an eclectic assortment of images.

I see Neil Armstrong. I see Henry VIII. I see the Horsehead Nebula. I see Warhol's 'Marilyn'. I see United Airlines Flight 175, a split second before it crashes into the South Tower of the World Trade Centre, forever frozen in a moment of doom. I see Van Gogh's sunflowers. I see the face of Jeffrey Dahmer. I see R. Budd Dwyer with a .357 Magnum in his mouth. I see John Lennon signing an autograph for Mark David Chapman. I see an advertisement for Pears Soap. I see Frame 150 of the Zapruder Footage. I see Constable's 'The Haywain'.

"Please, sit down," says Nigel. "Would you care for coffee? Or tea, perhaps?"

"Coffee, please."

"I'm afraid I don't have any sugar."

"That's… that's fine."

He enters the kitchen and sets about measuring spoonfuls of coffee into the filter and then filling the machine with water.

"I knew you'd come," he says once more, beaming this time. When he speaks it's with practised elocution, as if this isn't the way he's always spoken. "And don't think it isn't appreciated. I realise how hard it must have been for you."

I ask him what he means. He returns to the living room, resting in a suitably antique leather armchair which groans when he sits.

"This plague," he says, nodding sagely, as if there is already a silent agreement between us. "Outside these rooms. Outside this building."

"What do you mean by plague?" I ask. I think I know what he is about to say, but even so I want to hear him say it.

"Oh… there's no need to be bashful," says Nigel. "I think we both know what I'm talking about. You've seen the outside world. You've been on the front lines. Don't think I didn't recognise you. From your photograph in that newspaper. The plague is very real and very present. Not a disease, you understand. You know what I'm talking about?"

I shake my head.

"But you *do*," he says. "The world… outside these rooms, outside this building, is changing. But not the city. Not its geography. Its people. The people are changing. We are witnessing the complete collapse of the collective psyche. The end of morphic resonance."

Once more I ask him what he means.

"Our evolutionary impulse… our universal truths. The termite builds the termite nest not because it has chosen to do so, or even because it desires to do so, but because it has to, in the same way that you or I must eat, breathe, or engage in sexual intercourse. Oh, sure, we decorate these acts. If we breathe we must do so through exercise or meditation, or we must breathe clean and sweetly fragranced air. If we eat then we must eat in the finest restaurants, or we must eat fresh fruit and vegetables and free-range eggs. If we have sexual intercourse then it must be with someone we love, or with someone we find attractive, or with someone who will indulge our individual perversions. We make it seem as if we still have choice in each of these matters but we don't. Every single strand of genetic material in our clumsy, semi-evolved bodies is telling us to eat, breathe, and fuck."

I tell him that I still don't quite understand how this relates to his plague.

"The imperative is being forgotten, at best, and at worst confused. So many streams of information, so many options… people are losing track of what they need. A brand new C-Fish becomes a more important commodity than food. The rush of driving a stolen car encourages a flow of endorphins greater than that experienced after sexual intercourse. Likewise any act of violence or cruelty."

"But you called this a virus," I say. "How can it be a virus if you are just blaming it on the media?"

"Oh, it is a virus. It's simply a virus that has been fed back to us from technology. The first virus of its kind. I dare say doctors and scientists will never be able to identify it properly. Why should they? The symptoms are so broad, and yet they're so clear to even the most casual observer."

He pauses briefly to check the coffee-maker in the kitchen, before leaning close to me and whispering in conspiratorial tones, "A man was murdered at a furniture store the other day. Murdered. He had taken a parking space that another driver wanted… the ensuing fracas resulted in his murder. He was stabbed in the throat, while the children in *both* cars looked on in horror. At least I like to think they looked on in horror. It's entirely possible they watched the whole sorry spectacle unfold with dreary indifference.

"A young woman was pushed onto the tracks at White City underground station perhaps a week ago. A teenage boy pushed her onto the tracks, and was caught on CCTV. When asked why he did it he replied that he was just curious. The police found a video of the crime on the boy's C-Fish.

"There's talk of riots not far from here. Nobody knows why, but there *will* be riots. The summer's heat. The simple anxiety of living. Violence for the sake of violence. Who knows? But violence is more than just a physical act, you understand. It's become a language. Perhaps the only universal language of the new Babel. And with it we've found a new currency."

He looks to the kitchen once more.

"Oh… " he says, "the coffee's ready."

He walks to the kitchen and minutes later returns with two cups of black coffee.

"What do you mean, currency?" I ask him.

"Oh, you know," he says, pursing his lips to blow on the surface of his coffee and then smiling broadly. "You've been one of its most enthusiastic traders. Violence is the language. Celebrity, my friend, is the currency."

"Celebrity?"

"Yes. It's quite different from wealth, but I'm sure you already knew that. Celebrity is a self-contained economy, but one which violently disobeys all the rules of that oldest of professions, prostitution. Prostitution is indeed the oldest profession, because all professions since have been based upon it in some way. Every job is a variation on its theme. You perform a task or provide a service in exchange for the infinite abstraction of money. That money you then give to others so that they too can perform a task or provide a service. Celebrity is different. Our celebrities do not trade in service, they do not perform a task, as such, and they do not receive money. They simply exist, and their reward for existing is to be exposed. Like the Ouroboros. The snake swallowing its own tail. They are famous because they are exposed so we expose them because they are famous.

"We've used this rather sordid and unfathomable process to create a different class system, one to replace that faded and chipped antique of Victorian England that was well and truly shattered by the twentieth century. We lose our Gods and our Monarchs, our Lords, Ladies and Gentlemen, and we replace them with reality TV show winners and game show contestants, pop stars and actors from soap operas. What part of our evolutionary imperative does this serve? Answer… none. It doesn't serve us. We don't crave it for survival, or even to serve our base need for social inclusion. And yet we crave it all the same."

I am shaking my head and looking down into my coffee, trying to fathom what he is telling me.

"You say that violence is a language…" I say, "but that *celebrity* is the currency… what do you mean? None of this is making sense. What about sex? Does sex not count?"

"Not any more."

"What does *that* mean?"

"When the internet first started, its primary use was as a medium for transmitting pornography. This has changed. The most looked-at websites now are those showing video footage of real acts of violence or death. Every second of every day somebody, somewhere in the world, is watching planes crash into the World Trade Centre. Somebody is watching beheadings and hangings in the Middle East

"Violence is the new language. Celebrity is the new currency."

I look up at him. He is smiling as if to somehow imply my complicity in this.

"What's my role?" I ask. "You think I play a part in this because of the newspaper?"

"Absolutely," says Nigel. "We've waited a long time for somebody like you to come along."

"We?"

"I wouldn't say that we are an organisation. The word is meaningless these days. But we are a collective. A collective that has
monitored the spread of the plague. We always knew there would
be a like-minded soul who has operated within the system, within
the very source of the malaise."

"Me?"

"Of course you. We only witness the cult of celebrity through our
televisions and our computer screens. You have winced at the flash-
lights of the cameras and breathed the same air as these people. And
you have taken absence without leave from the front line, am I
right? I've seen you on your balcony. The way you watch the city,
as if you're looking for an answer. We can spot those who have
seen things for what they really are. You are one of us."

I put my cup down on Nigel's coffee table without having taken
a sip.

"No," I say, standing. "I… things have been getting on top of
me lately."

"Yes, of course they have. But only because you know."

"No… it's more than that… "

"Reality is failing you, Ed Raynes. Think of this as an open
invitation to do something about that. We are in the process of for-
mulating a plan to correct the problem."

"Correct it? But how?"

"One act. That's all it will take. It seems very clear to us now
that it was one act that started all this, so therefore it must be one
act that finishes it. Realigns this broken path we've been following for the past decade. Sets the broken bone of our existence and
mends it permanently."

"What act?"

"It will become clear in the coming days. Your active involvement with the currency of our times has accelerated the situation,
you might say. We have been paying particular attention to Mr
Curtis."

"Colin?"

"Yes. Colin Curtis. A very interesting character. Not so much a
person as a symptom." Nigel looks at the ground and shakes his
head, laughing as he does so. "He is not the cancer itself, but he

is the pain. He is the dark patch on the x-ray. He is the quiet and sensitive tone of voice adopted by a doctor giving you the terrible news."

"But what about him?"

"It *will* become clear in the coming days. You haven't touched your coffee. Oh, you *do* take sugar, don't you? I'm terribly sorry, but I'm unaccustomed to having visitors."

"What about the woman?" I ask him. "I saw her here, the other day."

He laughs softly. "Woman?" he says. "Oh, you mean Dee?"

"She looked like Diana," I say.

"Yes, she does, doesn't she? All by design. Dee is a little like you, though she never reached your lofty heights, nor has she experienced that world of celebrity at such close contact. She exists in the suburbs of celebrity… the run-down dilapidated slums of fame. She started as an impersonator in nightclubs… performing in a revue of transsexual lookalikes. There were no other famous females to whom she bore any kind of physical resemblance, and so when Diana died she assumed her career was over. *Au contraire*. She soon found herself very much in demand. A Belgian banker paid for her to travel to Brussels, where she was photographed sitting in the back of a Mercedes virtually identical to the one in which the Princess died. She quickly found herself on the fringes of a very new kind of prostitution. When she had achieved financial stability she quickly retreated from that world."

"But the clothes… her hair…"

"It's become second nature to her. For five or six years Dee had lived in the image of Diana. After her operation she realised she would always look that way, because as a woman she had only ever looked like Diana. It *does* give her a melancholy bent. It must be a disheartening experience to be forever dead."

"Are there others?" I ask.

"Oh yes," says Nigel. "Call us Legion, for we are many." He chuckles, sipping at his coffee and looking out toward the window and the city beyond. "In any other era we may have remained isolated, alone, but we are living in the greatest revolution of them all. One that enables communication without us ever having to meet. Dee is rare. I met her when she was at her lowest ebb, in the months before I chose to distance myself from the world of all-you-can-eat buffets, traffic jams, and 'mind the gap'."

I ask him what he did before he made that choice.

"It really doesn't matter," he says. "My life before was quite trivial. My father died, having said only four words to me in a decade, but left me a considerable inheritance. That enabled me to retire from any participation in the so-called rat race. It's become such a cliché, don't you think, that term? And yet, if one looks at it closely, it sums us up so perfectly. And so disturbingly. Rats were, of course, blamed for the plague of 1665.

"They say it was the Great Fire the following year which ended the plague. Sure, there were only six confirmed deaths in the fire, but the rats had been living in the thatched roofs of the old city's buildings. Their mass-extermination and the end of the plague are very probably related. I wonder, if we are the carriers of this new virus, what will our Great Fire be?"

There follows a long silence between us. Nigel's expression becomes wistful, contemplative, as if he is genuinely pondering this.

I look at the clock on the wall. It's late. Thoughts begin and end in nanoseconds; half-recollected memories crash into whatever feelings I have toward Nigel and his world. Everything has the quality of a dream when you choose to disconnect yourself from daily interaction with other people, and so, like a dream, you come to question the validity of what you see and hear.

I tell him I need to leave.

"So soon?" says Nigel. "But we were only just getting acquainted."

I say nothing. The confines of his apartment have become suddenly overbearing, as if every picture on every wall is moving inward; the rooms becoming smaller. I feel as if I am being bombarded with imagery. I get up and make my way to the door. As I enter the elevator I look back to see him standing in the doorway.

"I see your emptiness," he says, smiling. "Onwards and upwards."

The elevator doors close.

tv now – 11:33

…the body was found at approximately six o'clock this morning…

…continued until the early hours, leaving three dead and sixteen injured. Police say they are…

…airports across the country were on a high security alert this morning as…

You won't go wrong with Derekon…

…car-bomb which exploded at approximately…

…aerial bombardment throughout the night…

…have announced that they will be featuring *Lockdown* star Colin Curtis on the front cover of this week's issue.

I stop changing the channels and lean forward, sat on the edge of the sofa.

The image, which has caused some controversy, features Mr Curtis and a group of children who are pretending to be scared of him.

The image appears on screen. Colin Curtis stands before a group of theatrically cowering children, his hands raised in a parody of villainy, his mouth wide open in a snarling rictus. The children are all silently screaming, looking at the viewer as if pleading to be rescued from this monster. The whole thing is underpinned with comic exaggeration. We are meant to be laughing at this.

TV Now has said the image is not intended to cause offence, but is in fact an ironic commentary on the revelation that Mr Curtis is a convicted sex offender who sexually assaulted a six-year-old girl. Mr Curtis told press this morning that he was delighted with the photo, asking reporters, 'If I can see the funny side of it, why can't anyone else?'

Meanwhile, an insider at *Cosmopolitan* magazine told us Mr Curtis is a firm favourite to make the top ten in next month's countdown of the top one hundred British bachelors. Keith, it's back to you.

I cover my face with my hands. Back in the studio 'Keith' is now talking about weight loss pills and their side-effects. He cuts to an interview with a woman with no hair.

My telephone rings, and I jump up from the sofa, my hands falling to my sides. My telephone hasn't rung in perhaps a month. The landline exists only to allow access to the internet. The telephone itself is little more than an ornament. When I allowed the C-Fish to die and then hurled it into the rubbish I assumed I was virtually beyond contact; where I wanted to be.

When I lift the handset I hear my sister's voice.

"Thanks for my card."

I ask her what she means.

"My birthday. Thanks for my card. That you didn't send. You know I don't expect a present. It's too must hassle, the posting and the picking it up from the depot when I'm not here to collect it, and vouchers are just too impersonal. You might as well tell somebody how much they're worth to you in monetary terms. But a card would have been nice."

Her birthday. I'm not even sure what day it was, but I can safely assume from her tone of voice that it has passed. I can't remember the last time I thought of her.

"I'm sorry...?" I say.

"Okay, Ed. You're in London. We're down here in Hicksville. I'm sure you've got much more impressive things to be getting on with. Like your newspaper column." There's sarcasm in her voice now. I don't say anything in response. "Do mum and dad know you've been fired?"

"I haven't been fired."

"No, but you aren't writing the column at the moment. Why is that?"

"I'm taking a sabbatical."

"To do what?"

"A book," I tell her. "I'm writing a book."

"Oh *really*?" she says. I'm not sure whether she's impressed or whether she doesn't believe me. "And how is that working out for you?"

"It's going okay." I tell her. "I've written a hundred and one pages." I'm not even sure where that figure came from.

"And what kind of a book is it?" asks Lola.

She's good. And she doesn't believe me.

"Fiction." I reply, perhaps a little too abruptly.

"Right. You're kind of lucky mum and dad don't read your paper. I think they used to, when you started writing the column. They won't now, of course. For religious reasons. It's the page four models. They morally object to it. They won't even go round to the Barnetts' since their daughter got her lip pierced and coloured her hair."

"Lola... " I say. It's the beginning of a sentence I'll never finish.

Very suddenly, when I close my eyes, I can see us as a family, walking down toward the seafront of St Ives on Harbour Day. The four of us formed a chain, holding each other's hands, and we stopped for ice cream on the narrow cobbled street. I remember squinting against the sun as mum took a photo of us. That photograph would end up locked behind acetate in one of a dozen or more albums that lived on a shelf in their living room.

"What were you going to say?" she asks, her tone still abrupt.

"Nothing," I tell her. "It's nothing."

"No. What were you going to say?"

I say nothing. I see myself waving goodbye to a car filled with my family on my first day in university, and Lola in the backseat waving back at me but it's like something out of a soap opera now. As the car gets smaller I can hear strings.

"Ed... you're acting very strangely. Dad said you sounded funny when he spoke to you the other day. Mind you, he said that I was acting strangely before my birthday. Okay... so maybe I did panic a little, but I'm over that now. Besides which, the doctor's put me on a course of Derekon, and I've just gone through the fortnight barrier. Life is the proverbial bowl of cherries right now. Or it would have been if you'd sent me a birthday card."

I can still hear her voice and the words that she is saying but I am thinking about all those photographs behind acetate and wondering whether they have anything to do with events that actually took place. They seem so practised, so rehearsed; like those faux-spontaneous moments of enthusiasm and surprise you see in adverts.

Here's us being happy at the seaside.

Here's us being happy at the zoo.

Here's us being happy on a birthday.

Nobody ever takes photographs at funerals, and so I think it is safe to assume that the purpose of domestic photography is not to record a family history or to record the big, important events, but to create an image of happiness that one can display to one's friends and neighbours.

"Are you happy, Lola?" I ask, interrupting her mid-sentence.

"What's that?"

"Are you happy?"

"Yes, Ed. That's what I was just talking about. The tablets have begun to kick in and I'm very happy. What a weird question, Ed. Really."

"Is everyone happy?" I ask.

"Yes. Well... what do you mean? Are *you* taking drugs, Ed? And I'm not talking about the ones in packets that I pick up from Boots. I know you said you're taking a sabbatical and everything, but if you're just using it to get off your face on whatever the hell it is they're all taking in London these days I won't be impressed... "

"Is everyone happy?" I ask again.

"I suppose so," she replies. "As happy as they can be."

"Good," I say. I hear my own voice tremble, the words stuck in my throat. "I'm glad."

Then I hang up and cross the room to where the telephone is plugged into the wall. I pull out the plug and wrap the cable around the telephone itself before throwing it into the bin, on top of all the empty cartons and Styrofoam packaging. The sound of the bin lid snapping shut sounds for all the world like the slamming of an enormous door.

riots – 22:10

The riots have started, just as Nigel said they would, on the other side of the DLR tracks, in the estates of Canning Town. The exact cause of the riots isn't clear but they are said to have begun on Boreham Avenue and then spread further north, now reaching as far as the Lea Valley and the areas surrounding the site of the Olympic Village.

The night air is alive with the sound of sirens and helicopters. The sky glows with intense pools of fiery orange above the burning cars and skips full of burning refuse. Clouds of smoke, volcanically lit up by the flames, roll out over Custom House and the rooftop of ExCeL.

On television they are filming the looting of cornershops and the random acts of violence occurring in the streets. They interview people on this side of the tracks, possible neighbours of mine, all of whom are worried that the violence might just spill over and into our peacefully detached gated communities. There isn't a single person who doesn't believe the very existence of these communities is what triggered the riots in the first place. London's most affluent suburbs placed next to its most decaying hinterlands.

The gates of utopia are being rattled tonight.

I watch the fires and the flickering blue lights of the police cars, ambulances and fire engines for a while before realising that I want to be down there, witnessing this first hand. Why is this? I see images of glass bottles exploding against asphalt, and young faces snarling at police and cameras alike, but it isn't enough. I want to be able to smell petrol. I want my ears to pop with every broken bottle and be filled with the cacophonous wailing of every siren.

Nigel's words echo in my mind. Violence is the new language. Celebrity is the new currency. This mediated event; the on-screen violence happening only a few hundred metres from my apartment; is more a pageant than a crime. As another police car is engulfed in flames by a Molotov Cocktail, a group of youths leer at the camera, waving their fists, like the crowds at a football match in the immediate aftermath of a goal. This is not an emergency: it's a sporting event.

I am in the elevator and heading toward the ground floor before I have had a chance to realise the enormity of what I am doing. Only a few days ago I couldn't leave my apartment without feeling physically sick, and yet now I am walking through the vestibule and out into the smoky black night. Maybe this is different, this riot. There is less to read in a riot, fewer movies to decipher. The emotions are all on the surface; the snarls and the grimaces, the tears and the laughing. The cause and effect is all self-contained within the moment.

As I cross the western edge of Royal Victoria Dock I look back at my apartment to see dozens of people standing on their balconies, looking out over the inferno of Canning Town. A couple dressed in evening wear, perhaps for some kind of charity fundraiser, stand bracing themselves against their balcony. Her hair is pinned up like Audrey Hepburn in *Breakfast At Tiffany's*, and the white scarf around her neck billows on the breeze. Their faces are steely, rigid with concern. He has the square jaw of a matinée idol, and together they look like a couple from a disaster movie.

I walk on to the DLR station and cross the metal bridge. To my left, in the far distance, the untouchable towers of Canary Wharf stand unfazed by the violence erupting on streets less than two miles away. The bridge is now covered in graffiti and broken glass.

I cross a deserted Victoria Dock Road and walk into the estates of Canning Town. Here and there are the clues, the charred black memories of earlier acts of violence. The windows of an ancient block of flats have been put out and are covered now with sheets of plywood hastily tacked into place. A car with neither wheels nor windows sits in a circle of scorched tarmac, its paint burnt into a myriad of colours. Somewhere I can hear somebody screaming, but what strikes me first and foremost is the absence of people.

Overhead the helicopters swarm like vicious mechanical insects, their white prism search beams criss-crossing the estate, put into stark contrast against the night sky by writhing clouds of smoke. I can still hear screaming, but even that sounds mechanical; the same helpless, guttural cry, repeated at regular intervals. It's like a sound effect; a pre-recorded soundtrack of grief to accompany this film-set of destruction. By the time I come across my third burnt-out wreck of a car I realise that I am smiling.

On Radland Road I see a primary school ablaze, and the first humans; a team of firefighters spraying a thick fountain of water into the heart of the fire. A police car races past, lights flashing, siren blaring, and one of the officers, a young woman with a streak of soot on her face looks at me with bemusement.

Further into the estate and now, in the distance, I can see the ranks of police marching against the mob, carrying transparent shields and truncheons, cans of pepper spray at the ready.

I watch from a distance, and somewhere amongst the angry baying of the crowd and the shouted orders of the police I can hear television reporters yelling into their microphones. A window breaks. Another bottle explodes against the pavement. I can still hear that screaming.

As you can see, the rioting is still going on here in Canning Town, and police are being called in from all over the city to deal with the problem. There have been rumours of armed response units being called in, but as yet no incidents of gunfire have been reported…

I start laughing, and see the vague distraction this causes the reporter, who glances briefly in my direction. This experience is as bizarre as walking around the set of a familiar game-show (which I have done) or sitting in a room full of celebrities (which I have also done). There is something other-worldly about existing, however briefly, on the flip side of a television screen.

I walk across the road, presumably passing in and out of shot, an unidentifiable silhouette against all the orange fire and flashing blue light. Another contribution to my fifteen minutes.

The violence and the chaos are suddenly so beautiful. I feel the warmth from the nearby raging fires on my skin and I watch showers of glass fall from broken windows. A brick punches its way through both sides of a telephone booth and the glass atomises, tumbling to the ground like a thousand imitation diamonds.

The light reflected in all this broken glass is dazzling, hypnotic. I sit for a while on a wall and watch the flames, the angry faces, the flashing lights, and the incessant clouds of black smoke. Passing police officers and timid residents, hiding beneath their coats as if suddenly caught in a rainstorm, look at me, me with my beatific smile and my expression of wonder, and frown. They appear hostile, confused as to how somebody could be enjoying *this*.

Why shouldn't I enjoy this? This is all the evidence I needed. Nigel from Apartment 413 is right. The plague is spreading, and faster than anyone could have predicted. There are children throwing bottles full of petrol at the police, while television crews send it out live to every suburb in the country, while the affluent residents of London's Docklands watch from their balconies, terrified spectators in an arena of chaos. Why shouldn't this be funny? Why shouldn't this make me laugh until I'm sick?

Who said the revolution would not be televised?

girl time – 13:46

Okay, girls, so… Colin Curtis. What do we think?

Oh, he's just *lovely*, isn't he? I mean… he's kind of like the boy next door, but with that cheeky grin.

Really? You think? I mean, even after everything that was in the papers?

Well, yeah… us girls love a bit of a rough diamond, don't we?

The audience cheers in approval.

We like to get our hands on a man we can improve, don't we? And we hate goody-two-shoes. They're just too boring, isn't that right, ladies?

Another affirmative cheer.

Outside, beyond my balcony, there are still sirens. The suburbs of East London are still smouldering. Everything smells burnt. The sun beats down on all the blackened asphalt and broken glass. The streets are deserted and empty in a way they shouldn't be at midday. Over the sound of passing trains it is possible, every once in a while, to hear the sound of a can being kicked, or a dog barking.

Yeah… he has got that cheeky look about him. A bit of a jack-the-lad.

Well, I wouldn't kick him out of bed for eating crackers.

The audience screams. The panel on this all-female talk show put their hands on their chests in one collective gesture and start laughing uncontrollably. Well, uncontrollably until the show's producer yells at them through their earpieces to move on.

Oh, Sue, you're terrible.

…out of bed for eating crackers? That's… that's a new one on me…

They are talking about a paedophile. I don't need to remind myself of this, because it is a fact that I have been ruminating for more than three months. I wonder whether the audience in the studio, or the one at home, have forgotten this altogether.

He's got lovely arms.

Arms which he used to pin down his six-year-old niece before he forced her to perform "a sex act" on him. I've read the court transcripts. I don't know why. It was a little like staring at a crashed car or the person sprawled in the street being attended to by paramedics. You know it's wrong but you can't take your eyes away.

Well, he's young, free and single…

Yes, because prior to appearing on *Lockdown* he was in a genuine prison for five years. That didn't leave him much time to develop any meaningful relationships.

You don't have his number, do you?

No, but if I did, would I tell you?

The women verbally circle one another like vultures. And they are talking about a convicted paedophile. A paedophile for whom I am the architect of redemption. My words to Ondine echo inside my mind like something from a bad soap opera.
  "You could always try to make him look good."
  And here we are, days later, with a group of women sat around an improbably large table, against a backdrop of false windows and plastic flowers. They are made-up to appear normal under spotlights, and they are talking in double and single entendres about the man who practically raped his six-year-old niece. Had he actually raped her, of course, he would still be in prison right now, but the judiciary are very particular when it comes to orifices.

Shall we try to get him on the show? Shall we? We should try and get him on the show…

They are giggling and they are clapping their hands together and they are wilfully ignoring anything the newspapers might have told them only a few days ago. The tide has turned and I am the one who turned it. I should feel powerful right now, but I don't. I feel sick.
  They cut to a commercial break.

The new C-Fish 32-L. What do *you* see?

What do *I* see? What *do* I see? I can taste the smoke drifting in from the balcony. The air is thick, oily somehow. All this heat without the promise of rain has left the air dense with pollutants. You can feel them on your skin. My neighbours sit on their balconies wearing short trousers and sipping tall drinks decorated with slices of fresh lime and too many ice cubes. If it weren't for the sounds of the airport and the DLR I would probably be able to hear a hundred or more fans buzzing away in each apartment in support of the air conditioning units that are already humming a mechanical chorus across this part of the city. Radios give us tinny updates on the football, or on the riots, or on the latest act of barbarism to take place right on our doorstep.

…who is sixteen, was taken to St Thomas' Hospital in the early hours of this morning after neighbours called the police…

…shots were fired…

…fourteen injured…

…severe head injuries, while…

On screen the hosts of *Girl Time* laugh. Their audience laughs. I am trying to imagine what they would all look like eating shit.

As if on cue, the doorbell rings.

behold a gift designed to kill – 13:59

"Ed, I do hope you don't mind me intruding like this, I appreciate how much you must want to keep this space secure, but I simply had to speak to you.

"We believe the time is almost here.

"We've been monitoring media output, listening to the reports about the riots, about the other crimes. We've been watching with interest the developments in the international situation. We've been keeping an eye on Mr Curtis.

"You must understand that his very existence is fuelling the contagion, enabling it to spread with such voracity. His celebrity defies the logic of the modern age. I mean… what kind of post-modernism *is this*? There's only one thing that can correct this path. One thing that can prevent our freefall into the abyss.

"You see, it's a spell. It's like a bewitchment, an enchantment, a hypnotist's trickery. I watched black and white footage shot by the Soviets as they liberated the death camps. The German guards were crying as they described the horrors they had participated in. *Crying*. And yet only days before they had been burying the bodies of children dead from typhoid or gassed to death; treating their tiny pale corpses like refuse. What snapped them out of it? What made them see what they had done? Was it freedom? Freedom from the task at hand? Was it the barrel of a gun? Whatever it was, it appeared as if they had sleepwalked through every atrocity they had committed.

"People need to be woken. We are living in a country full of somnambulists, all of them dreaming of lotteries and talent shows while streets burn and paedophiles eat breakfast at the Savoy. This is nothing to do with morality. This isn't about right or wrong. It's about what it means to be human in an era when our evolutionary mission statement has been forgotten.

"Oh, we waited so long for you, Ed. We waited so very, very long for somebody with the right amount of access, and the right amount of understanding. You brought him to us, Ed. You brought Colin Curtis to us. You helped us to identify him.

"The world needs shocking acts, Ed. You understand that, don't you? We need these things to happen because they are the frames upon which the canvasses of life are mounted.

"Balzac talks about a generation so numbed by experience, 'so accustomed to terrible sensations, that only some unimaginable and well-nigh impossible woe could produce any lasting impression'.

"You don't have to wipe out a country to produce a lasting impression, Ed. When Rudolph Valentino died in 1926 the suicide rate amongst young women increased across the whole of the United States. The shooting of the Archduke Franz Ferdinand by Gavrilo Princip in 1914 resulted in the deaths of over sixteen and a half million people. These are revolutionary acts, Ed. Revolutionary acts.

"You see, the timing is so perfect. Do you know what this year is, Ed? In the Chinese zodiac it is the Year Of The Tiger. Karl Marx, Josef Stalin, Mohammed, Fidel Castro... they were all born in the Year Of The Tiger. The opening of the first cinema, World War One, the General Strike, the death of Harry Houdini, Orson Welles' radio broadcast of 'War Of The Worlds', Kristallnacht, the McCarthy witch hunts, the Korean War, the military coup in Burma, the death of Adolf Eichmann, the first transatlantic television signal, the death of Marilyn Monroe, Watergate, the kidnapping of Patty Hearst, Ali versus Foreman... all of these things happened in the Year Of The Tiger. It is a year of change. Disruption. Chaos. Revolution. All we are asking you to do is enact a revolution. Here. Now.

"Please... take this.

"Don't ask me how it came into my possession. As I said, we are a collective, and we are growing in number. We have made certain contacts. Contacts who are more than happy to offer us their patronage.

"This is a Makarov PM. It's a semi automatic hand gun. Have you ever fired a gun before? It really is as simple as it looks in the movies, Ed, trust me. If you are firing at close quarters you can't miss. The only thing the films don't prepare you for is the noise. It's like somebody punched a hole in reality and you were stood a little too close. It's so loud you almost don't hear it. But other than that it's easy. You aim, you fire. It feels almost like a magic trick, when you see that mark appear on your target. Of course you won't be firing at a target, Ed.

"You see… that's why we had to wait for someone like you. Someone like you has *access,* Ed. All those VIP passes, all those rooms in nightclubs that the rest of us just can't enter… We've waited so long, and now here you are. And here is the gun, Ed. It's a Makarov PM. Produced in Russia, though you *will* find variants produced throughout the former Eastern Bloc.

"I'll leave this with you, Ed. I'm sure you know what to do now. That's why we had to wait for you, you see? And we waited so very, very long."

animals who think they're people – 21:34

I have spent much of the day staring at the gun. Its very presence in my apartment is unreal. It looks so much like a prop. The *mise-en-scène* of it, placed on one corner of my coffee table at an angle, looks cinematic and contrived.

I have picked it up, and what shocked me at first was its weight. All those childhood games, running around with water pistols and cap guns, had given me the false impression that guns were light. This has a weight to it; the combined weight of the pistol and its full clip of 9mm rounds. Just holding it I feel deadly, all too aware of the fact that the slightest application of pressure on the trigger would fire one of those rounds at over three hundred metres a second into the floor. I wonder if it would pierce the floor, perhaps punching a hole through the ceiling of the apartment below. If I were to step out onto the balcony and fire it into the air, where would the bullet land, and what effect would a gunshot, rumbling and echoing out over East London, have upon the nearby blazing suburbs?

I have become gradually more and more fascinated with the concept of this machine. Its purpose is so pure, so lacking in ambiguity, that there is something beautiful about it. The idea that there are factories producing these is mind-boggling. Each component, each coiled spring, hammer, and trigger is cast and then assembled on a production line in a process that might seem abstract at first hand, until the finished product is there to see, in all its polished black glory.

I understand, without having fired it, what Nigel means by 'magic trick'. I hold the gun and point it at my reflection in the mirror, and imagine the mirror shattering into hundreds of pieces within 0.01 of a second of me pulling the trigger. I wouldn't even see the bullet, not even as a chrome flash or a streak of light. The exploding gases would erupt from the barrel, the shell case would be flung into the air, but before it had even touched the ground the mirror would be broken.

I turn on the television, and I see the face of Colin Curtis. He is posing for photographs with Trisha Smedley and Sebastian Keynsham. They are on a yacht, gliding down the Thames, sipping champagne. The reporter speaks in a drab monotone.

Mr Curtis has overcome the adversity of his paedophilia to become the nation's best-loved celebrity.

I've never met Colin Curtis, and yet I feel as though I have. His smile is so familiar. His laugh. His voice. His body language. We all know Colin Curtis. I know him better than most. I read the court transcripts, much as I didn't want to. Or did I? I read them, after all. I didn't need to, but I did.

I feel I know Colin Curtis so well I can form a photo-realistic image in my head of what he'll look like when I shoot him. The first shot might hit him in the chest, sending him reeling backwards, clutching the wound, blood spilling out between his fingers. The second shot might get him just below the chin, as his head cranes back and he's staring at the ceiling. It'll take off the top of his head and drop him to the ground where he will lie twitching for a few seconds before all movement stops and I'm left standing there in a cloud of gun smoke. Maybe I'll carry on shooting him just to see what happens when bullets sink into a lifeless corpse.

I lift the gun again, this time prepared for the weight, and point it at the television. I am one choice and a split second away from seeing my television explode in a cascade of sparks and glass.

...killing four people and injuring over a dozen more. Next we'll be looking at animals who think they're people, right after this break.

'Oh, I just can't take it any more. Everything is so grey and upsetting.'

'You need Derekon!'

'What's Derekon?'

'Derekon is packed full of mood enhancing 5-HT receptors that flood your synapses, while giving you a much needed boost of norepinephrine and dopamine.'

'But what does it all *mean*?'

'It means you'll feel great. Derekon comes in easy-to-swallow capsules, and now there's Honey And Lemon Junior Derekon which the kids will love. You can't go wrong with Derekon.'

Aaaaaaaaaaaaaaaaaaaaaaaaaahhhh! Has anyone seen my Joo-Joo?

The world is changing... every second... of every minute... of every day. The things we see are changing... every second... of every minute... of every day. Learn to change. The C-Fish 32-L. What do you see?

You know, I never could get enough of my mum's home cooking. That's why I buy Mum's Home Made Meal Paste. It contains all the flavour of a Sunday roast, dehydrated and vacuum-packed in foil to retain freshness. Just add water, and taste that home-made flavour. Mmm... carrots. And... and gravy... and succulent roast beef, all in an edible food paste. You won't believe how much Mum's Home Made Food Paste tastes just like real, home-made food.

'Oh, no... I don't think I can touch that. That's horrible. What is that?'

'That's the spleen, Carol.'

'Oh no... no, that's gross. I can't touch it. I think I'm going to be sick.'

'Just lift the spleen. We need to place it in this tray here...'

'No, I really am going to be sick.'

Celebrity Autopsy, tonight at nine!

The news report, with its footage of animals that think they are people, comes back, and I am about to change channels when I hear a familiar sound. It's the signature tune, the recognisable fanfare, of my C-Fish.

My C-Fish which died when I allowed the battery to run dry.

My C-Fish which I threw into a black plastic bag full of refuse which I then sent down the waste-disposal chute.

My C-Fish which should, right now, be sitting under tonnes of rotting food, used nappies and empty bottles in a seagull-infested landfill somewhere on the eastern edges of the city.

I look around the apartment, having to lift items of clothing and dirty plates in my search for the source of that infernal melody. The C-Fish is in the hallway. There is no way it could have been pushed under the door, and ten storeys up there's no need for a letter box. Somebody has entered my apartment and left it there.

I pick it up just as it rings off. Searching through the address book and the recent messages, I can confirm this isn't just *a* C-Fish, it's *my* C-Fish. From the slight scratch on the back of the outer casing to the 'down' arrow key, which needs to be pressed a little harder than any of the other buttons, this is mine, rescued from the refuse chute or the landfill, and returned to my apartment.

Seconds later it rings again, a withheld number. Reluctantly I answer it.

"Mr Raynes?" A heavily accented Asian voice, perhaps Indian. Strangely familiar.

"Yes. Who is this?" I ask.

"You have the gun, Mr Raynes?"

I tell him that I do.

"Mr Raynes… You must call Trisha Smedley in the morning and arrange with her to be interviewing Colin Curtis, with the view to ghost-writing his autobiography. There are rumours of a seven hundred and fifty thousand pound offer from Random House, and even of a million pounds from HarperCollins. These are dark times. The serial rights alone could be worth as much as seventy five thousand pounds."

"They'll never believe me… Brian Fenton must have ruined my reputation by now."

"No. This is not true. Brian Fenton does not speak of you at all. Brian Fenton *understands*."

"What do you mean, he understands?"

"I mean just that, Mr Raynes. He understands. Now I must be saying goodbye. Phone Miss Smedley in the morning. Tell her you wish to write the book. Arrange to meet Colin Curtis. You know what to do."

"Yes," I say, my voice shaking.

The line goes dead, and it is only now that I realise who the person at the other end of the line was.

It was Shardul. Shardul, with his brown/grey/bronze hair and his gypsy earring, pushing his vacuum cleaner around the office. Shardul, who probably hears more inside information at that newspaper than any member of K-Media's staff, including those spies who are on the payroll of other newspapers.

Shardul.

trisha smedley – 09:57

"Ed. Ed Ed Ed Ed Ed. Long time no speak. Brian said you're taking a sabbatical. Good move. It's great to do it once in a while, like when I wrote my book on Tuscany. Much needed break. Didn't have to see my zen coach for six months. It was heaven. So what can I do for you?"

I concentrate very hard on sounding normal.

"Well, Trisha, I was just wondering... Colin must be thinking of book deals right now."

"That's right, yes. And by the way, I think it's wonderful what you guys managed. Just wonderful. It just goes to show... the right words at the right time really can help the general public make up their minds. Colin's delighted."

"Right. Yes." I can taste bile. "Well... what I was going to ask was, um, whether you had anyone lined up to, you know, perform the writing duties."

"I see. Funny you should mention that. No... not at present. Well, we've had offers. Colin wanted to write it himself, but none of the potential publishers were keen on that. I can't say I blame them. I've read some of the poetry he put in with his *Lockdown* application... horrible isn't the word. Like William McGonagall but with more references to underage girls. Personally I have my doubts about that Scandinavian treatment he received but, hey... as long as we only invite over-eighteens to the book launch we'll be fine. Actually... the age of consent is sixteen here, isn't it? God... I've spent too much time in the States! Listen to me!"

"Right. Because I'd be quite interested in... in writing it. With me being on sabbatical and everything. And I did cover *Lockdown* for *The Voice*."

A long pause. I can hear her tapping the end of a biro against her teeth and clucking her tongue against the roof of her mouth.

"D'you know what, Ed, you might be on to something there. I guess we *do* owe you one. Sebastian was very impressed you managed to keep it quiet for so long. He's been talking to his father about it. Words have been said, Ed. Words have been said. This might be the perfect opportunity for us to, shall we say, thank you professionally for the last few months. Yes... that's a splendid idea, Ed. A splendid idea. We should do lunch."

"I was wondering whether I could meet Colin. Soon." I blurt out the words and cover my mouth with my hand. Could she *hear* my desperation?

"Absotively, Ed, absotively. He's very busy at the moment, of course. They're talking about him getting a single out for Christmas. That Maurice Chevalier song from *Gigi*. And then there's his TV show... I've got people thought-boxing that at the moment. Maybe some kind of travel thing... you know, like Michael Palin used to do. But yes... you'll have to meet up. We'll do lunch first. Catch up. I haven't seen you in *ages*. Let me just check my Fishary a second... "

Another long pause. The sound of keys being tapped.

"Right. I've actually got a window this Thursday. I *was* supposed to be in a meeting with the guys from *Oh The Humanity*, you know, the disaster video clip show, but they're in Toronto this week so I'm free. Well, for an hour. We should do Ground Zero. It's the new place just round the corner from us on Sloane Square. It's *mucho polémico*. Seb knows the owner so getting a table at short notice *won't* be a problem."

"Okay."

I'm thinking lunch. I'm thinking lunch with Trisha. I'm thinking lunch with Trisha in a new restaurant called Ground Zero that she has described in what I think was Spanish.

"Thursday, then," says Trisha.

"Yes. Thursday."

"Shall we say one?"

"Yes. One." My voice is flattening out to a stunned monotone.

"Great. Thursday at one."

She says goodbye and I think I say it back and then the line is quiet and I am left holding a silent piece of plastic to my ear.

preparations for leaving the building – 11:09

First it is important that I shave. For the first time since I was about nineteen I have gone more than two weeks without shaving. The result is a half-formed beard, better than any of my youthful attempts, but still not as impressive as anything sported by my father when he was my age.

Before I shave I sit in the shower and stick my fingers in my ears. This way I can hear the water drumming on the top of my skull. There's something child-like and comforting about it, something so internal. The sound that I'm hearing right now could never be heard by anyone else. This is *my* sound.

I stand in front of the mirror and I exfoliate with a facial scrub. I like the feeling of the microscopic plastic grains rubbing against my skin. It feels as though a layer of residue from all the smoke and the oily summer air is being stripped away. Then I wash my face and lather up with shaving gel. I pick a fresh disposable razor blade, attach it to my razor, and run it under the hot tap for about thirty seconds because I read somewhere that warming up the metal makes it sharper. Even so, when I apply it to my face it has a hard task, cutting through the dense black hairs. I shave one side to begin with, running my fingers over the skin. It feels brilliantly smooth, and pure. Like new skin. Then I shave the other half.

I brush my teeth and when I spit the stuff that swirls around the plug-hole is a dark shade of yellow. When was the last time I brushed my teeth?

I file the fingernails I haven't already bitten down to the quick and I style my hair with a waxy substance that costs fifteen pounds a tub. I should have had a haircut, but there isn't enough time now.

I put on the Vivienne Westwood shirt and Ozwald Boateng suit that I'm wearing in my old After Show picture. The trousers feel bigger and I need to wear a belt.

It seems I'll have to play the part of Ed Raynes at this restaurant. The truth is I've kind of forgotten how, these last few weeks. I even contemplate polishing my shoes but realise that a life being driven from location to location, or having to walk a maximum of two or three hundred yards to catch the next tube train leaves few scuffs on a pair of Bontonis.

By the time my shoes are on and I've straightened the collar of my shirt, my heart-rate must be around a hundred and twenty. I step out onto the balcony to stop myself from sweating. The air still smells of smoke.

The rioting stopped maybe two nights ago, but the police are treating it more as a ceasefire than a genuine end. It's still so hot. The suburbs are grumbling about hosepipe bans and there are fields of dry, cracked earth all across the countryside. The cities, meanwhile, are forever 'teetering on the brink', as they tell us on TV. The brink of what? Violence? There was always violence. There is always violence. As Nigel says, violence is a language. People have whole conversations using nothing but violence. So what is *this* city on the brink of?

I think I know.

The Makarov is still on my coffee table. It looks oddly quaint, now that I've become accustomed to it, as if it's there for purely ornamental purposes. It looks so small from the other side of the room and yet a single shot fired from it could change everything. Will change everything.

This city is on the brink of *something*.

docklands light railway – 12:08

Everything is sinister.

The man wearing thick NHS glasses and a sports jacket, a Daniel O'Donnell badge pinned to his lapel.

The clouds of steam rising from a dry-cleaning place in Limehouse.

The empty can of Dr Pepper that is rolling around under the seats.

The buzzing of a music file being played on somebody's C-Fish.

The voices of the German tourists sat behind me.

The facial twitch of the woman standing near the doors.

The sound of children laughing.

"Next stop Shadwell. Change here for the East London Line."

The fly that is crawling up the window.

The graffiti on the seat in front: *Kelly Francis has AIDS*.

This heat.

The C-Fish conversation of the man at the front of the carriage: "What you on about? What you on about? No... no... what you on about? I never seen him. I never fuckin' seen him. What you on about?"

The four baseball caps all pointed right at me from the left hand side doors and my occasional eye contact with their sullen wearers.

The jumble of rooftops and walkways in Shadwell, and the church spire, incongruous among the tenement buildings and tower blocks.

The girl in the wheelchair who makes involuntary grunting sounds every ten or fifteen seconds, and whose eyes roll around in their sockets as she cocks her head toward the ceiling.

The moment when we pause and wait for another DLR train to pass by slowly, the passengers briefly looking out from their carriage at us; a hundred split-second liaisons as people register the faces of strangers, forgetting them within seconds.

Everything is sinister.

And I realise that Hell isn't fire and brimstone, or even a cold, black emptiness. Hell isn't something out of a rock video, all pyrotechnics and women in black leather. Hell isn't even your worst nightmare, or physical pain. Hell isn't a painting by Hieronymus Bosch. Hell is a place where everything is sinister. Hell is a place where everything feels like a bad dream. Yes, it's other people, but it's more than that. It's other people, and it's their complete and utter indifference to you. It's other people, and it's the split second that it takes for them to turn back into the savage and feral creatures they always were, deep down inside. Hell is spotting that potential in a child sat next to you at a bus-stop or in the eyes of your best friend. Hell is reading a newspaper story about how a woman who has been in a coma for two years is pregnant and how the police are DNA testing hospital staff and relatives. Hell is seeing bunches of flowers tied to a lamp post. Hell is the foil and the needles left behind in a telephone box.

Everything is sinister.

ground zero – 12:53

The River Westbourne flows from Hampstead, through Hyde Park, and into the Thames at Chelsea. In its long and convoluted history it has been known variously as the Serpentine River, the Cye Bourn (which means Royal River), the Bayswater, and the Ranelagh. It once flowed into the Serpentine lake at Hyde Park, and beneath the eponymous bridge at Knightsbridge where, in 1141, the citizens of London met the apocryphal Queen Matilda. You will no longer be able to stroll along its banks, however. In the mid-nineteenth century the decision was made to drive the river underground, into a series of channels that would carry it below, and indeed above the citizens of Belgravia, Chelsea, and Paddington. Its most visible presence, over a hundred and fifty years since its babbling brooks were hidden from plain view, is at Sloane Square station.

There, it travels above the electrified tracks in a featureless grey conduit that looks like any other piece of anonymous and purely functional architecture, lost amongst the bricks, hoardings, and infinite cables and pipes. The city had no time and no nostalgia for the river; it could barely tolerate its necessity, and so it wrapped the river in clothes of stone and steel and buried it alive.

I walk beneath the River Westbourne, and out of Sloane Square station seven minutes before I have to meet Trisha Smedley in the restaurant. I decide to burn away the minutes by sitting on a bench next to a sign that says "DO NOT FEE THE PIG ONS" and pretend to read C-Fish messages. The trees provide a little respite from the sun.

An old woman shuffles her way across the square carrying at least half a dozen plastic shopping bags, each one filled with items of clothing, plastic cups, and other detritus. She's wearing a big floppy denim hat and a denim skirt that almost brushes the ground. On her feet she wears red flip-flops and grubby white socks. She walks with the aimless quality of someone who genuinely has no destination, ambling as if to remain stationary would kill her, as it would some types of shark. She's another movie; there are decades of back-story there. A childhood, maybe a marriage, she might have worked in a factory. A whole life-time building up to the moment when she would be dragging her feet across Sloane Square, serving little purpose other than as a cipher. I could try to engage with whatever that back-story was, but I have neither the time nor the empathy.

Trisha Smedley appears on the far corner of the square, walking briskly and chatting into her C-Fish. Even though it's not a video call she's still gesturing wildly as if to emphasise her point, very nearly blinding a passing courier. She's dressed in black which I guess would be intolerable in this heat if it weren't for the fact that her office will be nicely air-conditioned. But Trisha Smedley always wears black. Her husband, Sebastian Keynsham, also wears only black. They are a very colour co-ordinated couple, but it has earned them the nicknames Gomez and Morticia.

I suddenly find myself wondering whether I should have brought my gun. I haven't lost sight of the purpose of this meeting, but having it with me would have changed things. Every nanosecond must be charged with spontaneity when you are carrying a gun, your mind habitually at the crossroads of decision. Anything can happen when you're armed.

Trisha reaches the restaurant, which has one of those minimalist fronts; all tinted glass and white lettering on black.

GROUND ZERO.

I've heard of this place and I've looked it up online. It opened to a blaze of publicity:

Controversial chef Chester Samuels and conceptual artist Tracey Frampton have collaborated in a venture that combines the best in Ameropean cuisine and avante garde social commentary.

When Trisha enters the restaurant I get up from the bench and walk across the square. The bag lady looks up at me through lenses so thick they make her eyes look like pin-holes.

"I saw the bombs," she says, her voice hushed to near-silence.

The interior of Ground Zero is filled with bespoke minimalist furniture, courtesy of Tracey Frampton, and everything looks lacquered. From the bar, all the way around the restaurant, the walls are covered, floor to ceiling, with images of the terrorist attacks on September 11, 2001. They form a chronological narrative that begins with freeze frames from the Naudet brothers' footage of American Airlines Flight 11 crashing into the North Tower. Moving clockwise around the room we see the moment when United Airlines 175 crashed into the South Tower from every conceivable angle (except from within the building itself, of course). Then there are images of burning buildings, and silhouetted figures falling to their deaths, before this mural of despair ends with the iconic images of the World Trade Centre's jagged remains, stark against the smoke and floodlights.

The *maître d'* is maybe ten years older than me, with a perilously receding hairline and large, piercing eyes. He looks at me and purses his lips, shifting them over to one side of his face as if he is trying to recognise me.

"I'm with Trisha Smedley," I say, instantly realising how pathetic I sound.

"Ah, with Miss Smedley. Follow me."

He leads me across the restaurant. Trisha looks up from the wine list and notices me, switching on her best smile as she stands up.

"Ed!" she says. She kisses the air in front of my face and we sit. "So glad you could come. Been looking forward to this all week. No, really. Anton, would you be a darling and get us a bottle of Sancerre? Sancerre, Ed? Sancerre? I know it's only lunch time but this heat is just *intolerable*, and nothing quenches the thirst like Sancerre."

I shrug and nod noncommittally at the same time.

"Sancerre, Anton. That would be lovely."

"Sancerre, Madame," says Anton, pivoting on his heels and walking briskly toward the bar.

"I *do* love this place," says Trisha. "As I said, *très discuté. Et tres conflictuel aussi!*" She starts laughing and I laugh too but I'm all too aware that the mirth is probably absent from my eyes. I think I might even be frowning as I'm laughing, which may look strange from the other side of the table.

"So this book," she says. "What kind of an angle are you thinking, because we're thinking the whole kind of... you know... struggle against adversity thing... how he coped with prison, his treatment, life on the outside... that kind of thing."

I want to remind her that this is a man who sexually molested his six-year-old niece, but now is not the time.

"Yeah," I say, instead, "that could work."

"Yeah, well... I normally *hate* these kind of famous-for-fifteen-minutes autobiographies... I mean, you get these nineteen-year-old footballers and their Basildon girlfriends writing books about their lives, and... I mean... what have they got to write about? Really?

It's just so fucking cynical... but with Colin it's different. Colin's one of a kind."

You could say that.

"So that's where we're coming from... I mean, K-Media. We're thinking either Tower or Price Moggridge. We'll keep things in house, as it were."

"I want to meet him," I say. I haven't quite managed to use the correct tone of voice and it ends up sounding a little too aggressive; not that Trisha notices.

"And you will, Ed, you will. I'm sure you understand how it is at the moment... busy busy busy. Luckily all the nay-sayers have been painted as misguided bigots and kill-joys, so we're in the clear as far as the book is concerned. Besides... Hitler was fucking awful, and look how many books *he* sold."

I feel a wave of panic which I struggle to suppress as Anton returns with a frosted bottle of Sancerre in a transparent wine cooler. We go through the whole rigmarole of Trisha tasting the wine; a mere formality in this country, where nobody would even think of sending it back and asking for a different one, and Anton pours two half-glasses.

"Have you looked at the menu?" Trisha asks me, and I snap out of what was threatening to become an intense anxiety attack.

"Um, no... "

"Anton, if we could just have another five minutes?"

"Of course, Miss Smedley."

I open the menu, and for some reason that is when I notice that there is music playing, and that it is 'I Love New York' by Madonna, interspersed with sampled voices from 9/11 news broadcasts. My eyes are drawn to the mural again. The nausea returns.

"Yes," says Trisha, as if somehow capable of reading my thoughts. "They only play songs associated with or about New York. It's just *scandalous*. Caused quite a brouhaha when it opened. There were protests. You know... people who'd, I don't know, lost people or something. Christ... it's almost ten years ago. Get over it, d'you know what I mean?"

I look down at the menu. I see phrases like 'chilled Charentais melon soup with a Cornish crab vinaigrette' and 'salad of duck with truffle honey vinaigrette' and I make mental notes.

"Are we doing starters? Starters, Ed? Starters? Yeah? We're having starters?"

I shrug and nod.

"Great. They do these bite-size miniature burgers… like a cheeseburger, but with veal and mozzarella on focaccia. They're so cute."

We order food and I listen to her some more.

"Of course, once the book's been published we'll be looking at film rights. There's a *lot* of potential there. I know Seb's already spoken with Orlando Bloom's people. They're definitely interested, depending on schedule, of course. If we can look toward getting the book out by December, you know, in time for Christmas, we can start moving that forward in the new year. And of course the book will tie in with the single. We've got some great people working on that; these kids from somewhere down Walworth way, I think… You know, real street people. Not homeless, if you know what I mean. I'm talking about graffiti types with baseball caps and jewellery."

I use the first glass of wine to take the edge off. My muscles begin to relax and I stop grinding my teeth. I start talking to Trisha about the way I see the book developing, as if I'm reading from some prepared mental script, which in a way I am. I tell her that the prologue will deal with the night he won *Lockdown*.

"Oh yes, I'm liking that. I'm liking that."

I tell her that we'll emphasise key events in his childhood to evoke sympathy.

"Yeah. People love pain memoirs, don't they?"

I tell her that we'll paint the prison service as more cruel and barbaric than any of the people it detains.

"Controversial, yeah. That's good. Stick it to 'the man'!"

I tell her that we'll end the book on a note of optimism. He is a reformed character with a big bright future ahead of him.

"Excellent. Feel-good. That's so important these days, isn't it? All this doom and gloom every time you open a newspaper or turn on the telly. Redemption sells, Ed. Really, it does."

I don't tell her about Nigel. I don't tell her that there is a loaded gun in my apartment, placed on my coffee table next to the large, glossy books about Frank Lloyd Wright and East German packaging design of the 1960s and '70s. I don't tell her that when I meet Colin Curtis I am going to kill him, because in a world this fucked up it seems the only logical thing to do.

district line – 14:58

There is a bass-note beneath the rumble and clatter of the train, an ominous drone. It's like the sound the earth makes as it turns. Somewhere a child is screaming; not whining or crying, but *screaming*, and I feel both angry and frightened at the same time just listening to it. I'm not sure what disturbs me about that sound. Is it the child's inarticulacy? Its fear? I wonder whether that is the sound everyone will be making when the ground opens up or the meteors fall or the planes start dropping out of the sky.

Next stop... Victoria... change here for... the Victoria Line... and main-line rail services.

The pauses between sentences are where the pre-recorded voice has been digitally stitched together.

The train travels beneath the surface, under innumerable buildings, offices, streets, and emerges into a canyon between a jumble of old Victorian edifices. One day every mile of train track in this city will be subterranean. As space becomes sparse the canyon will get deeper, before all the tracks are covered to make room for further tower blocks and office buildings, and the underground will be just that, under ground, in its entirety. A city beneath the city, with breathing tunnels and percussive, rattling trains; commuters crucified in the aisles of over-crowded carriages, holding on to bars and straps, and everyone reading *Metro*. It's quite easy to imagine a world where there is no destination, where this subterranean population exists only in transit, forever avoiding eye contact, forever shifting from platform to platform, up and down escalators, standing on the right and minding the gap.

We are underground again, the windows filled with inky black and the spectral, distorted reflections of passengers. A station flickers into view, dozens of faces reduced to a blur as the train comes to a halt in Tower Hill.

I slowly climb the steps, behind a group of Chinese tourists and people dragging wheeled suitcases, and emerge amongst the ruins of the old city wall and more tourists.

I hear a tour guide with a French accent say, "The original London wall was built of Kentish ragstone and was between two and three metres wide, and five metres in height."

I walk through the underpass where a man sits against a wall clutching a Styrofoam cup, one eye open, his feet bare and caked in dirt. He doesn't speak. His silence unnerves me. I expect a slurred "Got any spare change", or some well practised greeting to catch me off guard, but there's nothing. He stares to the place where the ground meets the opposite wall through watery blue eyes, hardly moving, and not making a sound.

As I stand on the escalator at Tower Gateway DLR I hear perhaps half a dozen sirens and through the grimy glass of the sheltered stairwell I see crystallised flashing blue lights making their way along Tower Hill. It occurs to me that the sound of sirens is the sound of a city crying. Something bad is happening somewhere. Before opposable thumbs, speech, and numeracy that sound would have been the howling of monkeys, warning of an approaching predator or an impending storm.

Now that we've outsourced the sound of our own panic to a machine, we practise our indifference to its very presence: 'It's nothing to do with me,' we tell ourselves, and we focus straight ahead, not even bothering to look in the direction the sound came from. Part of that is a city thing, a cosmopolitan thing. Only country types and tourists look at the police cars, ambulances, and fire engines; because they are country types and they don't see this kind of thing all that often. But me? I'm a city type. This happens all the time, along with terror scares, shootings, and police signs appealing for witnesses on narrow flights of steps and under bridges. This is nothing new, nothing special. I'm indifferent to this brief moment of noisy, flashing melodrama.

In time, of course, the indifference ceases to be a practised conceit, and you no longer hear the sirens, or the blades of the police helicopter, just as you don't see the guy in the underpass, and he no longer sees you. Everything fades into white noise. Everything becomes the high-pitched whine of tinnitus that you've had so long you can no longer hear it.

But not for me.

Now I'm hearing everything. I'm seeing everything. I see the expressions on strangers' faces and even the slightest gesture becomes imbued with something operatic, something epic in scale.

Now I'm feeling nothing. I watch and I listen to these things and I wait for an internal response but there's nothing. Everything might as well be happening on television. Everything is so artfully shot and rendered in slow motion that it's little more than a music video inside my head.

Why do I notice these things? I notice them because they are real. More real than my colleagues, or whatever friends I was meant to have. More real than my emotions. More real than anything that has happened to me. The faces of strangers, the howling of sirens, the artificial lights and the flickering display screens of the DLR are everything and all that I have.

when i kill colin curtis – 20:21

When I kill Colin Curtis I will shoot him in the face and I will point the gun right at his face and I will pull the trigger and the bullet will hit him just below his left eye and it will make an entrance wound little bigger than the end of your little finger and it will send a great big shower of blood, bone, and lumps of his occipital lobe out through the back of his head.

When I kill Colin Curtis I will shoot him in the eye and his eye will vanish and all there will be is blood and the bullet will shatter the inside of the orbital crater and tear through his brain like a juggernaut through a playground and it will crack his head open like a bloody melon and it will kill him.

When I kill Colin Curtis I will shoot him in the throat and he will reach up and grasp the great big gaping hole in his trachea from which he's making this horrible wet gurgling sound and blood will start to trickle from the corner of his mouth and he will lose all co-ordination because the bullet will have punched a hole out through the back of his spinal cord and he will drop to the ground gurgling and unable to move and I will stand over him laughing.

When I kill Colin Curtis I will shoot him in the groin because it seems like poetic justice and the papers will have a field day with it and he will fall down clutching the bleeding mush that used to be his genitals as blood pours out of both sides of his midriff and then I will shoot him once in the gut because I think the person who kills him *this* way wants him to feel pain and I will shoot him once in the chest and then in the throat and then in the head as if I'm trying to blow away his chakras or something and he will lie there bleeding and screaming but I'll have shot him in such a way that it will take him minutes to die.

When I kill Colin Curtis I will begin by shooting him in both shoulders and the bullets will pulverise his subscapularis and shatter the glenohumeral joint and I will shoot him in both knees and both patella will crack like china plates and he will fall down and then I will hold his head in both my hands and I will crush his head like that scene in *Blade Runner* and put his eyes out with my thumbs while he screams and screams but can't move and I won't stop until I'm up to my elbows in blood and bits of his head.

When I kill Colin Curtis we will be sat in a restaurant in Mayfair and when the waiter or waitress asks us if we would care for some wine I will nod and ask for a bottle of Sancerre and then I will draw the gun and I will shoot Colin Curtis in the forehead and then I will turn to the waiter or waitress and say I've changed my mind and could I please have a bottle of Chablis.

When I kill Colin Curtis I will piss on his corpse.

When I kill Colin Curtis I will shoot him several times, sending him reeling backwards with gory squibs exploding inside his shirt until he topples back over a coffee table because in this scenario I'm shooting him in a sitting room and he might crash through the glass top of the coffee table and then I will leave one bullet in the chamber and I will put the gun inside my mouth making sure to angle it just so, so that the bullet travels right through my brain and opens up the top of my head like a great big fucking Jack-in-the-box.

When I kill Colin Curtis I won't shoot myself but I will photograph his body in all manner of amusing positions and possibly play dress-up and then I will C-Fish the photographs to my friends and relatives perhaps with quirky Christmas-themed frames featuring snowmen or penguins or glittery stars.

When I kill Colin Curtis I will film it on my C-Fish and then I will upload the video onto galactusvideo.co.uk and by the time those monitoring the website realise that what they have on their hands is a real life snuff film it will have had ten thousand hits and people will have saved it and they will be emailing it to their friends and colleagues and everyone will be talking about the video where Colin Curtis gets shot on camera and they might complain about the picture or the sound quality or the fact that the picture jerks every time I fire the gun but they'll watch it nonetheless.

When I kill Colin Curtis everyone will hate me but that will be okay because I'll hate them too.

the news – 22:00

The arrests were made in the early hours of this morning at addresses in Canning Town, West Ham, and Plaistow. Fourteen men and three women have been arrested in connection with what the police are calling a 'campaign to inflict terror and carnage upon the people of London'.

It doesn't currently appear that this group has any connection with any known terrorist organisation. Indeed the police have been quick to point out that none of those arrested are Muslim and that, of the seventeen people arrested, twelve are white, and that all of those arrested are British.

Details about the alleged terror plot are very thin on the ground, but it would appear that it involved a series of suicide bombings to be carried out on London transport, in nightclubs, and on the site of the Olympic Village in East London.

The nihilism is spreading. The madness seems to drip from the television screen. In Los Angeles a film producer has been arrested following a shooting at his home. In Paris a group of academics committed seppuku in honour of Yukio Mishima. In Milan a famous model has set fire to herself during a catwalk show. The nuclear stand-off in the Far East is at a "critical point". The bombs continue to rain down over Azadi Square, the white marble tower in its centre shattered and left looking like a giant chipped tooth. Phillip Mackenzie has finally resigned.

Even though it has gone ten, the temperature outside is twenty-seven degrees centigrade and it hasn't rained in over a month.

My C-Fish rings. I expect it to be Nigel, or maybe Shardul. My heart beats a little faster. The name I see on the screen is

ONDINE

"What's happening?" she says, without saying hello.

"What do you mean?"

"At the newspaper. Something's happening."

"Ondine… what are you talking about? I haven't been at the paper for weeks. You know this."

"No… I know you haven't. But something's happening. Brian

told me you're ghost-writing Colin Curtis' autobiography. And now they're sending me on holiday."

"What?"

"Brian's sending me on holiday. I had holidays left, and he's told me I have to use them up starting tomorrow. What's going on, Ed?"

I tell her that nothing's going on. My voice trembles and my throat is dry.

"Don't give me that, Ed. What's going on? Phillip Mackenzie resigned today. Only an idiot would take the person who broke the whole story and put them on enforced leave the day after it came to a head."

I tell her that I don't know what she's talking about.

"I asked him about you, and Trisha Smedley, and the whole fucking Colin Curtis thing and he said that was the plan from day one. He said you were on a sabbatical, and that it was to allow you to focus on the book, but I could tell he was lying. I can always tell when Brian's lying. It's in his eyes, Ed, *it's in his fucking eyes*. You aren't on sabbatical. I saw you the other day… I saw what you were like… and then you suggested we try and turn the whole thing around… so I did… I can't believe I actually said it. We were desperate. none of us had slept. So I just said exactly what you said… and they bought it, Ed. They actually fucking bought it. And this man… Colin Curtis… he's a fucking rapist. He is a rapist of children. And now we've turned him into Elvis or something. And Brian says you're writing the book, and everyone else seems to have known about this all along. Why am I out of the loop, Ed? What's going on?"

I tell her again that nothing is going on.

"Don't give me that. I can tell… I can just tell. Nihad says it's the coke talking. He *would* say that, wouldn't he? He's got a nose like a fucking Hoover, but *I'm* the one with the coke problem. That's why I'm going sober, Ed. As of today I'm not drinking and I'm not doing coke or anything else for that matter. I need my head to be clear about this.

"On holiday! Can you believe it? What's happening next week? What don't they want me to know about?"

"There's nothing," I say, suddenly aware that I'm breathing loudly.

"No," says Ondine. "No… no… Phillip Mackenzie has just resigned, and Brian tells me he doesn't need me to cover the story, because we've got Kevin Selby to do all that. I don't buy it for a second. I saw what you were like Ed. Something is happening to you, and Brian's acting like nothing's happened."

"Really, Ondine." I say. "You're over-reacting. I know how I was when you came to see me, but I'm okay now. Really, I am. I was just... a little... I don't know... *stressed*."

"That wasn't stress, Ed. You were having some sort of nervous breakdown. Everyone is having some sort of nervous breakdown. Do you know what I mean? There is something *wrong* with people. I'm going to find out what's happening, Ed. Holiday be fucked. I am going to find out what is going on."

"Really," I say, my voice finally composed, my tone sincere, "it's nothing, Ondine. Nothing is going on. Everything is going to be okay."

"Whatever, Ed. Whatever," says Ondine, hanging up.

On the television there are advertisements.

Some people say that technology and religion are separate things. Some people think that God would not want us to be burdened with all our inventions and labour-saving devices. At the Technostics Church Of Great Britain we like to think a little differently.

We believe that science and technology are gifts from God. Jesus was, after all, a carpenter, and carpenters were the technicians of the ancient world. If Jesus were alive today he may well have invented the hand-held computer or the hybrid motor car. He may have invented the nano-oven or the retinal bank scanner.

The Technostics Church of Great Britain. Where technology is our God, and God is our technology.

Join The Music Bank today and you can download every UK top forty single since the charts began for just twenty-nine ninety-nine. That's over two thousand songs for less than thirty pounds! From Kenny Rogers to the Sex Pistols, from Louis Armstrong to the Prodigy, there's something for everyone! Join The Music Bank today!

Download the latest C-Fish editing software for your pics and movies from Demonweb and you can win the chance to win one of these great Sonicronic Games Consoles. All you have to do is call this number...

These teenagers are doing symph because they think it's cool. All the kids are doing it these days; so why shouldn't they?

Here's why!

Symph affects those parts of the brain which regulate time. Advanced research being carried out in America has shown that those who regularly misuse symph run the risk of not only forgetting about the past, but of remembering the future. That's right. Friends, loved ones, cherished moments, all forgotten, replaced with the dizzying nightmare of events that haven't happened yet, and might never even occur.

Don't be a fucking idiot. Say no to symph.

I am on my knees in front of the television, my hand over the gun on the coffee table, and I am laughing. For the first time in I don't know how long I am laughing, and with my free hand I am reaching out toward the television as if touching the screen will end the stream of images and sounds spilling out of it. This moment of hysteria is brought to an abrupt end when my C-Fish rings for the second time this evening. The number is withheld but I answer it anyway.

"Ed." It's Nigel.

"Yes?"

"Everything is in place," he says.

"What do you mean?"

"I mean everything is in place. The time is now. You will see."

He hangs up before I can ask another question, and for a moment I contemplate calling the number back, until I realise that I can't. The C-Fish rings again. This time it's Trisha Smedley.

"Ed, hi... sorry to be calling you so late, but I know what you journos are like... up all hours... just to let you know that Colin would *love* to meet you so we were thinking Saturday. Just you two, *mano a mano* as it were. You can go out for drinks. Nothing formal. Just to see if you hit it off, because that's so important, I think, if you're going to be his ghost writer."

"Saturday?" I say. I don't sound too surprised. If anything I sound horrified.

"Yes. Saturday."

"Trisha... do you know Nigel?" The words leave my mouth so quickly, it is as if they are generated by pure impulse. There is a long silence at the other end of the line.

"Nigel?" she says, a hint of saccharine in her voice that sounds like faux-naivety.

"Yes. Nigel," I tell her. "From four one three? He's a neighbour of mine."

She chuckles girlishly.

"Why would I know him?" she asks.

"Nothing," I reply, hurriedly covering my tracks. "It's nothing."

"No, Ed. I don't know Nigel. So shall we pencil you in for Saturday? Colin has suggested you meet at a bar first, maybe move on to a few clubs. I'll give him your number. Well... I've already given him your number. Hope you don't mind, but it's so much better if we can get the wheels in motion as soon as possible. Do you agree?"

"About what?"

"The wheels, Ed. It's so much better if we can get the wheels in motion, yes?"

"What wheels?"

"It's a metaphor, Ed. An analogy. Whatever you want to call it. I think everyone at K-Media and the newspaper will be happier once we can get this thing off the ground."

"What thing?"

Another long pause. I can hear her sighing and then it sounds as if she is whispering to somebody who is in the same room as her.

"The book, darling," she says eventually. "I'm talking about the book. So shall we say Saturday? About seven-ish? Cocktails? You're a darling, you know that, don't you Ed? An eighteen-carat darling. Speak to you soon. Kisses. Byee."

soho – 18:49

A drunk dances with the Hare Krishnas beneath the arch on Gerrard Street. He's holding a can of beer above his head and following them round and round in circles, trying to sing along with them.

"Hare Krishna... Hare Krishna... Krishna Krishna... Hare Hare... Hare Rama... Hare Rama... Rama Rama... Hare Hare..."

I stand at the turn-off from Wardour Street for what might be

minutes, watching this spectacle. The Hare Krishnas dance in
their circle oblivious to him, or maybe humouring him, beating
their tambourines and singing without harmony. A part of me
wants to be offended, though I am not sure on whose behalf. Am
I angry that this drunk is making a mockery of their faith, or that
they are allowing him to do so?

On the corner of Shaftesbury Avenue and Frith Street an old
man with sloping shoulders and grey hair is shouting into a mega-
phone, "Jesus Christ has taken us off the broad road of sin that
leads to hell and given to us eternal life, and we shall never perish,
but you have to come to him, for though when he died on the
cross he paid the price of sin and opened heaven's door, he
doesn't force you in, there's no automatic entry into heaven, you
must come the way I came, and the way I came is God's way… "

His voice is a drone without proper punctuation, his sermon a
rolling liturgy without hope of an end, as if he's all too aware that
should he pause for breath he will lose the attention of the few
passing tourists who are listening to him. They will move on, to
the nearest bar, or nightclub, or whichever den of iniquity he is
trying to save them from.

Before I pass the preacher I hear a pin-stripe suited guy with a
C-Fish video monocle shout, "Fuck Jesus, and fuck you!"

I walk down Frith Street and into Soho.

Soho, named after an ancient hunting call from the days when
this was all fields. A different kind of hunting can be had now, of
course. Just about anything can be tracked down in Soho.

The rickshaw boys, almost all of them handsome with jet black
curls and olive skin, snake their way with ringing bells through
the dense, plodding traffic of merrily drunk office workers, ultra-
groomed queens, and families queuing for West End shows. If the
Earth were flat and it had an edge I like to think it would be Soho;
a sprawling, cluttered marketplace filled with disparate crowds,
music and sirens.

On Old Compton Street a man with a face like death stands
holding a sign pointing the way to an all-you-can-eat buffet.

A man in a white tuxedo and bow tie pushes himself across the
junction in a wheelchair.

A threadbare transsexual in a green Adidas jacket and fishnet
tights is selling The Big Issue.

He's waiting for me on Greek Street.

Colin Curtis.

He's sitting near the bar in a place called Kenji Urada, his back
to the wall, scanning everyone who walks in. I see him doing this
through the open windows. Almost every bar on Greek Street has
its windows open. All the air conditioning in the world can't shift
this oppressive, sickly heat. When I enter the room he scans my
face and in the dim, red-tinted light he recognises me and smiles.

Colin Curtis is yet another person who looks exactly the same as
they do on television. The idea that most celebrities are somehow
taller, shorter, fatter or thinner than they look on TV is a myth.
There may be one or two exceptions to the rule, of course; those
celebrities who pay good money to be lit the right way or spend
hours in make-up, but television is, generally, a remarkably honest
medium. The only people who ever think they look or sound different on TV are those people who are on TV themselves.

He's a little shorter than I am, with dark hair, a St Tropez tan,
and big doe-eyes that tell you he couldn't possibly be a paedophile. He looks nothing like Orlando Bloom, but that's not to
say he's ugly. Rather, he looks slightly worn beneath the tan and
the recently styled hair. Prison has drained something of him. We
should have known it all along. Something behind the eyes speaks
of isolation.

"You must be Ed," he says, in a non-specific Estuary accent, all
'muss' instead of 'must'.

I shake his hand. It's wet with what I hope is condensation from
his pint of Kirin.

"It's alright, this place, isn't it?" he says, looking about himself.
"I mean… I'm talking about a boy from Basildon, know what I
mean? I could get quite used to all this."

A waiter in black arrives at the table and asks if we would like
more drinks.

"Yeah, two more pints of this and we'll have a bottle of that
sake stuff 'n' all."

Colin Curtis laughs and shakes his head.

"Honestly… if you'd told me five years ago I'd be sitting in
some posh Japanese bar in the West End talking to some geezer
who was just about to write my life story I'd have told you, 'You
must be fucking mad'. But now… here I am.

"I mean, it's alright inside for all the bank robbers and gangsters
and all the rest of it. They can sell their stories like *that*." He clicks
his fingers. "But when you're a nonce… not a fucking chance.
Well, not for most of them, anyway. I suppose I'm different."

The two glasses of Kirin and the bottle of cold sake arrive and are delicately placed before us. I become aware that I am tapping my right foot very quickly, my knee jerking up and down under the table.

The gun is heavy inside my jacket.

"So what d'you fancy doing, then?" says Colin. "I mean… you fancy going to a few clubs, getting a few jars down us, or what?"

I shrug and tell him I'm easy. It's pretty much the first thing I've said since I walked in.

"I just found out about this place round the corner," Colin continues. "It's called Naughty. They've got all these girls, eighteen, nineteen years old, all done up as schoolgirls. All of them. I mean… *fuck me*… you spend five years in prison for you-know-what, and you come out and everyone's at it. It just goes to show, see, it's like I always said, it's not unnatural. All these people who say it's unnatural… it's not. Look at fucking chimps and that. They're fucking their kids and they're fucking their mate's kids when they're barely able to climb about the fucking trees. That's not unnatural. It's all part of nature, isn't it?"

For a moment I visualise unloading the gun into his face and watching the wall get plastered with bits of his head. Instead I nod and smile awkwardly.

"It's alright, I know you're not into that kind of thing. Trisha told me. She's a good girl, isn't she? I mean, I *wouldn't*, but she's a lovely girl. Been a diamond with me, she has. A diamond."

I finally take a deep enough breath to speak, and ask him, in vague staccato half-sentences, whether he is still into 'all that'.

"Well… " he grimaces, "I mean, I had a load of counselling and that, but… you know… that's just given me a bit of self control. It's like a compulsion, see? Common sense goes out the window. That's what they taught me. Self control. But it's like I always used to say… what's the number one cause of paedophilia?"

I shrug.

"Sexy children!" he yells, slapping his hand against the table and causing the drinks to jump noisily. He doubles over laughing and I giggle without sincerity. The denizens at neighbouring tables are looking at Colin, some with disdain, some with vague curiosity. *He doesn't belong here*, say their derisory glances. *His voice is too loud, his jokes too vulgar. His territory is the chain pub, branches of which can be found in every clone town in the country, or perhaps the kind of place that serves tapas and olives but which never quite attracts the right kind of crowd. What is he doing in* our *place?*

Colin Curtis leans across the table and pours the sake into its shallow cups.

"Go on," he says, passing one to me. "Get that down your neck."

I sip the drink and feel it trickle down my throat like poison. My stomach lurches. I think I'm sweating. Of course I'm sweating in this heat, in this bar, with *him*. His eyes scan the room as if he owns the place. Perhaps he can sense those supercilious looks and now he's looking back at them all with defiance.

First I'm on your televisions, now I'm in your fucking bar.

I tell him I need to use the toilet.

"Knock yourself out," he says, taking another slurp of sake before washing it back with a mouthful of beer.

As with virtually every West End bar the toilets are subterranean, down a creaking flight of stairs that are flanked on either side by black walls. I stand in a cubicle and listen to the strangely threatening sound of thunder that is coming up from the ground. The tube, perhaps? But there are no shallow, sub-surface tunnels here. I close my eyes and feel the only slightly less warm air belching out of an overhead vent. It feels like I'm standing on the rooftop of hell.

I draw the gun from my inside pocket. It is literally a pocket-sized gun; a novelty almost; but its weight has been a constant reminder of the reason I'm here. Throughout my journey I expected it to fall, clattering to the ground; sudden evidence of some violent act not yet committed for all my fellow passengers to see. What could I have done in that situation? Picked it up and run? Turned it on myself?

Suicide is a constant and easy option when you are armed. The decision to put a bullet through your own head is much more open to spontaneity than cutting open your wrists in a bath or even hanging yourself. Those methods need preparation. Shooting yourself is different. It's instant. From the moment you have a gun your capacity to kill yourself increases a hundredfold.

I put the tip of the barrel against the side of my head, just to try it out for size. Even in this heat the metal is surprisingly cold. I allow my finger to curl around the trigger. It might sound like a paradox, but I've never felt more alive. A part of me wants to run out into the bar right now and open fire. I don't care who I hit.

Waiters, the clientele, Colin Curtis. I'll fire blindly, as if I'm trying to shoot the whole world. I'll watch their bodies slump over cups of sake and rectangular plates of sashimi and I'll keep shooting until there are no more bullets and the only sound I can hear is screaming.

I take the gun away from my head and put it back in my inside pocket. Then I leave the toilet cubicle and I catch a glimpse of myself in the mirror. I look deadly. The stairs groan under my feet and I'm back in the bar and back at the table where Colin Curtis is grinning to himself.

He knocks back inches of beer and he tells me how he sees the book developing and how he thinks it will make a great film but he's not too keen on being played by Orlando Bloom.

"Well, he's just a bit posh and that, isn't he? I mean, *Orlando*. Who calls their kid Orlando? Nah, you want someone a bit more real. Like that whatsisname out of *The Transporter*. He'd be alright. Doesn't look like me or anything, but he's got the right accent. Can you imagine Orlando fucking Bloom trying to put on a Basildon accent? He'd sound like a fucking joke."

We finish the beers and the sake and he suggests we move on. We step out of the bar and the waiter says goodbye and I'm pretty sure I can see relief on the faces of the other customers. It's relief that Colin Curtis has left the building, but they don't know how close they came to being gunned down in the middle of a Saturday night. They don't know how close they came to being a vaguely blurred photograph on the front page of tomorrow's tabloids under a great big sans serif headline like Death in Soho or In Cold Blood. People in the business of creating front pages love massacres and atrocities. You don't have to think of anything particularly clever or witty; something hard and minimal will do, the less fussy the better.

Soho is people and noise. Stumbling junkies and girls in cowboy hats. Families bunched together like circled wagons trying to avert the gaze of their children from anything that speaks of an underworld. Taxis crawl out across the junction of Bateman Street and middle-aged men smoking French cigarettes sit at chrome tables scanning the youthful crowds with lustful eyes. Anything can be found and had in Soho.

The exterior of Naughty is like every London strip club with delusions of grandeur. A cordon to guide the clientele toward the door. Rectangular Russian doormen in black shirts and black ties with spiral cords leading to ear pieces and NASA style crew-cuts. When they see Colin Curtis they nod stoically before lifting the rope and letting us in.

Nothing quite prepares me for what happens next.

In the vestibule we are greeted by Rob Rascal. Rob Rascal, former singer with Belsen Beat, last seen propping up the bar and begging for money at the premier of *Something's Got To Give*.

He smiles warmly, and in a perfectly coherent voice says, "Good evening gentlemen, and welcome to Naughty. Just the two of you?"

We both nod.

"Excellent. If you'd just like to follow me, I'll take you to your table and introduce you to your waitress for the evening."

I'm starting to feel woozy. My face is burning up. My stomach lurches. We enter the club, which is red, like all strip clubs should be, and are taken to a table at the edge of the stage. We are then introduced to Katerina.

"This is Katerina, she will be your waitress for the evening. I'm sure you are already well-versed in the house rules. No touching and no lewd comments, please gents. This is a respectable establishment."

A respectable establishment? Yes. I look around the room and see the narrow eyes of weekender businessmen and out-of-towners. Stag nights and Saturday nights 'away from the missus'. The air bristles with a kind of static sexual tension; a charge which is going nowhere, generating nothing except more charge.

Katerina takes our order, a bottle of Krug Clos du Mesnil, which Colin Curtis picks out from the menu not by name but by price.

"We'll have that one," he says, handing her a platinum Amex and waving her goodbye.

"It's the only thing they understand," he says, his eyes on the empty stage. He chews his lower lip in anticipation, and I ask him what he means.

"Well, places like this. It's not about your manners or how posh you talk or the clothes you're wearing. Oh, of course, they're not going to let you in wearing a t-shirt and shorts, looking like you just stepped off the beach in Maga-fucking-luf, but the only thing they *really* care about is money. You give 'em the Platinum Amex and they're all, 'Yes sir, no sir three bags full, sir'."

I think about Nigel's words. Celebrity is the new currency. What Colin Curtis said is right, of course, but the only reason he is right is because he's a celebrity. The only reason we were able to walk right in here without paying is because he's a celebrity. We aren't some out-of-town stretch limo full of wide-boys who will try and run out of the club the minute the bill arrives. Colin Curtis has a Platinum Amex.

The bottle of Krug arrives and Katerina pours a little into each glass. I've had a lot of champagne in my life, but this is exceptional. This tastes how I thought champagne would taste when I was a child, rather than the surprisingly tart, arid muck I would eventually taste at weddings, film premieres, and the occasional book launch.

"That's alright, that is," says Colin Curtis, after knocking back perhaps three quarters of the glass in one go. By my estimation he's just downed almost a hundred pounds worth of champagne without really tasting it. "It's quite refreshing, isn't it?"

I nod and sip mine, practically able to taste the money. My stomach lurches again. The room isn't spinning, but it has a fluidity; as if the red walls and the red curtain on the stage and the tables and the chairs were all somehow liquid. I put my glass against my forehead.

"What's the matter?" says Colin Curtis, laughing. "Feeling a bit under the weather?"

"I think I need some fresh air," I say.

"Bollocks. This place has got the best air-con in Soho. You'd hardly know there was a fucking heatwave outside. What's the matter with you?"

"I don't know… "

I take another sip of champagne and feel something trigger in the back of my throat. With my hand over my mouth I stifle the first warning signals that I might just vomit at any moment.

"Sorry, Ed… " says Colin Curtis. "I probably should have given you a half. I wasn't sure whether you'd had any before."

"Had any what?" I ask. My voice sounds like I'm standing inside a metal tube.

"Symph," says Colin Curtis. "I put a symph in your pint back in that Japanese bar. It fizzed up like an Alka Seltzer. I had to stir it round with a chopstick before you got back. Sorry mate… are you feeling alright?"

He's trying to sound concerned but he's laughing the whole time, and his laughter seems to rise in pitch, until it's this horrible braying sound in my ears.

"It's always like this the first time," he says, putting one hand on my shoulder. "I just thought it might be a bit of an icebreaker. You seemed a bit stressed, that's all. Thought you might like a bit of a pick-me-up. Or a put-me-down. Whichever way it goes."

"You gave me drugs...?" I slur, holding onto the stem of my champagne flute as if it were some kind of handrail.

"Not drugs. A drug. You're just coming up off it, that's all. Give it five and you'll be fine. I took mine about two minutes ago. Everything's going to be fine. Just chill... let it wash over you..."

His voice is fading. The curtain moves and the MC takes to the stage. He is a tall and angular man with hair like a 1970s quiz show host.

"Good evening, and welcome to Naughty," he says, in a knowingly plummy BBC World Service voice, half way between Nicholas Parsons and Giles Brandreth. The men in the club cheer. The light shifts. Everything seems to melt. "We've got some lovely girls for you tonight. All the way from the finest finishing schools in Europe." Another cheer. "And what they're just *dying* to know is, have you all been naughty? Well... *have you*?"

By now the audience is baying, howling like a pack of ravenous dogs at feeding time. The curtain opens, and the MC steps down from the stage and makes his way to the large Scotch and soda that is waiting for him on the bar. The music starts: 'Joe le Taxi' by Hanayo and Jurgen Pappe. I'd recognise that bass line anywhere, even if I'm hearing it from inside what sounds like a metal box.

Three girls in school uniform step out onto the stage. They look so young. This isn't like the kind of strip show I've seen before on awful corporate trips to Peppermint Rhino and the Shoreditch Triangle. These girls aren't made up in a Manga cartoon version of adolescence; all knowing winks, bubble-gum and lollypops; they look like they've just been scooped up off the street at hometime. The uniforms aren't stylishly customised to expose pierced navels and small-but-tasteful tattoos, they look like real school uniforms, and they aren't wearing any make-up. They look out at the audience as if they're genuinely scared.

Colin Curtis is loving this. He looks at me and nods as if waiting for my approval, smiling from ear to ear. I try and steady myself by placing one hand on the table but it feels like the whole thing is vibrating with that heavy, sleazy bass line.

Tout les p'tits bars… Tout les coins noirs…

Slowly they begin to undress, but in that awkward way of somebody taking their clothes off for the very first time with someone
watching them. There's nothing artful or graceful about it. No
attempt is made to make it provocative or arousing, but aroused
they are: around me men are leaning forward in their seats, slack-
jawed and wide-eyed.

Through the haze of the drug I wonder whether this is, in fact,
the ultimate act. Maybe they're pretending that they aren't pretending, maybe that is it. This brings some comfort, it's what I hold
onto. The market for the artificial is gone. People want real. This
club gives them real, or the illusion of it. It gives them a simulacra
of the illicit that would be fascinating if it weren't so disturbing.

My vision blurs and I see us, Colin and I, stepping out of a cab
somewhere. The street is that kind of rain-washed London street
with cobbles that you only get in movies. The rainwater on the
cobbles is lit up orange by the street lights. There's a neon sign for
a chip shop or a kebab shop somewhere in the background, out of
focus. The cab pulls away (I think I paid) and as it does I pin
Colin Curtis against the wall and I shoot him in the stomach. It's
clumsier than I planned and he just curls up in a ball, drunk and
in pain, clutching the wound as if he's still not sure what it is.

But none of that has happened yet. It's just the drug, I tell
myself. It's just the drug.

I try to hold on to something from the past because I've heard
about this happening and I won't let this happen and I'm trying
for the life of me to remember what relevance the monkey puzzle
tree has but I can't even think what the fucking thing looks like.
The girls on the stage seem to be so far away, and I can hear Colin
Curtis saying something to me but I can't hear what it is.

One girl nervously takes off her bra while another artlessly
removes her knickers and all I can hear is the sound of men
whistling and cheering.

I'm sat in a cell in a police station while a very stern officer who
looks no older than twenty asks me if I realise what I've done and
I tell him I'm not really sure and he tells me in a dead-serious
voice, "You've robbed this country of one of its best-loved
celebrities".

He bites his lip and he looks like he's about to start crying. I
laugh in his face and that's when the cell is full of other officers

all beating me with truncheons, and the worst thing is I love it.

But none of this has happened, yet. None of this is real.

We were in West India Quay. I remind myself of that. We were in West India Quay, and there was an insect. I remember the insect. But what colour was it? There was an insect. And somebody was talking about China. And then there was Phillip Mackenzie. I remember Phillip Mackenzie. But why? Do I *know* him?

Colin Curtis is biting his lower lip and grinding his hips back and forth while watching the girls on the stage undress.

I don't know Phillip Mackenzie. I don't *think* I know Phillip Mackenzie. Who the fuck is Phillip Mackenzie? I'm in a club. I'm in a strip club. What the fuck am I doing in here? There are girls on the stage. And Colin Curtis, the celebrity Colin Curtis, is sat next to me, and he's licking his lips and smiling and shaking his head softly as if he can't believe how happy he is.

And suddenly everything is okay.

I've been covering my hands with my eyes and somewhere deep down worrying that this might draw attention to us and that we might get ejected, but of course I'm worrying about nothing. Nobody is looking at *us*. All eyes, from the MC to Rob Rascal, are on the stage.

And suddenly everything is okay.

I take my hands away from my eyes and look around me at the movie version of my life. I hear the music, and I see the soft electric throb of the lights, and everything is caught up in such a beautiful slow motion I could almost weep.

Detachment. This is the lesson. None of this is real. I repeat it like a mantra to myself, momentarily worried I might be saying it out loud until I realise I'm holding my breath.

None of this is real.

After a while just the thought of each word becomes amusing.

None of this is reel.

Nun of this is reel.

Nun of this Israel.

Nun of the scissor eel.

I start laughing and Colin Curtis looks at me and makes 'crazy eyes' before holding up his glass of champagne and shouting "cheers" over the din of the music.

On stage one of the girls cagily touches the breasts of another girl, who responds by wincing. There is an audible gasp from the

audience. They breathe in as one. I imagine that they are all con-
joined, linked beneath the tables as part of one sprawling fleshy
mass; like the end of the film *Society*. They breathe in as one.
They slurp their over-priced drinks as one. They are erect as one.
Colin Curtis smiles at me once more and his eyes look black, like
eightballs. I can hear him laughing and laughing.

One of the girls is on her knees, tentatively lowering the knickers of another girl, looking at the audience every now and then
with a fearful expression, as if to ask, 'is this what you want?' The
other girl's eyes are closed and she bites her lower lip as if she's
hating every second of this. And I keep telling myself that none
of this is real. None of this is real. None of this is real.

On stage the girls are mutating. Their physical forms become
fluid, flesh against flesh; tongues and orifices meeting in head-on
collisions like raindrops on a windshield. The music snaps them
into strange contortions. I can't see where one person ends and
another begins. Over the music I can hear them gasping.

And none of this is real.

The room gets darker. Everything is in slow motion now. I'm
not moving. My body feels like stone. It occurs to me that my
entire body could shut down, my heart could stop beating, my
lungs could stop taking in air, and there wouldn't be a thing I
could do about it. Perhaps this is it. The final moments. A strange
and sinister death.

I remember police cars and ambulances. I remember paramedics and the girls on stage wrapped in towels watching in
horror as they take me away. I remember the police interviewing
the MC and Rob Rascal, and them shaking their heads and saying
they don't know what happened. I remember Colin Curtis, his
eyes bulging and his face shiny with sweat telling them he thinks
I may have taken drugs. I remember the ambulance's journey
through the city, and the strange perspective that lying on a
gurney in a moving vehicle gives you. Familiar buildings flicker
past the windows at strange angles. It almost feels like flying.

And I remember dying.

But none of this has happened yet. I remember none of these
things. I am in the nightclub Naughty, with Colin Curtis, and he
nudges me with his elbow, and he is laughing, and pointing at the
stage.

"I think I need to leave," I say, but he doesn't hear me and so I
say it again, only louder this time.

"What?" he says. "But it's only just starting. It gets proper hard core after this bit. They've got an Alsatian and everything."

"I need to leave."

"Oh, for fuck's sake."

"I can't remember things… "

"What?"

"I said I can't remember things. I can't remember what my mum looks like."

He leans across the table, still holding his champagne flute, his big doe eyes still as black as obsidian.

"What the fuck are you talking about?"

"I'm talking about everything. I can't remember *anything*… It's all… it's all going…"

"Jesus… you're having a fucking symph-out. Shit… we'll have to go. I can't have you freaking out in here. You might get me banned. You're not going to be sick, are you?"

"No. I don't think so."

"You're not going to shit yourself?"

What does he mean, shit myself? Could I shit myself?

"No," I tell him. "I just need fresh air. I can see things… terrible things… "

Colin Curtis stands and he helps me to my feet. The rest of the room fails to notice this. They are watching two girls performing simultaneous oral sex on one another in an act that's played out to look amateurish and clumsy and forced.

Colin Curtis leads me through the club and all about me the lights and the furniture and the faces are dripping off one another and I feel like I'm walking through treacle.

Rob Rascal is at the bar and when he smiles it's like his whole face is about to crack open. He nods in my direction and as I pass him he whispers something to me.

"Make it quick and don't look at his eyes. It's easier that way."

We step out through the entrance of the club and the first thing I notice is the sky.

Above the streets of Soho a sky that was fading blue when we entered the club is now a violent grey, heavy and black in places, bursting at the seams with the promise of thunder and rain. The air smells different, electrified, like a warning.

"What's happened to the sky?" I ask.

Colin Curtis looks up. His footsteps are awkward, as if the sudden change in atmospherics has affected his reaction to the drug.

"Clouds," he says in awe. "There are clouds."

We step out into a Soho Square that's full of hipsters, queens and skateboarders. A dwarf walks past in a pin-striped suit, his jacket tossed casually over one shoulder. I can hear boom-boxes and C-Fish music, helicopters and distant police sirens, the braying of taxi horns. Everything has that underwater quality. I know I'm in Soho Square because this is where Soho Square is, but it could be any square in the world. Its dimensions have changed. The trees in the centre of the square are like a jungle. The buildings on every side look like ancient ruins, and the statue of Charles II is crawling with insects.

"Oh fuck..." says Colin Curtis. "I think it's starting to kick in. The symph, I mean. Are you feeling anything yet?"

What does he mean, am I feeling anything yet? My legs are rigid and I can still hear the music from that club. What was the name of that club? What club?

"I think we need to get in a cab," says Colin Curtis. "Everything will be alright if we get in a cab. We'll go to Greenwich or something. Stand on the whatjamacallit... the line... where the time is. If we stand on that line everything'll be okay."

I see adverts plastered on the faces of passers by. I hear music coming from the drains. In the sky there are buildings on fire. Chunks of burning masonry are raining down on London. The steeple of St Patrick's church crumbles as if it were made of sand. There are animals in the gutters. The natives are restless in the trees. When I close my eyes I see the figure 5 in gold.

We stagger down Sutton Row and out into the carnival of Charing Cross Road. Looming over us, the brutal slab of Centre Point stabs the clouds like a half-buried knife. Colin Curtis stumbles out into the road, waving his arms frantically as if he were stranded in the desert and had just spotted distant headlights.

A cab pulls up. The door unlocks with a loud clunk. We get in and we leave Soho.

cab – 21:06

"'Ere... you're that bloke off the telly."

Colin Curtis and I are sat in the cab, pressing ourselves back against black leather seats. The cab driver, a man who seems to occupy most of the space in the front of the cab, his mountainous frame topped off with a flat cap, is little more than a pair of eyes in the rear-view mirror.

"Yeah... I am," says Colin Curtis. He breathes loudly, sweat pouring down his face, as we drive down Charing Cross Road and back into the heart of the West End.

"What was that programme called? What was it? *Locked In*? *Locked Out*? 'Ere... what was it called?"

"*Lockdown*."

"Nah. That wasn't it. What was it called?"

"*Lockdown*. It was called *Lockdown*," says Colin Curtis.

"Yeah, that might be it. I never watched it. The missus used to watch it all the time. She used to like that Scottish bloke. Ronny. Was that his name? The *love rat*. She used to like him."

"Right... yeah... "

The West End feels like a safari park on a Saturday night. Occasional hands, spread flat, slap against the windows, as if the drunken revellers think they can hold back the metal tide as they spill out onto the roads. The pavements are so crowded that the people hardly seem to move. Luminous placards float above their heads.

2-4-1 ON BOTTLES

COMEDY NITE HAPPY HOUR 8-10

SUBWAY 200 YRDS

The people carrying these signs seem to have replaced those people who would once wander the streets telling you the end of the world was nigh. Once upon a time they would have carried standards painted with blood red crosses or quotes from the Old Testament or the Book of Revelation. Now it's all happy hours and fast-food restaurants.

We drive along the eastern edge of Trafalgar Square, where the tourists are pouring out of the National Gallery and down the steps into the square itself. They sit around the fountains and on the steps and around its belvedere; European students smoking cigarettes and vagrants drinking from dented cans. Families chasing after hyperactive toddlers and little clusters of alternatively-dressed teenagers sitting moodily around the lions.

"So… you must be absolutely loaded now, mate," says the cab driver.

"Well… " says Colin Curtis, looking vaguely awkward.

"And I tell you something… " the driver continues, "I mean… all that blah-blah-blah in the papers about what you done before you went in there. I mean, prison and all that. It's like I've always said, if you've done your time, you've done your bleeding time, d'you know what I mean? Let sleeping dogs lie and that. Besides which, them who lives in glass houses shouldn't throw stones."

"What d'you mean?" asks Colin Curtis.

"Well, I'm only saying… you went away for doing what you done, but I don't think there's a red-blooded man alive who wouldn't admit to, you know… having a bit of an eye for the younger ladies."

I want to say something. I want to remind our driver that the girl Colin Curtis violated was six years old, but I can't even form the words.

"Really?" says Colin Curtis, leaning forward in his seat.

"Oh yeah. I mean… it's only natural, isn't it? If you've got to choose between some lovely young thing with pigtails and some fat old boiler who looks like a pig… who're you going to pick? Eh? Eh? Who're you going to pick?"

"Yeah, I know," says Colin Curtis, grinning. "Exactly."

This is wrong. This is wrong. This is wrong. This is wrong.

"And the only thing with you was you got caught."

I look out of the window and start praying for a high speed collision; the kind that would tear this taxi in half like an aluminium can and leave bits of me all over Victoria Embankment. The kind that would leave our bodies in such a state that photos of us would end up on all manner of websites, next to decapitation videos from the Middle East and photographs of shark attack victims.

"I know," says Colin Curtis, dolefully. "That *was* the thing."

"I mean… there's loads of blokes like you who don't get caught. And nobody even talks about it. I mean… if I'm honest, things *have* happened."

Oh please, God, not now. Not here. The taxi cab confessional played out in reverse. I remember reading somewhere that taxi drivers give more testimonies in murder and rape cases than doctors. Taxi drivers are the ones people tell. Cabs are little more than confessional booths on wheels. People try out their psychoses for size on taxi drivers. They tell them what they've just done, and what they're about to do. They open up their hearts and share their life stories, and sometimes, just sometimes, the taxi driver does the same back.

"I mean, not for a long time, you know? But things have happened. Nothing much. Just... uh... just..."

He pauses for concentration as we leave Victoria Embankment.

"Just... my niece, it was. Pretty little thing. I got drunk one Christmas party. Things happened, after she'd gone to bed, and that. But, you know... she was being all flirty with me. So... well... it's all in the past. And she's married with kids now, all settled down. Nothing wrong with her."

Colin Curtis is smiling. His eyes are like puddles of ink. I look down briefly and see that he's got an erection.

We drive over Tower Bridge, past Japanese couples photographing one another at the exact point where the two sides of the bridge meet. Viewed from the bridge the north and south banks open out like limbs of stone and glass and concrete, preparing for an embrace.

"My family's lived in London two hundred years. D'you know that? Two hundred years? We traced the family tree back. Well, my son did. On the internet and that. Two hundred years... Whitechapel. Bow. Plaistow. Always been over the east side of the Fleet, we have.

"My great-grandmother lived to be ninety-one, and she used to tell us, when we was kids, that she saw Jack the Ripper. No word of a lie. Her family was living on Bucks Row when the first one, Mary Ann Nichols her name was, had her throat cut. My great-grandmother said she was trying to get her baby sister to sleep... their mum had died of consumption about six months earlier... and as she looked out of the window, my great-grandmother, she saw him. There in the street! Black as night! Jack the Ripper."

Throughout the cab driver's monologue I find myself looking out of the window at the streets, the twenty-four-hour cornershops, the gastro pubs, the flocks of Asian women in saris, the strutting boys in pastel-coloured Ben Sherman shirts; anything solid, anything real. My mind is littered, soiled with images of blood on rain-washed streets, and the Ripper, dressed like a pantomime villain; a top hat and cape, an outlandish handlebar moustache and lamb chop sideburns; but spattered with real blood.

"'He had eyes like the fires of hell,' the old dear used to say. Still… never knew whether she was making it all up, personally."

We take a left onto Curlew Street and stop at the end of Shad Thames.

"Well, 'ere we are. Shad Thames."

Colin Curtis pays him, and as we're stepping out of the cab our driver says, "'Ere, mate… you wouldn't mind signing this for the missus, would you? She loved your show. It'd make her day, that would."

He hands Colin Curtis a scrap of paper and a ballpoint pen.

"Of course," says Colin Curtis, beaming.

shad thames – 21:32

"You live here?" I ask Colin Curtis as we enter the deep, man-made canyon of Shad Thames.

"Yeah… moved out of the Savoy last week. One of the girls who works for Trisha helped me pick the place. It's really nice. Really posh, like… "

He's walking in a zig-zag, looking up at the high walls to either side of us, and the rickety-looking wooden bridges that link one gentrified warehouse to the next.

No matter how many estate agents, coffee bars or restaurants occupy these buildings, no matter how many square feet of these once-upon-a-time warehouses are converted into open-plan apartments, they'll never scrub away the last traces of old London from the place. It's the sheer verticality of its edifices, reducing the sky to a narrow gash of grey light; the arched windows like despairing eyes. No matter how polished and quaint the cobbled street might look, there is still something malevolent in the darkness between each stone.

The street and the walls and the rickety wooden bridges speak of an ancient London that stank of fog and damp and spilt liquor. The brightly lit doorways of the delicatessens and coffee shops still remember the shadows in which sinister figures once stood, smoking clay pipes and snarling at passers by.

All the gentrification in the world can't exorcise the ghosts of this street, and certainly not under the brooding cauldron of the sky above.

I'm sure I can hear thunder.

We come to a gate in an archway at the side of one of the old warehouses, and Colin Curtis swipes a card to let us in. We climb steps that look out over the murky river and I focus on the simple act of moving. It's so alien to have to concentrate on something as simple as climbing a flight of steps, but I do. I can hear Colin Curtis talking but I don't know what he's saying. Every time I blink, the world seems to change.

Another roll of what could be thunder.

"What time is it?" says Colin Curtis. I look at my C-Fish, but the numbers seem to be changing, over and over.

"I don't know," I reply.

We enter Colin Curtis' apartment. His sitting room is larger than my apartment, with a balcony overlooking Tower Bridge, Butlers Wharf, and the River. It looks exactly like the kind of apartment I always thought I'd live in but never did.

"Drink?" Colin Curtis asks, staggering toward the bar that resides in one corner of the room, next to a vast and sprawling home entertainment system. "I've got... well... I've got everything really. I've got some coke round here, too. Maybe that would sort our heads out. A line of sniff. Clear things up a little. Then we can talk about that fucking book."

I have stepped no more than four or five feet into his apartment. Nobody I know will ever live like this, nobody I *really* know. Oh, sure, there are people I've met at parties and people I've had to interview, but nobody I've ever loved or been intimate with will ever live in an apartment like this. They won't have a well-stocked bar, and they probably won't have some cocaine put to one side for just this kind of emergency. This is the other side of the looking glass. This is where celebrity lives.

I wonder whether the money that pays for this is real, or whether it's celebrity money. They are not the same thing. Celebrity money is based on promises and maybes. It floats in the ether as figures talked about but never made physical. Is Colin Curtis paying for this place? Is Trisha Smedley? How much money did he win on that show? How much for all the magazine covers? The products he will end up selling? The after-dinner talks? The Christmas Number One? The film? The book?

"You know the most fucked-up thing," he says, apropos of

nothing, pouring two large Zubrowkas and spilling most of it over the bar. "The most fucked up thing is this… when you're famous, everyone smiles at you."

I ask him what he means, still not moving from my position near the doorway.

"Everyone smiles at you," he says again. "Like… like you're a monkey in a zoo or something. Like it's funny, you just being there. They don't speak. They don't come up and say hello, not most people. They just fucking *smile* at you. And they just stand there and do it. And if they *do* speak to you they hang on your every word, even if you've got nothing to say. They actually *listen* to you, and then they smile some more, or they laugh, even if what you said wasn't all that funny. Why is that, Ed? Why… why do people do that?"

I tell him I don't know.

"They reckon everyone wants to be famous, don't they?" he says, dropping ice cubes into the glasses and sloshing them around. "What was it that bloke said… that one, the famous one… what was it he said? Everyone'll be famous for fifteen minutes?"

"Andy Warhol," I say softly.

"Yeah. That's him. Andy Warhol. Everyone'll be famous for fifteen minutes. I wonder whether that's true. 'Cause this feels longer than fifteen minutes. This feels like it's never going to stop. And all I really want is for people to stop fucking smiling at me. Because… " He shakes his head. For a moment I am perilously close to feeling some sort of sympathy, or maybe even pity for Colin Curtis. I brace myself until my stomach hurts and I'm almost biting through my lip, until the feeling has gone away.

"Because of what?" I ask him.

"Because if this doesn't stop then I won't stop, will I?"

I ask him what he means. He steps out from behind the bar and. almost tripping over the edge of a rug. he walks toward me carrying both glasses of vodka.

"When you're normal," he says, "there's rules, and there's laws, and if you fuck it up you get caught, most of the time anyway. But when you're famous… when you're really, *really* famous, there's nothing. Everyone just smiles at you and lets you do it, because they like you, and the worst thing is, they don't even know why."

And that's when I shoot him.

My hand has been on the gun for maybe a minute and a half and it's out of my jacket pocket in a split second. He's perhaps eight feet away from me when I shoot him. The glass of vodka in his right hand shatters and his thumb just seems to explode and the right side of his chest buckles, like someone's dented it with an invisible hammer.

All these things happen at exactly the same time.

"Oh, fuck… " says Colin Curtis, dropping the other glass and stumbling backward before hitting the ground with a loud thud.

There's blood leaking out between his fingers and, when he coughs, a little dribbles from the corner of his mouth, just like in a film. I've dropped the gun, and I'm walking toward him, my hand over my mouth, waiting for an emotion that doesn't come.

"Fuck… fuck… " says Colin Curtis. "Aw, man… I can hardly see anything… everything's blurry… where are you?"

I tell him I'm still there.

"Did you *shoot* me?" he asks, his voice dampened by his shallow breathing and the blood in his throat.

"Yes," I tell him.

"Fuck… " says Colin Curtis. "I thought so. D'you know something, though? It doesn't hurt. I can't… I can't feel it properly. Well, I can and I can't. It's… fuck… is the window open or something… it's fucking freezing in here… and it's so dark." He laughs softly. "I'm just lying here in the dark waiting to fucking die."

I crouch down beside him, making sure I don't step in the blood. He's looking straight up at me, but I don't think he can see me. He laughs again with a mouthful of blood, and in a voice that's little more than a whisper says: "The irony… the irony…"

I sit with his body for a while, in the quiet of his apartment. London looks at us through twinkling neon eyes as the sky bruises over. Each time I hear sirens I brace myself and wait for them to draw nearer but they don't. The gunshot was so loud I practically didn't hear it, just like Nigel said, and yet nobody seems to have noticed.

Colin Curtis is smiling up at the ceiling of his enormous luxury apartment in a puddle of blood, vodka and his own piss and all I can smell is gunpowder. I want there to be more than this. I want there to be more than the complete absence of meaning that surrounds a dead body. They always mean something in paintings, whether it's a *pietà* or the Death of Marat. In the flesh they are just that: flesh. Without *mise en scène* they are no more loaded with meaning than road kill or a carcass in a butcher's window.

I get up and walk away from Colin Curtis' dead body and I leave the gun where I dropped it. The police will come here and they will take fingerprints and they will ask questions and they will find out I was with him and they will take my fingerprints and then they will arrest me, and maybe then all this will begin to mean something.

I walk down the steps and let myself out through the gates, and I walk back down Shad Thames, climbing the steps up onto Tower Bridge. It has started to rain. The rain beats the surface of the river and hisses under the passing traffic as if the whole city were one giant hotplate.

As I cross the bridge my C-Fish rings and I answer it to hear Shardul's voice.

"Mr Curtis… " he says, "he dead?"

"Yes, Shardul," I say. "He's dead."

the next day – 11:01

I sit in front of the television eating breakfast cereal with UHT milk.

Mr Curtis, who only weeks ago was the winner of the latest series of *Lockdown*, was found by police in the early hours of this morning. Early reports suggest that he died as the result of a gunshot wound to the chest, though this has not yet been confirmed.

Shocking news, of course, this morning… Colin Curtis, who won this year's series of *Lockdown*, shot dead in his own home. Can you believe it?

I can't believe it.

Can you believe it?

No, I can't believe it either.

I can't believe it.

No… No… I just can't believe it.

…the winner of the reality show *Lockdown* had been shot dead in his apartment some time last night. Police were alerted by an anonymous phone call telling them there had been a shooting at Mr Curtis' address at Shad Thames in central London.

Well, I suppose once again it comes down to the whole issue of celebrity, doesn't it? I mean... John Lennon is a classic example.

...shot dead some time last night, at his apartment on Shad Thames near Tower Bridge...

Mr Curtis was born on this council estate in Basildon, in 1977. Raised a catholic, he attended this school in the town, before...

...had served five years in a *real* prison. Mr Curtis, who was released in...

...winning this year's series by over a million votes...

...in his apartment. Police are carrying out a detailed examination of the crime scene, and are appealing to...

They'll find me. They have to find me. I left the gun. He had two glasses of vodka. That's the kind of thing they pick up on in TV movies and detective shows: "He was carrying two glasses of vodka... that must mean he knew his killer."

They'll find me. And when they find me I won't lie, or try to cover it up, or tell them a far-fetched story about how I saw some black guy coming up the stairs as I was walking out, and he looked like maybe he was holding a gun under his hooded top. I won't tell them I was brainwashed by MI6 or that I did it because he was a paedophile and all paedophiles are evil. I won't really give them a reason. This has to be thought out, planned, to reach the maximum desired impact. This has to be shocking.

I think about the newsroom at *The Voice of the People*, where everyone will be sat at their desks; half dumb with shock after my arrest, but also fixed upon the task at hand.

The headline.

Because what kind of a headline can a newspaper write after one of its own has just shot and killed the most famous person in the country? They'd be fine if it was the other way around, of course, but not this.

I still haven't heard from Nigel. I thought maybe he would have called me by now, or at least left a note under the door, but there's been nothing. I am back in my apartment and it seems smaller, now, than when I left it. A sense of scale, of normality, has returned. It is an apartment once more. For so many weeks I came to think of it as my landscape. A place of deserts, and seas; tropical in the heat wave, balmy in the moonlit evenings.

It's strangely quiet now. I can't even hear the planes at City Airport. It hasn't stopped raining since I left Shad Thames. Even from ten storeys up I can see the surface of the water in Royal Victoria Dock jumping and dancing with every raindrop, as if it's boiling.

I wait for sirens.

I wait for armed police.

I wait for all the things that should have happened in the TV movie version of my life, but which haven't.

The after-effects of the symph can still be felt. Movement is still strange; my footsteps feel heavy and my hands stiff. The light shifts with whatever residue the drug has left behind. I find my memory jarred by things on television, and I wonder if they happened.

Colin Curtis… yes, I remember Colin Curtis.

And sometimes, every so often, I have to remind myself that I shot him.

Police arrived to find Mr Curtis in his apartment, having been shot just once, though they really aren't telling us any more than that. Back to you, Diane.

The day is beginning to pass, and still nothing has happened. On the television there are multiple camera crews in Shad Thames filming nothing but police ribbons and police cars. Multiple reporters form a human wall that marks the outer edge of the exclusion zone. Bystanders mill around in the background of each shot. A man in a blue raincoat talking into his C-Fish waves at the camera. Half way through the afternoon one of the channels cancels the episode of *Columbo* it was about to show, and when I check online it turns out that the episode involved a television celebrity being shot. We are treated instead to almost an hour and a half of Tom and Jerry cartoons, including *Yankee Doodle Mouse, Mouse Trouble, The Cat Concerto,* and *Dr Jekyll and Mr Mouse*.

And still nothing has happened.

Indeed, nothing happens for another six hours, as I watch more cartoons fill the spaces where programmes now deemed inappropriate should have gone. All the crime thrillers have been cancelled tonight. All the murder mysteries. Anything with violence. Anything that might have mentioned guns. And in the place of all this absent programming: cartoon after cartoon after cartoon.

Duck Dodgers in the 24½ th Century.

Duck! Rabbit! Duck!

One Froggy Morning.

Don't Give Up The Sheep.

By nine pm I'm starting to remember the moment when I shot Colin Curtis, only now it's with cartoon sound effects.

Whizz! Bang! Ka-Blam! Splat! Kerr-Ash!

When he hits the ground it sounds like a bass drum and the sudden crash of a cymbal, followed by a muffled trumpet.

Wa Wa Wa Waaaaa.

Why did I leave the gun in his apartment? If I had the gun with me now I could put it in my mouth and I could fire a bullet up through the hard palate, sending the contents of my head out through the top of my skull like soggy confetti.

This time they'd hear. They would have to hear. One of the neighbours would call the police and they would get here and they would find the weapon and they would *have* to put two and two together because if they couldn't then what the fuck am I paying my taxes for?

On television a cartoon sheepdog and a cartoon wolf are clocking off after a day of trying to kill one another.

And nothing has happened.

the arrest – 12:13

Three days later something happens.

I am still watching television, after taking another delivery of supplies from the supermarket's driver, and the newsreader says something that very nearly makes me choke on my meal of energy bar and caffeine-based soft drink.

Police have this morning arrested a thirty-four-year-old man in connection with the murder of *Lockdown* star Colin Curtis. The man, who has not yet been named, was arrested by armed officers at an address on Abbey Street in Bermondsey at around seven o'clock this morning.

Thinking this to be perhaps some trick of the mind or an aftershock of my experience with symph I begin changing channels, and on each and every one of them it is the same story.

…arrested at around seven o'clock…

…armed officers arrested the man, who has not yet been named, at…

…Street in Bermondsey, less than half a mile from where Mr Curtis was found dead on Sunday morning…

…that they have arrested a thirty-four-year-old man in connection with the murder, which has left the world of show business stunned these last four days.

Okay, so tell us a little about the arrest…

Well, Diane, the arrest was carried out by armed officers, we can confirm that, but no shots were fired during the arrest, and the gentleman in question does not appear to have been armed himself when arrested…

…Curtis, who was found dead in his apartment on Sunday morning. Mr Curtis, the winner of the reality TV show *Lockdown*, had only recently moved in to the apartment in London's fashionable…

…nection with the murder of Colin Curtis…

I turn off the television, my free hand over my mouth, my thoughts sloshing about in my head like too much wine in an empty stomach. I begin to wonder if it's me they've arrested. Could I be *that* delusional? Could it be that I am, right now, sat in a cell somewhere while others observe me and wonder where my mind is?

Nigel will know. Nigel knows all about this. He is possibly the only person who knows all about this.

I get up and put on a pair of shoes for the first time in three days and I leave my apartment quickly so as to avoid any further panic than I'm already experiencing. The corridor is filled with the noise from the other apartments but the elevator is cool and calm, and the ethereal pre-recorded voice that tells me I am going down is strangely soothing. I get out on the fourth floor and I walk to Apartment 413, and I rap my knuckles against the door three times. There is a long pause. I can hear motion inside the apartment, the sound of footsteps nearing the door. The chain being slotted, the handle turned.

When the door opens a few inches I see a young woman, no older than twenty-five, holding a baby. Beyond her, the apartment looks completely different. Nigel's pictures, his museum of images, is gone. I can smell lilies and freshly baked bread.

"Can I help you?" the woman asks, smiling sweetly.

"I-is Nigel here?" I ask, even though my lurching stomach already knows the answer.

"Who's Nigel?"

"Nigel." I say. "He lives here."

"Oh, I think you must have the wrong apartment."

I look at the number on the door: 413.

"No… Nigel *does* live here," I tell her. "I know that he lives here."

"Well… he doesn't *now*," says the woman, still smiling. The baby looks at me in that vaguely distrustful way that babies do and blows bubbles out between its lips.

"How long have you lived here?" I ask. I feel angry but driving the anger is a kind of fear, or some other emotion that I'm not entirely sure I've felt before. If I have, it's been within the claustrophobic confines of a dream.

"A year and a half," says the woman, her tone now a little more anxious. "I can get my husband," she says. It's not an offer, it's a threat.

"No," I tell her. "It's okay. I… I must have the wrong apartment."

She closes the door and I am alone in the corridor. The journey back to my apartment is cold and desolate. I sit back on my leather couch and I turn on the television.

…at some point on Saturday night. Mr Curtis, who was thirty-three, had recently moved into the apartment in London's…

Clearly another psychopath. Clearly another… another *nutter* who wanted him dead. I mean… that's the trouble with fame, isn't it? It's like John Lennon… Dimebag Darrell… all these famous people. They're in the spotlight, in the public eye, and people can't cope with it. It drives people crazy.

I leave the news channels. There may be other things happening in the world today but you wouldn't know it from watching TV. All they seem to know is that a man has been arrested in connection with the murder of the television celebrity Colin Curtis, and all I know is that it wasn't me.

I spend minutes or maybe hours waiting for some sort of contact. I check my emails, my galactus profile, my C-Fish, but there is nothing. Perhaps this is it. Perhaps I am being filtered out of existence.

On the television there are soap operas and more cartoons. There are game shows with 'fabulous cash prizes'. There are make-over shows and documentaries about the world's biggest tumours and children born without limbs. There are sitcoms with live studio audiences and programmes which show me the holidays I could be having in places much sunnier than grey London with its aura of madness and death.

And once more I wait for something to happen.

the fever (i see the future) – 02:31

I see the future. Through the rivers of rain that pour down my window, through the canopy of clouds lit a fiery orange by the city, through the haze of my thoughts and the grim dreamscapes of a fever, I see the future.

It is a future in which nobody leaves their apartment, in which the city is transformed into a landscape of endless tower blocks, each one a Babel in its own right, housing disparate communities of warring isolationists, all of them screaming in tongues. A whole subclass of drivers delivers food to the citizens while they toil at computers linked by bio-software plugged directly into the cerebral cortex. Their thoughts control the data they are paid to process; their minds hired out by global conglomerates as virtual space into which billions of gigabytes of information can be downloaded in a split second. The people on television are computer-generated images, based upon ideas and concepts we once found reassuring; a pearly white smile, blonde hair, and regional accents that are non-threatening.

I see a future in which sexual congress is carried out in public by rapists of both sexes and willing victims who need the experience of being utterly brutalised just to feel human. The streets are otherwise empty, but for the occasional car with windows so heavily tinted that nobody can see in or out. These self-driving capsules move from building to building without ever exposing the passengers to fresh air or direct sunlight.

I see a future in which abattoirs exist alongside schools and tenement buildings, slaughtering animals and processing their remains into pre-packaged food that is driven by conveyor belt directly to the apartments.

I see a future in which the workers are given doses of pornography, fed directly into their thoughts first thing every morning. A future in which time becomes meaningless as the process of living becomes truly twenty-four hour. Day and night mean nothing. There is awake, and there is asleep, but in this world those consciously unused parts of the brain can still be used, sleeping but not dormant. A reservoir of more virtual space.

I'm not sure how long this fever has lasted, or what has caused it. I like to think this is my body shutting down, as if my physical and mental well-being are somehow trying to align themselves. The oppressive heat of the last month has gone, replaced by an endless rain.

I have vague memories of writing an essay in school called 'The day it rained forever'. I would have been eleven, perhaps twelve. Every other child in the class wrote a story about an actual day when it seemed to rain forever and they were forced to play indoors. My essay was about a boy my age standing on the rooftop of the tallest building in a town that was slowly being submerged in water. There were no other survivors, just this boy, watching the grey surface of the deluge inching its way upward, swallowing each building in turn. The story ended with the narrator standing in the middle of what looked like an infinite lake, as the water rose above the rooftop of the building on which he stood. For one messianic moment he was able to enjoy the illusion that he was indeed walking on water, but that was where the story ended. My teacher was disturbed.

"And what happens next?" she asked, gripping the A4 sheets in one hand and a red biro in the other.

"Nothing," I replied. "The water will keep rising."

I wonder, if I was to leave my temporary place of rest and make my way to the window, is that what I would see? Royal Victoria Dock, and the surrounding area, lost beneath a sea of grey water. Hotels and apartment buildings like a man-made archipelago rising above the surface.

It just doesn't stop raining.

On the television they are talking about Colin Curtis again.

Police have named the man charged with the murder of Colin Curtis as thirty-six-year-old Wayne Connery from Bermondsey in South London. Mr Connery was born Wayne Roynan but changed his name by deed-poll six years ago, naming himself after the actor Sean Connery. Neighbours say Mr Connery told them he was in fact the illegitimate son of Sean Connery and that he had changed his name after re-establishing contact with his biological father. There has been no confirmation yet on whether any of these allegations are in fact true...

I close my eyes and I see the future. I see galleries full of paintings sealed and buried beneath mountains of lead as if they contained nuclear waste with a half life of a thousand years. I see whole body transplants and operations in which brains are spliced together in host bodies to form hybrid personalities. I see human bodies being used as fuel and fertiliser in factory farms that surround, like a vast green sea, the island cities filled with workers.

I see landmark buildings towering above a deserted city, covered with vines, like the ruins of Washington DC in *Logan's Run*, and packs of wild dogs gnawing at the bleached bones of the dead.

There has been no contact in days, maybe weeks. Time has become immaterial. Day and night are distinct only in shades of darkness and light. I watch fuzzy shadows, rendered shapeless by the clouds outside, shift across the room. I watch the lights of distant buildings flicker into life. I wonder, on more than one occasion, whether I am actually dead and this is the purgatory to which I've been consigned. Endless news stories about Colin Curtis. Endless re-runs of sitcoms that have dated horribly in such short spaces of time; the jokes ill-timed, the one-liners like cargo containers dropped from a great height, the incessant mugging and outlandish physical gestures offensive and ugly.

Appearing in front of the court Mr Connery's lawyers pleaded not guilty to the charge of murder on the grounds of mental illness. Mr Connery will undergo further psychological evaluation to see if he is fit to stand trial...

Time means nothing. Time could suddenly flip into reverse and I doubt that I would notice if it weren't for the narrative of television. The American dramas that begin with the narration "Previously on... " before offering a recap of the previous episode. The tantalising previews of next week's episode as the end credits roll. The soap opera of world news, part war game, part Shakespearean melodrama, part satire. The audience at home casts public figures as heroes and villains based upon the colour of the tie they are wearing or the tone of voice they use. An epilogue of a weather forecast to tell us whether it will rain or not in two days time, even though it hasn't stopped raining in *weeks*.

Time means nothing. Take away the super-narrative and we are left with repetition after repetition after repetition after...

You don't need me to go on.

We buy into the super-narrative of celebrities, adulterous politicians, and war because if we didn't, it would just be the same thing every single fucking day.

Judge Justice Polsom-Grey ruled that Mr Connery would not stand trial but would instead be moved to Broadmoor Psychiatric Hospital.

Guilty but not guilty. The evidence for the prosecution is now played out on the evening news. His obsession with celebrities. The photographs they found in his one-bedroom flat in Bermondsey. The letters he had written to a well-known game-show host. The previous arrest near the home of a celebrity chef.

Wayne Connery shot Colin Curtis.

Nobody is quite sure where he bought the Makarov PM but there are murmurings of 'eastern Europeans' and 'arms smuggling'.

That's just how easy it is to buy a gun these days,

says a senior police officer, shaking his head with dismay.

That a loner like Wayne Roynan

(They've started calling him Wayne Roynan, which means Sean

Connery's people have said something.)

could buy a gun with such ease is not really surprising. Not to us, anyhow. We've been aware of this growing problem for some time.

The photographs of Wayne Roynan show a dishevelled man with badly cut hair and three days worth of stubble. A man who doesn't sleep much. A man who might just have a single bedroom flat filled with photographs of celebrities and celebrity magazines.

Wayne Roynan shot Colin Curtis.

galactus.co.uk – 11:45

Created by Marvel Comics' Stan Lee and Jack Kirby, Galactus first appeared in Fantastic Four Issue #48 in 1966. Heralded by Silver Surfer, he arrived in our world bent on devouring the planet, because that's who Galactus is. He is the Devourer Of Worlds. He achieves this with the aid of his Elemental Converter, which can drain the life force of an entire planet. In Issue #50, the Fantastic Four (with the aid of Silver Surfer, who had turned against his master) threatened Galactus with the Ultimate Nullifier, a device capable of destroying entire time-lines from beginning to end. Galactus left, promising never to return.

The website galactus.co.uk, named after the Devourer Of Worlds, was begun in 2003 by Greg Barnaby, an Oxford graduate from Boston, Massachusetts, and Tristan Sumner, a graduate of the London School Of Economics, from Hove, in East Sussex. Initially starting life as a networking/dating site, it became part of the K-Media group in 2007, quickly expanding to become the UK's 'first complete online community'. It now includes email facilities, television, video and music downloads, online gaming, networking and dating, shopping and gambling, travel agents, banking, insurance, and news.

It is currently estimated that two out of three people in the United Kingdom are members of galactus (always a lower case 'g') and that over ten million regularly contribute blogs to the site.

I am one of those people.

The writing of blogs is an unusual habit. Part confessional, part emotional vent, it allows the writer to be more than they normally are, or less, depending on their degree of self-censorship. In addition to the forty million UK members with profiles of themselves, there are an estimated two-and-a-half million profiles of fictional characters from computer games, films, television programmes, and novels. There are an additional four hundred thousand profiles purporting to be those of celebrities which are, in fact, put together by members of the general public.

I am not one of those people.

Everything I write in my blog is true, exactly as it happens, or as I experience it. It is important that you know that.

Of course, I could have fictionalised everything. Given everyone make-believe names, changed the locations, written everything in a snidely knowing way that would have left little to the imagination. But I didn't want to do that.

Everything I write in my blog is true.

I get the call through in the morning, while the rest of the country, if not the world, is still watching the news in the deluded hope that anything as interesting as the death of Colin Curtis is going to come along. It is a symptom of the aftermath of a news 'event'. Everyone sits, glued to the television, in the hope that something just as big is about to break, live while they are watching.

The call is from Trisha Smedley. I haven't spoken to her in maybe a month. In the time since we last spoke I have killed a man, and I have thought that I was about to die.

"Ed... fantastic news. You are the talk of the net."

I ask her what she means.

"I mean you're the zeitgeist, darling. You are the name on everyone's lips."

Again, I ask her what she means.

"Oh God, darling, don't you read *any* of the papers? You are the next big thing. Like the dancing baby... Numa Numa... Chocolate Rain... the Singing Nazi... you are the biggest internet sensation this country's ever had."

I feel my heart sink. I think I know what she's going to say next.

"Galactus, darling, galactus," she says. "You must have seen how many hits you've had in the last couple of weeks? Surely?"

I haven't actually. My apathy has reached a near Zen-like state, monotonous, a precursor to a virtual kind of death.

"We are talking tens of thousands. *Tens of thousands*. Of course,

the buzz started with all those people searching Colin Curtis'
name on galactus, and soon enough finding the link to your blog."

My blog.

The blog I have written for the last two years.

The blog you are reading right now.

"*The Independent* is running a piece on it next Sunday and
they're just dying to get an interview. It's the kind of thing they
love. Tabloid hack with hidden depths. They're announcing it as
the return of post-modern irony."

"They're what?" I ask.

"Oh yes. The way you weave fact and fiction. I mean… it's
been done before, but this is the razor's edge, Ed. This is the
razor's edge. Most people wait years before going for the
jugular like you have… writing about Colin Curtis' death the
next day. It's all *mucho polémico*."

That term again. The Spanish one she used to describe *Ground
Zero*.

"Now what we were thinking," Trisha continues, barely pausing
for breath, "is that K-Media part owns the rights to the blog
anyway, so we don't have to worry about any complications in
getting a publishing deal. We can simply package it up with
Tower or Price Moggridge and get it out in a matter of months.
It's going to be huge, Ed. *Huge*. It's going to outsell the fucking
Bible or something. Seb is very happy about all this."

I want to tell her that I shot Colin Curtis. I want to tell her that I
shot him and I watched him bleed to death, but what's the point?
Wayne Connery/Roynan is now a patient at Broadmoor
Psychiatric Hospital, barely able to string coherent sentences
together once they have dosed him up with a cocktail of
Thorazine, Seroquel, and Stelazine. Anything I say right now will
simply be interpreted as yet another outburst of post-modern irony.

That word. I can hear Colin's voice rasping it with his last
breath.

"I'll be handing all this over to Dexter Wong some time this
week. He's wonderful, Ed. You'll just *love* him. He can arrange
all the interviews, and then he'll be teaming up with either
Eurydice at Tower or Skee and Galba at Price Moggridge to do
the publicity. But… as I was saying to Dexter this morning…
what publicity? It sells itself!"

She blows a kiss down the line ("Mwah!") and says goodbye
and the line goes quiet, and somewhere I am sure I can hear the

sound of my soul screaming in the infinite night. Surely *now* this will all begin to unravel. Oh, sure, right now they think it's funny, they think it's satire, but at some point they are going to join the dots and realise that I was telling the truth. Tens of thousands, she said. *Tens of thousands*. And they must have all had a good laugh at just how tasteless the joke seemed, and they're probably still laughing, but sooner or later somebody, one of the investigating police officers perhaps, or a witness who saw me walking along Shad Thames, will make the connection, and the joke will end abruptly.

Surely.

dexter wong – 15:49

Dexter Wong sits on the other side of the table. In his left hand he holds a pencil that's painted to look like a cigarette. When he speaks it is with a broad, some might say coarse, Liverpudlian accent that seems at odds with his looks (inherited from his Chinese father), his purple Gieves & Hawkes suit, and his yellow cravat. When the waiter brings us a bottle of Chablis and pours a little into his glass, Dexter sips it, grimaces, and says, "It'll do," without looking at him once.

"So Ed… " he says, "Trisha hasn't got a bad word to say about you. It's like the sun shines out of your frigging arse or something. Not that I blame her. I've read the book, and I've got to say, it's great. It's like a fucking nail bomb going off in a convent or something. This is exactly what we've been looking for. No more chick lit. No more celebrity autobiographies. No more SAS memoirs. No more dirt-dishing post-divorce sob stories. No more frigging pain memoirs. We need something that's real, but not real. Something that'll wake people up. Something that'll make people gasp. What are we going to call it?"

I tell him I haven't given it much thought.

"What about *Psychoville*?" he asks. I frown. "Yeah… I wasn't sure about that. It just popped into my head during my reiki session this morning. What about, *The Man Who Shot Colin Curtis*… you know, like that one with John Wayne and whatsisname in it? No? D'you know something? There's a good reason I don't come up with titles for a living. I can get you on a sofa with David fucking Letterman like *that…* " he clicks his fingers dramatically, "but ask me to come up with a name for something and I haven't got a fucking clue. I think Skee and Galba are on the case. They're usually good at that sort of thing.

"Now are we thinking paperback? Hardback? How many words are there?"

I tell him there are more than sixty six thousand words.

"Okay… Well, I guess we *could* do a hardback. Let's face it… they'll sell. This book is so *now*, Ed, it's like I want to fuck it or something."

He knocks back a mouthful of wine and takes a phantom drag on the cigarette-coloured pencil.

"Do you know what I mean?"

I shake my head.

"It's like I want to have the book, right here, right now, and I want to fuck it."

I hold my wine glass but don't drink from it. Memories of the symph and Colin Curtis' final hours have given me an aversion to alcohol, something Dexter Wong hasn't noticed as he finishes his glass and refills it.

"Fucking service in here," he says, shaking his head. "You have to fill your own fucking glass. Maybe I *will* fuck your book when I've got it. Yeah. I think that would be dead good."

I ask him what he means, suddenly feeling a tingling discomfort in my stomach and on the back of my neck.

"Oh, you think I'm talking metaphorically, but I'm not. Fucking books is a very sensual experience. I'm sorry… I'm just being me. D'you know, they don't even have a name for it."

Nervously I ask him what he means.

"It's my turn-on. Inanimate objects," he says. "You can look it up in any book you like. Oh, sure, they'll tell you about fetishes, but fetishes are always about the sensual relationship the object has with the human body and blah blah frigging blah blah… you know… shoes. Leather. Hand-cuffs. It's not like that. I just like fucking inanimate objects. It did start with shoes. I remember when I was about fourteen sticking my cock inside one of my trainers and… you know… it all kind of went from there. Any object I could fuck I'd fuck. Bottles. Jars. Sofas. Anything. I just like objects. And I still haven't found a name for it. There must be a name for it, what do you think?"

I tell him I don't know what the name for his turn-on would be.

"Objectophilia, maybe? I was thinking of putting a book together. You know. A coffee table book, mostly photographs. *Objects I'd Like To Fuck* or something. Anyway… listen to me, yakking on. This is about you. This is about *your* book."

My book. This is about my book.

Dexter Wong takes out his C-Fish and starts tapping at the buttons.

"I'm going to call Galba. Lovely boy. The kind you'd like to wear his knees as earrings… d'you know what I mean? Hang on…" He places the C-Fish next to his ear and waits. "Galba… Hiya, Galba, it's Dexter. I'm with Ed Raynes talking about his book. Yeah, that's the one. We were trying to think of a title. Have you guys got any ideas? Oh, she did? Excellent. So… any thoughts?" A long pause. Dexter Wong's whole face lights up and he starts giggling uncontrollably. "That's fucking genius, Galba. We should give you a pay rise for that. Don't tell Skee I said that. Thanks, love. Thanks, Galba. Bye."

He puts his C-Fish away and leans close to me over the table, a conspiratorial smile spread across his face.

"Celebricide," he says, leaning back in self-satisfaction.

"Celebricide?" I ask.

"Yeah. Celebricide. You know… like homicide, matricide… Celebricide. Murdering a celebrity."

"That's the title they've come up with?"

"Yeah. You don't like?"

I don't say anything. I'm not sure what I think of it. I stare at some point perhaps five metres behind Dexter's left shoulder, possibly frowning.

"Well, we can work all this out later. What's in a name, ay?" he says, pouring himself another glass of wine.

book launch – 21:15

On the table the flutes of champagne look like installation art. Some commentary on decadence, perhaps. Something that's meant to turn our stomachs, but doesn't.

All I can see is people holding those self-same flutes of champagne and they're all smiling. Everyone is smiling. They are smiling and talking, but the individual words they are saying are mashed together to form a continuous murmuring over which can be heard the latest ever-so-cool instrumental chill-out music and the clinking of glasses. Seb Keynsham is here, dressed in black, just like his wife, Trisha Smedley. Brian Fenton is here. Dexter Wong is here. Tracey Frampton is here. Hector Q is here.

Rob Rascal is here.

There are people I have interviewed here, but now *they* are here for *me*. Everyone wants to talk to me. It's how I imagine getting married must feel. I haven't moved from this spot in almost an hour and every so often another face will emerge from the chattering crowd, usually escorted by Dexter Wong, or Galba, or Skee, or any one of their entourage, and I'll be introduced as if I were a minor royal and this were some sort of fucking garden party.

"Ed, I'd like you to meet Maris Kramer of Oregon Films. Maris, this is Ed Raynes."

"Hi, Ed... great book. Dexter sent me a copy a few weeks back. Loved it. Listen, has anyone spoken to you yet about possible adaptations? You see, we're very interested in web-films and we're thinking of... "

Maris Kramer's voice turns to mush. I can see her mouth opening and closing and every so often she smiles sweetly, if insincerely, and she laughs, and so I laugh back, but I'm not listening.

"Give it some thought," she says, her hand on my arm. Another sweet smile and she walks away.

My parents and my sister are here, the only delegates from my family. They don't look happy. They all have their coats.

"We're going now," my mother says, tight-lipped. "Your father has a long drive in the morning so he'll need an early night."

I say something along the lines of, "But it's early, you can stay a few more hours, surely?"

"No, Ed. We need an early start. It'll be a long drive. Thank you very much for inviting us." None of this is said with any warmth. She kisses me on the cheek, nods without saying goodbye, and walks away. My father shakes my hand, nods stoically, and joins her.

"They're not happy," says my sister. "*I'm* not happy. We've read the book. Why did you make up all those things? I mean, about *us*? About them converting to Islam and me having some sort of nervous breakdown before my thirtieth? Was it meant to be funny, Ed? Because we're not laughing."

I shrug and try to tell her that it's all a work of fiction.

"Really? Really, Ed? Is that the best you can come up with? You use people's real names and then you say it's a work of fiction? Oh, I'm sure that washes with your post-modernist, deconstructuralist friends but it doesn't wash with us. We're your family, but it's like we don't even know you any more. You're just this person we see on the cover of your book or on TV or in the paper. I mean, who the fuck *are* you these days?"

I ask her what that's supposed to mean, but it's soft, without any aggression.

"Goodbye, Ed," she says, kissing me on the cheek and walking away.

I'd like to say this is the moment when I run after them and apologise to them for everything I've done. I'd like to say this is the moment in the movie version when there is a swelling of strings and we all hug and maybe I quit this crazy life because it isn't for me, and I join them back in their provincial little corner of the country, and we all live happily ever after. I'd like to say this is *not* the moment when I wonder what would happen if their car left the motorway during their journey home, and landed upside down on train tracks in the path of an oncoming train. I'd like to say I'm not wondering whether I'd inherit their house and, if I did, whether I'd redecorate.

"Ed, this is Oliver Gladwell. He's in the new Matt Walsh film. Oliver, this is Ed Raynes," another voice, another face.

Oliver Gladwell, perhaps twenty-five years old, shakes my hand and holds eye contact a little longer than I'd normally expect. He smiles and he tells me how much he can't wait to read my book. I've realised there are two types of response at a book launch: those people who have read the book already, or say they've read the book already, and are always full of glittering praise, and those who can't wait to read it. Again, I'm phasing in and out of what Oliver Gladwell is saying, catching occasional words here and there, and he says something about the chapter in which we are all 'doing coke in the bar'. He asks whether I really do coke or whether that's just the character in the book.

I'd like to lean close to him and tell him it's all real, every last bit of it, and that I watched Colin Curtis bleed to death without the slightest flicker of emotion. Instead I put on my best knowing smile and I say, "Well, that would be telling".

"Only I've got some," he says, his demeanour changing at once to one of boyish conspiracy. "I mean… if you'd like some."

And so Oliver Gladwell (who, according to Red Carpet in *The Voice of the People* is dating teen singing sensation Qelli Mai) and I leave the bar of The Paraffin Club and walk down the stairs and into the gents toilets while trying not to look like we're about to take illegal drugs.

The cubicle is claustrophobic and humid. Ten years ago the toilet would have been more crowded than the bar upstairs and you could have counted on there already being a dusting of white powder on the nearest flat surface. Times have changed and now there isn't a flat surface in sight; an attempt by the club's management to be seen to be doing the right thing.

Oliver opens his wallet as quietly as he can and takes out a small sealed plastic bag inside which is a tiny silver spoon and what looks like two grams of cocaine. He lifts a spoonful of the coke out of the bag and puts it under my nose, nodding enthusiastically. I take some, and then he takes some.

"It's good shit," he says, his voice a little too public schoolboy to be convincing when he's trying to talk 'street'. He folds the bag and puts it back in his wallet and then he kisses me on the mouth and I feel his tongue touch mine. His hand is over my crotch and unbuckling my belt and popping the button and then lowering the zip in a single, frantic movement. A part of me can still register this as erotic, but there's a displacement here, a distance from the act that leaves me feeling like an observer.

"I really want you to fuck me," he says. "Now. Here. Fuck me, while the coke's still working."

And so I fuck him. The first sexual contact I've had with anyone in months, since all *this* began, and it feels like nothing more than a rudimentary set of bodily functions. I wonder whether he's really enjoying this as much as he appears to be, or whether his barely contained gasps and moans are simply an extension of his art, brought into this cubicle for an audience of one. I groan and then he groans. He whispers things, like telling me he's about to cum, and then he cums, and I pretend to cum, and the whole thing is over, and as if to demonstrate how quickly his passion has faded and been replaced by cocaine paranoia he quickly buckles up his belt and is out of the cubicle without saying another word.

Before leaving the toilets I pause in front of the mirror above the wash basins and look myself in the eyes. My pupils are dilated. Nobody wants to believe all that stuff about the eyes being the windows of the soul when they look this black. I have that momentary feeling when you look at yourself in the mirror and it's almost like you're seeing your face for the first time. When you realise that this bundle of thoughts and feelings that walks round, observes things, listens to things, feels, tastes and smells things, does so in this packaging, with this face.

"It should have been me, you know."

I hear a gruff, northern accent and turn to see Bruce Albion stood beside me at the wash basins. He looks like he hasn't been home in days; his face covered with a growth of stubble, his tie undone, the collar of his shirt stained with either soup or blood. He smells like sherry. I ask him what he means.

"All this. It should have been me. Not sure why they didn't pick me. Not the right chemistry, maybe. Or maybe I pushed it too far." He shakes his head dolefully from side to side. "I don't know." He says, and then bellows: "Was I just too shocking for them? Or was I just not shocking enough? Never mind. Good luck, Raynes. I couldn't have wished it for a better guy."

As I back away from the sinks Albion blearily looks across at me, breaking the stare-out competition he had been having with his own reflection, and mimes the action of shooting two pistols in my direction.

I walk out of the toilets and scan the crowd; the faces of rising stars and fading stars, of media darlings and those people you only ever see or hear about at parties like this. The number of people here I don't know outnumber those I do by perhaps ten to one. But they're all here for *me*.

As I scan the faces I see two that I *do* recognise. It's only for a nanosecond, whatever a nanosecond is, but I see them; like a sub-liminal image beamed directly to my retina; and they're lost in the crowd as soon as I've seen them. I look out at the crowd and at all those faces, and the two that I know I've seen are Nigel from Apartment 413, and Dee, his Princess Diana lookalike friend.

I'm about to cross the room and search for them when I am stopped in my tracks by Seb Keynsham. He shakes my hand with a vice-like grip and beams from ear to ear. When he talks it's with a mid-Atlantic drawl that I've always thought affected, since his days at Yale, no doubt.

"Ed… " he says. "Great book. And great work these last few months. I heard about your ideas concerning the aftermath of

Lockdown, Brian told me all about them. Great work. And the book is amazing. You know, this all ties in with my vision for K-Media. I don't want people to think of K-Media as a media empire. Those words... they're... I don't know, people think empire they think Rome, they think Genghis Khan, they think Ottomans, they think Hitler. It's not good. I want people to think of us as a gathering of ideas. A central nervous system feeding the brain of the country. Fuck it... the world. Lots of branches going out into all the limbs, all the organs, and feeding back to the brain. D'you see what I'm saying?"

I want to correct his grammar. I want to tell him that it is impossible to see what somebody is saying, but he *is* talking about a 'vision' so I suppose it's to be expected. I nod and try to do 'thoughtful'.

"Anyway, Ed... enjoy tonight," says Seb Keynsham, shaking my hand one more bone-crushing time before moving on, waving to somebody on the other side of the room. I am about to resume my search for Nigel and Dee when I hear another voice.

"You did it, didn't you?"

I turn around and see Ondine. Her eyes are glowing and the tendons in her neck are sticking out like the strings on a double bass.

"What do you mean?" I ask her.

"Colin Curtis. You did it, didn't you?"

"What are you talking about?"

"You shot him. Everyone thinks this is like some kind of massive joke, don't they? Some post-modern satire kind of thing, but I know it's not. I *saw* what you were like. And then I got a phone call. Wayne Roynan was nowhere near Shad Thames that night because he was in hospital. He'd cut his thumb on broken glass and it needed stitches so he went to the nearest A & E and he was there for six hours waiting to be seen to. Oh, sure, you can check all the records but you won't find a thing. No Wayne Roynan, no Wayne Connery. It was one of the nurses, the one who did his stitches, who called me. She said the records had vanished, so she spoke to the police and they said that she must be mistaken, but she knew it was him because he told her the whole story about how his father was Sean Connery. It stuck in her mind, as it would, and when he was on the news a week later she knew it couldn't have been him who killed Colin Curtis. He'd left the hospital at six am. It would have taken him an hour and a half to get from the hospital to Shad Thames.

"I sat on it for a while. I didn't know what to make of it. Maybe this nurse was just looking for her fifteen minutes, trying to get her name in the papers. It's happened before. And then I read the book. How can nobody know about this, Ed? How can nobody know you were with him that night? I mean... there must have been witnesses. What about the witnesses Ed?"

She's leaning in close to me now and talking loudly, but none of the guests appear to be paying any attention.

"The scale of this... " says Ondine, "I mean, the sheer bloody scale of it. And why? To sell a book? To shift a few more papers? Why, Ed? What's wrong with you people?"

"I'm sorry, Miss, but we're going to have to ask you to leave."

We have been joined by two bouncers in black ties.

"I'm going nowhere," says Ondine. "I'm the only person who knows. How can I be the only person who knows?"

They take her away, each one holding an arm, and she starts shouting, but by now she is incoherent with rage. Some people look at her. Some people raise eyebrows. A few people laugh. Ondine is dragged through the reception of the club and pushed out into the street. Everyone starts talking again.

Brian Fenton is at my side.

"I'm sorry about that, Ed," he says. "She's been under a lot of stress lately. We all have. But don't worry. It's all taken care of now."

He smiles, that spout-lipped, all-gums smile, and nods.

"This is going to be spectacular," he says.

I ask him what he means.

"The book. Everything," he says. "I can just imagine the head-lines."

And then he's gone, walking toward Trisha Smedley, and still smiling that smile.

celebricide – 23:09

The journalist Edgar Raynes is, perhaps, more famous for his tabloid exposés of celebrity scandals than for his literary skills, but this week sees the publication of his first novel, *Celebricide*. Part memoir, part post-modern dissection of twenty-first-century mores, *Celebricide*, so the publisher Price Moggridge promises us, 'deftly straddles the dividing line between autobiography and satire'. It is being touted as a worthy successor to Swift's *A Modest Proposal* and Vonnegut's *Slaughterhouse Five*.

Already there is talk of its title being recognised in the next edition of the Oxford dictionary, its definition being 'the murder of a celebrity of no political importance'. John Lennon as opposed to John F Kennedy. Jill Dando as opposed to Benazir Bhutto.

In addition to this there have been calls from some corners for celebricide to be recognised as a crime in its own right, similar to hate-crime. But what of the book itself? Tom… what did you think?

Well, I thought it was *abysmal*. I mean, the characters are based on real people, but they're sketchy and ill-formed. They're like characters in a cartoon or something, though that's being unfair to cartoons. And quite frankly I thought we'd put post-modernism in its most clunky, ironic, shallow form to bed a long time ago. The humour in it, well… what I took to be humour, was far too broad to have any real bite to it. It was all shock for shock's sake. And talk about convoluted. The whole thing twisted and turned, but without any real pace, sometimes sluggish, sometimes racing along like some kind of epileptic race-horse. I came away from it feeling like I'd taken drugs or something.

Germaine?

Mmm… I think I agree with Tom on this, but I'd go further. For one thing, the *misogyny* in the book just leaps off the page. There are three female characters in the whole book, and all of them are unhinged, whether it be the mother, the sister, or the colleague.

But you could argue that *everyone* in the book is unhinged.

Well, I suppose, but then that would be a rather dismal view of humanity. And I think that's another thing that annoyed me so much about this book – its pessimism. I mean, is the world *really* this bad? Are people *really* this bad? Where is the hope?

Tracey… you wanted to say something?

Well, I couldn't disagree more. I thought this was a fantastic book. And you say it was pessimistic, Germaine, well… I'd disagree. I don't think we are *meant* to view this book as a reflection of the real world in any shape or form. I think this draws more upon Bakhtin's notion of the carnivalesque; the deliberately obscene humour, the grotesque characters. We know they're based on real people, but it's the exaggeration of those people that makes them entertaining. Furthermore, we only ever see the characters from the narrator's point of view, and one of the points I think the book is trying to make is that we are, as a society, becoming increasingly isolated and self-obsessed, and so the other characters are always going to be ill-defined.

That's an interesting point, Tracey, but what about the accusation of bad taste? I mean, it's only a few months since the murder of Colin Curtis, and already we have a book which uses that as a focal point for satire. Is that in poor taste?

Well, I think it was Albert Camus who said 'always go too far, because that is where you will find the truth'.

What do you think, Tom?

Well it's funny you should mention that Mark, because that's the one thing I *didn't* object to. The whole process by which Colin Curtis became a celebrity was grotesque in itself, so this seems the fitting coda for that obscene circus of events. I don't think *taste* comes into it.

Germaine...

Yes. And I suppose this book started life as a blog, where such material would be less open to censorship. It's just a shame it was less open to a little judicious editing and re-writing.

Re-writing? They should have scrapped the whole thing altogether.

Yes, Tom... I think you're right there. I just felt it was a wasted opportunity. Ed Raynes clearly has the upper hand on any other writer when it comes to exposure to and experience with that whole celebrity world, and I suppose the idea that it's the writer, the person who crafts the fact and fiction of celebrity, who kills the celebrity... I suppose that's an interesting conceit, but I'm not entirely sure it ever develops any further than that.

Well... that's *Celebricide* by Edgar Raynes. It's out next week from Price Moggridge in hardback.

The name Takashi Miike is synonymous with the word prolific, having directed over forty films since his debut, *Shinjuku Triad Society*. Fans of the eccentric director have come to expect the unexpected, but even they were surprised when he announced plans to remake the classic MGM musical *Meet Me In St Louis*…

overdose blue – 12:41

I'm sat above Canary Wharf underground, on a bench in the park that has been planted between the great glass domes of each entrance. It's curiously peaceful here, at any time of day, even in the middle of the week. I've come here as part of what I'm beginning to think of as my rehabilitation.

My mind is clearer now. Everything seems a little less clouded. I'm leaving the apartment more and more often; buying my supplies in supermarkets. Sometimes I even wander around at night, listening in on the conversations of strangers on the DLR or sat outside the bars and restaurants of Docklands.

I still haven't been back to Soho.

A squirrel leaps out from under a bush opposite the bench on which I'm sat, and scurries along the edge of the path before leaping across to the other side and vanishing beneath another bush. How on earth, I wonder, did squirrels get *here*? What kind of journey must nature have made to have found its way to this little green oasis in the middle of so much concrete and glass? Something about the presence of the squirrel makes me smile, and then laugh almost silently through my nose with a puff.

"Ed!" I hear my name and turn in the direction from which the voice came. It's Nihad. He's carrying a brown paper deli bag and drinking from a bottle of mineral water. He looks different somehow. More controlled. A little less wired than usual. He sits next to me on the bench and firmly pats me on the back.

"Well done with the book, mate," he says. "Fantastic news. And the launch was just great. Any plans to come back to the paper?"

I shrug and tell him I'm not sure. I'll have to see how the book pans out.

"Of course… of course… " he says, nodding thoughtfully.

"Well, so long as you still remember us when you're rich and famous, ay?" He belly laughs. "But we'd love to have you back in the newsroom," he adds. "It's getting so dull, what with you leaving, and then Ondine."

"Ondine?" I ask.

"Oh fuck," says Nihad. "You... I thought someone would have said something. Man... fuck... "

I ask him what he's talking about.

"Fucking hell... I'm sorry, man. I thought maybe Brian or somebody would have called you to let you know. Ondine died. It was a few days after your book launch. Sleeping tablets. Vodka. Totally did a *Janis Joplin...* "

My rural idyll between the skyscrapers might as well be on fire right now. The incongruous tranquillity might as well be torn to shreds by the roaring of a jet engine or the deafening boom of an atomic bomb. It might as well be raining broken glass.

"Fuck... Ed... are you okay?"

I tell him I think so but all I'm thinking of is Ondine on the floor of her living room, a foam of vomit on her blue lips. Overdose blue, just like that night in the bar.

"I thought it was odd you weren't at the funeral," says Nihad. "I mean, you and Ondine were mates. You were sat opposite each other for two years. Shit.... I can't believe no-one told you. I'm sorry... anyway... listen... I've really got to fly. I'm just finishing off a piece on that business up in Birmingham and then I'm playing squash with Brian. I'll tell him I saw you. Take care of yourself, yeah?"

Another firm pat on the back, and he's gone.

signing off – 18:03

Oxford Street is all rain and Christmas lights, the flickering red and green reflecting up off the wet tarmac, a soft focus city in reverse. The buses and taxis hiss and the pavements are dense with umbrellas.

I can smell coffee, from the Starbucks on the second floor, and I remember a time when book shops smelled of books and not coffee. The queue snakes this way and that around the ground floor of the shop, kept in place by the kind of barriers they have in airports. They stand with their wet coats and their folded umbrellas, each one of them holding a hardback copy of *Celebricide*, the new novel by Ed Raynes, and they are all looking at me.

Dexter Wong is here somewhere, talking to photographers and the two or three film crews who are prowling around the shop looking for the best angles.

I think about autographs, and signed copies, and what it all means. Is it the autograph these people are after? Is it the black squiggle that means I've held that book and touched it with my hands? Does it make the book more real? Does it enhance the reading experience? What will they want me to write?

Maybe it's something more cynical than that. In an era of e-Bay and comic book conventions perhaps they want my signature in that book because then it'll be worth just a little bit more than the price on the cover.

In the window of the shop there are giant cardboard renditions of that cover; a blurred close-up of a television screen depicting Colin Curtis' face; his eyes and mouth blocked out with my name and the title, like the Sex Pistols' image of the Queen. Plastered across the cardboard signs are notices advertising my presence here tonight.

Edgar Raynes will be signing copies of *Celebricide* on…

When I look at my name in big bold print it's like that moment when you don't recognise your own face. They call face blindness *prosopagnosia*. I wonder what they call it with names. It's not words I'm not seeing, it's my name. I'm looking at my name, on those signs, on my books, but it means nothing. I hear my name on TV, I hear people talking about me, and the book, and it means nothing. It seems like a coincidence. Like there's another Ed Raynes out there.

The staff at the book shop look at me, and they look at Dexter Wong, and Dexter nods, and the queue begins to shuffle forward, with the first two people walking toward me, each brandishing a copy of the book.

One is the kind of girl who still chews gum and the other is a boy wearing eye shadow and a t-shirt that reveals a pale famine belly.

And they're both smiling at me.

They don't say anything, they simply put their books on the table and open them, and never once take their eyes off me while they're smiling.

"Who do you want me to make this out to?" I ask. I think that's the line I'm meant to say. If there's a script to all this, and there's a script to *everything*, then I'm meant to ask who they want me to make it out to, and they either tell me their own names or the names of the people they are buying the book for.

"Kelly," says the girl.

"Dane," says the boy.

To Kelly, best wishes… my signature.

To Dane, best wishes… my signature.

They thank me and they giggle and they walk away as the next person steps forward: an elderly woman with a transparent plastic headscarf and a walking stick.

"Who do you want me to make this out to?"

"Me, love," she says. "Frances Spitzer. Frannie. Write Frannie."

To Frannie, best wishes… my signature.

"Thanks, love. Is it full of swearing?"

"I'm sorry?"

"The book. Is it full of swearing, and all that sex and violence?"

"Umm… " I shrug, "a little."

"Oh, lovely. I likes a bit of sex and violence. Bye, love."

She chuckles saucily and walks away and the next people step forward. I find myself reciting Tennyson's 'Coming Of Arthur' inside my head.

Wave after wave, each mightier than the last.

Dexter Wong smiles at me from the stairwell, where he stands next to a cameraman. Somewhere a camera flashes. I hear another name and I sign another autograph.

In the fleeting seconds between each signing I feel the pulse of my life, a metronomic throbbing, the machinery of my existence ticking on. Those long, sultry days trapped in my apartment seem like another existence. I think of the mornings spent on my balcony, watching the commuters, like grains of sand, spilling out into the city. I remember the haughty derision with which I watched them. Now it seems I am a part of the machine once more, but my purpose is pared down, reduced to its essentials.

I sit here, the face of the author, and I sign books. Anyone could do this. I remember hearing about Warhol having stand-ins; a brilliant exploitation of his increasingly unusual appearance. All people needed to see was the shock wig and shades. If the picture on the back cover of the book were someone else, would it matter to these people who was signing it?

"Who do I make this out to?"

"Carrie. It's for my girlfriend."

Would it matter to any of us? We see celebrities in shopping malls and airports and we tell our friends, as if it is somehow outlandish that these people should exist off the screen or the page. But all that really mattered was that we saw them. We saw their faces. We might not have spoken to them or even said hello, but we saw them. Would it *really* matter if it wasn't them? If we didn't *know* it wasn't them?

"Who do I make this out to?"

"Trevor. You can write Trev if you like. Everyone calls me Trev."

He wants me to know that everyone calls him Trev. It's not like we'll meet again, but that informality is all important to Trev. It implies a moment, just a split second, of intimacy between us. A moment when he looked me in the eyes, and he saw my face, my actual face, and just for that moment I knew his name. Never mind the fact that I've forgotten the names of each and every person who came before him.

"Who do I make this out to?"

"Can you write, 'to Mandy, happy birthday', and then your name?"

Because it's Mandy's birthday. And to Mandy, who clearly isn't here, it will seem as if I knew it was her birthday already, and I cared. And Mandy, upon opening the book, will think perhaps I am thinking of her, and her birthday, while she is opening her cards and gifts.

"Who do I make this out to?"

"Jenny, and can you add kisses?"

Because Jenny wants to feel special. Jenny wants to feel affection. Jenny wants to know that somebody, somewhere kissed her, even if it was just on paper. And when the kisses are marked x x on the title page Jenny limps away in her leg braces and steps out into the rain.

I scan the queue and they are still smiling at me. Some of them are talking to one another, but they never look away from me, and they don't stop smiling. One woman walks toward me with the lens of her C-Fish's camera aimed at me, but her hand is shaking. Her eyes are filled with tears and she's breathing as if in the middle of a panic attack.

"I think you're amazing," she says. "I've loved you since you wrote for *The Voice of the People*. You're amazing. Oh my God…

I can't believe it's actually you. You're amazing."

She takes a photo of me on her C-Fish and then leans across the table and throws her arm around me and takes another photo of us together; me looking vaguely stunned, her a mess of tears and snot. Dexter Wong is signalling to two security guards with a 'cut throat' gesture and the guards are doing their best to gently separate us, but she's holding on tight. She puts the book down on the table with her free hand and puts her other arm around me.

"I love you," she says. "You're amazing. You're amazing."

"Who do I make this out to?" I ask. The security guards are prising her fingers from my back.

"K-K-K-K-Kate," she says, and then, to the guards, "Please... no... please... he's amazing."

They pull her away and I hurriedly sign the book. One of the guards is leading her toward the exit, and she still hasn't taken her bloodshot eyes off me. I hand the book to the second guard, who follows them.

This should have vexed me. I should be worried, or maybe even scared. I should be rigid with distaste for this meaningless circus, faced by a crowd of grinning skulls, listening to K-K-K-K-Kate still screaming in the street, but instead I love it. My heart feels like a balloon inside my chest and I realise that I'm smiling, beaming even. I love this. I love every aspect of it. They're all here for me. Each and every one of them is here for me.

The next person steps forward and places another copy of the book, my book, on the table.

"Who do I make this out to?" I ask, looking down at the open book.

"Make it out to Nigel."

It's the first time I've heard her voice properly, without it being drowned out by the sound of descending planes and the distant electric hum of the DLR, and yet I recognise it instantly.

I look up from the open copy of *Celebricide* by Ed Raynes, and I see the face of Princess Diana. The hair is just right, the beige trouser suit a dead ringer for something I'm sure I've seen in countless photographs. Only the voice gives the game away; that husky voice with its revealing bass note and its lack of grace.

I look at Dee and I smile, and she smiles back, and she lifts the gun, the Makarov PM, from her purse, and points it at my chest.

"It is accomplished," she says, still smiling.

The first shot turns everything into an echoing cacophony. I feel the impact of the bullet, but only briefly. It knocks the air out of my lungs and turns the world black, and through the fog of what is happening to me I see the queue breaking past the barriers and running away in all directions. I think I can hear screaming.

The second shot hits me in the chest once more and now I can see blood, everywhere blood. On my suit, on my hands, on the table, on the book.

Dee looks down at me, still smiling, and fires the gun again and again. My view is tipped backwards, the screaming crowds vanish and are replaced by the ceiling. My head explodes with pain as it strikes the floor, and I feel the dull warm punch of another bullet ripping through the front and back of my Poole & Co suit before burying itself in the ground beneath me.

Dee is kneeling on the table now, her expression crazed, defiant. She laughs, though I can't hear it, puts the gun under her chin, and ends her final thoughts in one blinding, bloody instant. Her body tips forward, lurching in gravity's embrace until she falls at my feet with a heavy thud.

In one corner of my eye Dexter Wong ushers the cameras closer. His expression is one of excitement, the thrill of the moment, like a film director bewitched by the accidental glory of a sunset. The cameras lean in close, their spotlights forming half a dozen tunnels of light for me to choose from.

I'm trying to laugh but my mouth is full of blood.

I'm trying to tell them how funny this is but I can't quite catch my breath.

The room begins to fade. The ceiling, and the screams of all those bystanders, the sound of Dexter Wong telling the cameras to "get closer... get closer... "

I think about the insect on the table. I think about Nicki Santos pretending to dance. I think about a digital Marilyn Monroe, and Rob Rascal asking me for money. I think about Nigel. I think about Colin Curtis' last gasp. I think about the newsroom tomorrow morning. I think about Brian Fenton. I think about the paper.

And I can just imagine the headlines.

Thanks to the following:

Penny, Simon and everyone at Seren for their tireless help in getting this thing from concept to book; Ceri Radford and Co at *The Daily Telegraph*, for allowing me to sit in on their morning conference (fortunately it was nothing like the one in this book); and Jason Kennedy for a very helpful transatlantic feedback session on the first draft. Thanks also to everyone who listened to or read certain chapters while I was writing this, including Myspacers and everyone at Homotopia in Liverpool.

A personal shout also to my family and friends: the Gaits, the Llewellyns, everyone who was at Benbury, the Bailey Street Massive, the Wub Group, the Glam-organs (past present and future), the Llandaff North Crew, the Woods family, my colleagues, and everyone who's ever cooked dinner for me. There are too many names to list without this looking like the inside of a hip-hop album, but you all know who you are.

Eleven
David Llewellyn

Tuesday, September 11, 2001, is just another boring day at the office for the young professionals of corporate Cardiff, as they email each other their gossip, jokes, requirements for the weekend and, occasionally, work. At the centre of this online world is 'process accountant' and would-be author Martin Davies. Martin is frustrated by his job, in denial over his break up with his girlfriend and baffled by the triviality of his life. When, just after lunch, people start flying airliners into New York office blocks, Martin feels he is rapidly losing the plot...

Part *The Office*, part Beckett, *Eleven* is a striking debut novel. Smart, funny and brutally sad, it opens up the inhumanity of throwaway 21st century society. *Eleven* is for anyone who has ever clicked SEND when they should be doing something else.

Eleven £6.99, Seren, 2006, ISBN 1-85411-415-8

Praise for *Eleven*:

In its juxtaposition of the petty bickering of office politics, the frustrated immensity of individual needs, and a physical event that might just shatter the world, it conveys an almost unbearable poignancy. Much, much power is crammed into this short novel.

Niall Griffiths

In offering a dark comedy, Llewellyn shows more taste than do many more earnest seekers of artistic relevance... a funny and disturbing view of a disaffected age.   Nicholas Clee, *The Guardian*

Eleven is a compulsive read, and I devoured it at one sitting, unable to put it down... It's easy to imagine this becoming a cult book for the disillusioned younger generation.   Ray French, *Planet*

A micro-mezze of human emotion, *Eleven* thrusts snippets of love, trust and disappointment into the mix and proves that the knock-on effect of petty office politics can be disastrous.   *Gay Times*